T0354498

The Game

The Game

Stephanie Bergen

THE GAME

This is a work of fiction. All of the characters, names, incidents, organizations, and dialogue in this novel are either the products of the author's imagination or are used fictitiously.

iUniverse books may be ordered through booksellers or by contacting:

iUniverse
1663 Liberty Drive
Bloomington, IN 47403
www.iuniverse.com
1-800-Authors (1-800-288-4677)

ISBN: 978-1-5320-5685-7 (sc)
ISBN: 978-1-5320-5686-4 (e)

Library of Congress Control Number: 2018910443

Print information available on the last page.

iUniverse rev. date: 08/31/2018

To Jennifer Lynn,
The reason I started this journey.

❧ *Prologue* ❧

natalie liese

"What's the plan?" I asked as I slammed the car door shut. I couldn't believe that this was happening. This kind of thing usually only happened in movies. Secret car meetings like this, between two people that wanted to meet and scheme. Not that I felt good about scheming.

"The plan is simple. You just have to get Janessa to agree to it. That's all. I'll handle the rest, I told you."

James. His plan was to set up my best friend — my sweet, innocent, ambitious best friend — with his horrible and conniving one, in the hopes that my friend, Janessa, could change him. I didn't think that it would work. People like Bryan *didn't* change. Their pure black hearts were incurable.

"She won't," I muttered. "She's much too smart for that." Or at least, I hoped she was.

He let out a heavy sigh and ran his hand across his face, as frustrated with me as I was with him. "Natalie.."

"James, we can't play cupid and set these two up. They're *too* different. You're just going to have to find someone else to set him up with," I snapped. I closed my mouth for a second, waiting for him to respond, but he didn't. "I get that you want what's best for Bryan, but you have to understand that, as Janessa's best friend, I *have* to protect her. I can't do what you're asking and *not* feel guilty about it. He's *going* to hurt her."

"Not if I have anything to say about it."

"I don't think there is anything you *can* say to change who he is. He's hurt a lot of people, you said so yourself. Why would you want to make Janessa suffer?"

"Because I truly believe that she can change him."

"Maybe, maybe not." I didn't think there was anything he could say to change my mind.

"We all used to be friends once, or don't you remember that?"

"Oh, *I* remember." I looked at him. "I *also* remember the two of you icing me out around the second grade. Why was that? Afraid you'd catch cooties?"

"It wasn't like that and you know it."

"Do I?" My tone was harsh but I didn't take it back. I couldn't. The pain of losing the two of them was suddenly coming up again.

"Natalie," he spoke softly, reaching for my hand but I snapped it back, intertwining my fingers and holding them in my lap. "I never wanted to stop being friends." I just sat there, silently looking out the window. He sighed, pulling his hand back to the steering wheel. "Back to the point: you and I *both* know that there is a human side of Bryan."

"Not anymore."

"I know we have issues — and we can work on those later if you want — but right now, we can help our friends." He paused, for just a minute. An annoying minute. "She can *change* Bryan."

"And in the process, she'll get hurt! Not just a little bit either, this could *kill* her. She believes in the power of love but she's been through a lot. I don't want to see her crushed." I looked at him, hoping that some of what I was saying was getting through to him. "This plan of yours is going to *ruin* her."

"And that's where we come in. You'll help her and I'll help him. Come on, Nat. Please?" He begged. "Please, help me with this."

"If things go sour between Janessa and Bryan…" I turned in the passenger seat and jam a finger into James' chest. "I will personally blame you." I poke him again, hard and he winced. "And there will be no going back. I will never *ever* talk to you again. *Ever.*"

He thought about that, almost hesitating. "Deal."

"Okay." I hesitated. We shook hands, like we were making a bet. "So what's the plan?"

"Just get her to agree. That's it."

❧ One ❧

Is this really _how you_ envisioned ending your senior year?"

"Actually, yes," I answered my best friend, Natalie Liese. We were in between classes, stopping by my locker so I could grab a textbook that I'd forgotten this morning. "This is exactly how I'd imagined it. I didn't spend my entire high school career studying to the point of exhaustion just to throw it away at the last minute."

"Then, don't think of it as throwing it away," she suggested as I closed my locker and turned the dial up to zero.

I looked at her confused. "How _else_ should I think of it?"

"Branching out?"

What?

She must have seen the confusion on my face because she added, "Making memories?"

"Making memories," I repeated. "You mean breaking rules and getting busted by the police when they raid parties for illegal substances?"

"Exactly!" She exclaimed as we started heading toward my math class, where she would leave me. "All I am saying is that you could use a bit of excitement, laugh a little. I'm worried about those stress lines that are making grooves on your forehead."

"I don't have stress lines!" I smacked her gently with my textbook.

She chuckled. "I'm just saying, what could it hurt?" She shrugged like it was nothing. "You've worked so hard, you deserve a bit of fun."

"Yeah, maybe when July comes. Not now."

"No, _now_," she insisted. Shocked by the clipped tone she used, I just stared at her. She had never been a great liar so I hoped her expression would give something away. Natalie refused to look at me as she averted her gaze to the ground. She picked at her cuticles as she spoke, "Look, with everything going on at home, I just wanted to do something fun with my best friend before school is over. Before we graduate."

I could already feel myself softening to her demand. As much as I didn't want to abandon my studies completely, on some level, I understood what she meant.

"Just think about it."

We stopped in front of my math class and at this point, I wasn't sure what else to say on the subject. I wanted to stand my ground and say no because, again, I didn't want to abandon my studies. But at the same time, the next three months suddenly felt like three days, like there wasn't enough time to spend with her and go crazy. So I promised I would think about it and we would talk later.

Then she left and I went to find my desk in the front of the room.

For the first few minutes of class, I got myself situated. My textbook was open in front of me with today's lesson staring at me in the face with my notebook open to a blank page. I glanced at the clock on the wall. There were a few more minutes before class started. With my favourite pink pen in my hand, I started to think about this summer.

What did I want to do?

I couldn't remember the last time I went to the movies with Natalie. I think it had been so long that when we had gone, we were accompanied by her parents. I couldn't remember how it had felt to be in that kind of environment. So I uncapped my pen and wrote:

See 5 movies

I looked around the classroom as my mind blanked. I saw two couples in the back, leaning toward each other and talking in hushed tones. It was hard not to deny the chemistry they had and a part of me yearned for that now too. Did I really want to go into a relationship with someone from high school? A relationship that would be doomed from the start? Did I really want to put myself through that?

I couldn't say with absolute certainty, as I dug through my pencil case for a pencil. I know I had a couple. There was one, right in the very bottom, that had been chewed down so far that it was now the size of my thumb. It also happened to be my favourite pencil. I jotted down:

Have a doomed relationship

There was always something on someone's to-do list that could not be accomplished. I guess that one would be mine.

By lunchtime, I had added three more things to my list.

Try alcohol
Stay out past curfew
Befriend someone new

With everything on my list, the doomed relationship one still seemed to be the most unlikely to happen. But for some reason, Natalie disagreed. She also had some ideas for a potential contender. As we were sitting down at our table in the cafeteria, she looked over my list and approved of all the things I had written down. She also insisted that she could help with a couple of them. But it was when she dug through her own pencil case and pulled out a purple ballpoint pen that I got nervous. She jotted one name in the margin — Bryan O'Donald — and added an arrow toward the relationship point.

"Whoa, whoa, whoa," I protested. With my pen that I quickly whipped out of my bag, I stroked it out. Twice. "That is not happening."

"Why not?" She asked, lifting her eyebrows, challenging me to do it again when she rewrote his name. "Are you backing out already?"

"No, I'm not," I told her. "But I am also not going to be going after *him*."

I couldn't, even if I wanted to — which I don't, — still I couldn't go after him. For the small fact that half the population of this school has already been in a relationship with the guy. I didn't need the drama they would create, nor did I need to be just another girl. God knows he has more experience in every area of the dating life, and I? Well, I don't have any.

"Hey, if you want to accomplish that point, it needs to be Bryan," Natalie remarked, cheerfully. "You won't have to do anything. He'll come up to you and ask you out. All you have to do," she grinned, "is say yes."

"You make it sound so easy." I rolled my eyes.

"Make what sound so easy?" My foster brother, André, asked, pulling out a chair and sitting down quickly. He was one of those people that looked *okay* in black and knew it, so they made it apart of their everyday wardrobe. He also had long shaggy hair that he wore up in a bun, that always looks greasy even though I *know* he showers.

Natalie tells him, asking for his opinion as if I actually cared to hear it.

"I think that sounds like a good idea," André said. "Your first relationship should be easy."

"No, your first relationship ends in heartbreak," I retorted. "Everyone knows that, except you guys. Apparently." I looked at them pointedly. I ripped my list out of their hands and shoved it into my bag along with my pen. I excused myself and headed to the bathroom.

I washed my face, hoping the cold water would help but for some reason, it didn't work and trickled down my shirt instead. I splashed my face once more, before drying it and that's when I heard the bathroom door open. "Nat, could we..." I trailed off as I turned around and found Bryan standing there instead, but I finished it anyway, "...not."

There is a moment in everyone's life when you know you're screwed. This was my moment when I turned around and felt the full effects of his gaze as it was firmly placed on me. As I had admitted many times before, silently to myself, he looked gorgeous, even as he stood in the girls' bathroom. He was leaning against the wall with his arms were crossed across his chest, his broad shoulders squared. His ankles were crossed. He looked so casual.

I opened my mouth to say something, anything that could possibly feel like the right thing to say. But my mind blanked. What could be said in such a situation? I closed my mouth and this time, Bryan stepped forward, cleared his throat.

"Janessa, right?"

I nodded. I had thought that no one knew my name. It shocked me, *baffled* me even, that he did. He was the quarterback, the best player on every team that he'd ever played for. Not to mention that his stare could silence women so fast. I'm sure he could also make them do whatever. He had power, enough confidence to be the most wanted guy in the school, which continued to beg the question: *How did he know my name?*

"I've never seen you around school before," he commented. I wasn't surprised, I had been able to conceal myself pretty well. If I had wanted him to know my existence, I may have tried to gain his attention, but I had been a little preoccupied. "And there's no way I would forget a face as beautiful as yours."

Now I had read enough romance novels to recognize this line. And knowing what kind of womanizing male god he was, it snapped me right back to the present. "Wow," I breathed. "Does that line really work for you?"

I may have sounded fearless but my heart was pounding painfully in my chest, knocking against my ribcage so much that I thought it might break free. He stepped even closer, and for a second I forgot to breathe. Natalie was right about one thing, being with Bryan would be so damn easy. But giving in to their request, *his* intense stare, would mean putting my heart on the line.

"Usually," Bryan admitted, grinning, "yes, it does." He paused. "Is it working with you?"

Was he serious? Did he actually think that the line, he had used with all those other girls, would work with me? I fought the urge to raise an eyebrow. I'm sure he would just find that hilarious. "I think you'd have to come up with something more original than that."

"A challenge, huh?" He asked rhetorically. "I like it." He winked. "What do you say to you and me? Getting away? Tonight?"

And there it was, my invitation. I could already hear Natalie's voice in my head. *Just say yes.* The word was on the tip of my tongue, but then I felt the weight of my English and math homework and I didn't know what to say. She had said it would be so easy. That all I would have to do is say yes. But having a relationship was supposed to be the one thing that I would not be able to accomplish, right?

But now, staring into his beautiful green eyes, I was just at a loss for words.

"Think about it," he said. Then told me to meet him at the Dropoff if I changed my mind. The Dropoff was a cliff that overlooked the town. It was the designated sex spot. With that thought alone, blood rushed to my face.

Then Bryan disappeared out the bathroom door, leaving me standing there, wondering what I wanted.

Just standing there, in the wake of his departure, I started thinking about all the things I had to have missed out on while my nose had been stuck in a book. Was there really a whole other world beyond the ones I knew? Did I want to venture into it? Learn what they had to offer?

Apparently, the answer to that was yes, because five hours later, I found myself next to Bryan on a picnic blanket in silence. I wasn't sure what to say. And he had to be used to girls that talked for hours about nail polish and the difference between two different shades. That wasn't me. So I didn't know what to say or even what to bring up.

"Can I ask you something?" He suddenly asked, taking my hand and gently holding it in between his two big ones. His touch had to be one of the best things I had ever felt. Like the biggest, softest caress in the world.

"Sure," I said, the words barely above a hum but he heard it anyway.

"Wanna hear a joke?" He looked at me. "I told my sister this joke and she thought it was hilarious. I was just wondering if it would have the same effect on you."

Oh, so he had a sister. That was good to know. I thought I would file that away for later conversation topics. I adjusted in my spot enough to face him more directly without forcing him to let go of my hand. I really didn't want him to and he didn't look like he wanted to either. "Sure. Who doesn't like a good joke?"

"What has many keys but cannot open any doors?"

I had heard the joke before. "Ah, I know this one. A piano."

"Well, look at that," he spoke sarcastically. "I'm in the presence of a genius."

I shrugged. "So, you have a sister, do you?" I asked. I looked up at him. Never in a million years would I have pictured him with a sibling. A lot of the time he acted as selfish and snobbish as a single child that has spent their whole life getting whatever they wanted.

Bryan nodded. "Yeah. I do."

"How old is she?"

"Seven," he answered.

"Wow." I don't know why, but knowing that, it gave me a new picture of him that I never thought I would see. I figured he would have to be good with kids if he had a sister that young. It was almost surprising.

"What?" He was smiling. He almost seemed completely at ease with himself and at this moment, he also seemed very happy.

"Nothing. I just never expected — I mean, that from all that I know about you from the gossipers at school, I never would have thought that you had a sister that young. Much less that there would be a possibility that you would be good with kids," I said it all very quickly. I wanted to get it out before I lost my nerve.

Bryan chuckled. "Are you kidding? I love kids."

"Really?" That was pleasantly surprising to hear.

He nodded. "Do you have any siblings?"

"Sort of," I said. "I mean, I have had foster siblings, but there had always only been one at a time and they never stuck around long enough for me to really get to know them." I wasn't sure how much I wanted to tell him, or how much he really wanted to know; but looking into his beautiful green eyes, so inviting, so curious, so intrigued, I kept going. "A lot of the girls that my mom fostered had difficult childhoods. So did the guys. Not all of them, but some of the girls resorted to theft whereas a few of the guys had... their own techniques."

He just nodded. He didn't try to pry for more answers. "Alright, so now that we know about each other's siblings, let's back up, shall we?"

"Back up?"

"Yes." He nodded. "What do you prefer? Coffee, tea, water, or juice?"

I chuckled. "Seriously?" Bryan took my hand in his, turning my hand, palm up. I watched him as he begins to slowly draw circles. The motions shot sparks through my body, which could have just been a reaction to the ticklish feeling I got. "Well, I don't like coffee. I only drink tea when I'm sick, and only green tea. I couldn't try to pick between water and juice if I tried."

He nodded, taking it in.

"What about you?"

"Love coffee, cannot live with it. I am not a huge fan of tea, love water. Who doesn't? And juice, it depends on the type of juice."

꧁❦꧂

As he was dropping me off that night, we sat in his car, talking for a little while longer when André stepped out of the house. Bryan noticed him first.

"Is that your foster brother now?"

I turned in my seat. "Yeah. That's André."

"He looks nice."

"They all looked nice," I told him, unbuckling my seatbelt. "I have come to learn that looks can be deceiving." A tight-lipped smile crossed Bryan's face then. I smiled as well. "Well, I should go inside. I'll see you later."

He nodded and I got out of the car.

I got to the porch, turned just as I saw him start to drive away, watching until he reached the stop sign at the end of the street, where he turned left. Then it was just me and André. I'm sure he had something to say about it. I just wasn't sure if I wanted to hear it.

When I looked at him, I knew for certain that I didn't want to hear it. His eyebrows were raised, his eyes shone with a teasing curiosity and he wore a huge grin. An *I-got-you* grin. "So?" He urged.

"So, what?"

When he didn't say anything more, I pushed past him and headed into the house. It was late, mom was still up, I could tell from the pots banging around in the kitchen. "What's my mom up to?"

"I have no idea. She was mumbling something to herself, I couldn't hear what though," André told me.

I gave a small nod and then went in to let my mom know that I had returned. "Hey, you okay?"

In the kitchen, my mom looked as though she were rearranging. But at this hour? Currently, she was kneeling on the floor in front of the cupboard in the corner and she was moving the pots further into the back. As far back as they could, but it was already full and organized from the last time it had been cleaned out. What was I missing?

"Yeah, I'm okay," mom told me but she didn't sound so sure. "It's just, I was looking for a pot today when I was making dinner and I couldn't find it. So I decided to do a bit of rearranging. It's nothing."

She sounded so insistent, so why did I get a bad feeling in the pit of my stomach that told me something bad was going to happen?

"Anyway, how was your date?" She asked, coming up and taking a seat next to me at the island.

"Well, one, it wasn't a date. Two, it was good," I reveal. "I learned a lot about him. There is a whole other side of him that the kids at school don't know about."

"Like what?"

"The little things."

So I told her everything I had learned, outright and indirectly. The things that I had inferred were the things that I was a whole lot more interested in. He had to be good with kids. He was very gentle, I learned that by how he held my hand or how he had held me close to him when the wind had picked up a little. He had been so gentle and kind. He was also honest. When I asked him questions about his past, embarrassing stories, for the most part, he told me each one of them. In detail. Those things, the little things that I learned about him had me starting to feel something for him that I would never have thought I would.

I, now, knew what the other girls felt when they had started to fall for him.

"Awe," mom crooned when I finished.

I couldn't help feeling the blush as it graced my cheeks and highlighted them a deep shade of red.

Mom chuckled. "Alright, well, you must be tired. I'll let you get to sleep. I'll be done soon and then I'll go to sleep too. I promise."

"Okay."

We bid each other good night and then I headed up the stairs and got ready for bed. I put on a pair of pyjama shorts and a pink cami, brushed my teeth and hair, before slipping under my covers. That night, sleep came to me slowly, but when it finally came, it was peaceful.

❦ Two ❧

The next morning, I was woken by the sound of someone knocking on my door. Hard pounds that sound very close. "What?" I groaned aloud, jerking up to a half sitting, half lying down position. I glared at the door, at whoever was behind it.

"Honey, I'm sorry to wake you so early but I was just wondering if you could take André around town so he can deliver his résumés."

Sleepily, I groaned again, looking over at my alarm clock. 7:03.

"Janessa?" Mom asked again when I didn't say anything.

"Fine. Can I go back to sleep now?"

"Sure."

I thought I heard a chuckle from the other side of the door but I let it go, as I nestled my head on my pillow again. I fell asleep.

Beep! Beep!

It was my alarm. This time I was able to suppress a groan as my hand came out and smacked the snooze button. I rubbed my face, checked the time — 8:01, — and looked up at my ceiling. The first thought I had was that I hadn't finished all of my homework last night. I remember having finished my English and the majority of my math homework in the free period, but there was still a stack on my desk that I knew I needed to tackle today.

So I climbed out of bed and began to get ready for what the morning may hold.

I pulled out a pair of skinny jeans from my closet, a crimson blouse that I needed to tie at the front and a pair of white ankle socks. Only on weekends did I decide to dress up a little bit more, something that Natalie had begun to berate me for. She thought I should dress a little fancier at school as well. Show people that I am more than my brain. Or at least that's what she says. I didn't agree.

When I was dressed and ready for the day, I headed downstairs and found André sitting at the dining room table with a bowl of cereal. He barely looked up at me as I entered. "I was meaning to ask, how was your date last night?"

Startled, I jumped about a foot in the air at the sound of his voice. With a hand on my heart and the other gripping the edge of the counter behind me, I waited for a beat. Long enough for my heart rate to go back to normal.

"You're jumpy today," he noted, scooping cereal into his mouth.

I shook my head a little, he laughed. I ignored the *jumpy* comment. "You know, I wish people would stop calling it that." I got a bowl from the cupboard behind me. "It wasn't a date and it was good."

"That's all I get?" He looked almost offended as if he had actually expected me to give him more details.

"Well, what more do you want to know?" I asked, pouring Froot Loops into my bowl; then adding milk to it.

"What did you guys do?"

"We hung out at the Dropoff and we just talked."

He raised an eyebrow. "The Dropoff?" His face lit with recognition then. "You mean the cliff where people go to have sex?"

I didn't need to respond to give him all the answers he wanted. It was strange how quickly he had become accustomed to this town and the popular hangouts. Especially, considering he didn't have any friends. He hadn't tried to make any and spent more time having lunch with Natalie and me than he did going out and being the friendly person that I know he is, deep deep *deep* down.

"I am going to assume that you guys didn't do anything that's worth my time, right?"

"If it's not worth your time, stop asking about it," I spat.

On my way to the table, I noticed a sticky note on the fridge in my mom's handwriting.

Janessa,
Don't forget to take André out today. He's got his résumés all ready to go. Thanks. -Mom

Great, I had that to look forward to, I thought, plucking the note from the fridge and taking it with me. "Apparently I am taking you to the businesses in town," I said, not expecting a response. I stuck the note on the table in between us.

He just nodded. "Apparently. I told her I could just go out on my bike but she thought I needed you to take me around. Give me the tour, or something." He rolled his eyes and lifted his bowl to his lips to drink the milk. Or rather, slurp the milk. Noisily.

"Is that really necessary?" I glared at him.

"Well, since it bothers you," he said, noting my reaction, "yes. It is definitely necessary." He finished slurping his milk and then got up to dispose of the bowl and spoon. "Let me know when you're ready to go."

I gave him a two finger salute as he disappeared up the stairs. I went back to my breakfast, enjoying it in peace.

❦

By noon, André and I had gone all over town. To every business that was hiring. He had spent most of the time sulking in my car as I drove, even when I gave him the so-called tour. Showing him where the movie theatre was — on the edge of town, — the road to the Dropoff, the school — he already knew where that was, but we were driving past it, — *A Slice of Heaven*, etc. He huffed and puffed every now and again, and that seemed to be the only evidence I had that he was even still alive.

At noon, I pulled into the *A Slice of Heaven* parking lot and headed inside with André.

A Slice of Heaven was owned by Natalie's mom, Olivia. The four of us — Olivia, Natalie, my mom, and I — work here together, along with a couple others. Some were great, others were less motivated. I learned that it wouldn't matter where you go, you would always find one person in an establishment to have more enthusiasm and then there were those that made it obvious that there are hundreds of other places they would rather be.

A Slice of Heaven was a cross between a cute little bakery and a sandwich shop, which seemed like an odd combination but it soon became the norm. Its interior was painted the lightest of yellows with pictures on the walls of some of Mrs. Liese favourite paintings. Natalie had told me that when Olivia was first opening the shop, she would go to every secondhand store, vintage shop, garage sale just to see if they had any paintings worth her time. And for cheap. There were five booths, three along one wall and two on the other. There were several little tables littering the floor, with customers sitting in them enjoying a sandwich or a slice of delicacy.

There was also a karaoke station on one side of the wall that was empty now, but most nights it was the most favoured hotspot to our loyal customers.

I peeked around the lineup into the back to see if I could see my mom. Sure enough, she was there, flattening a slab of dough with a rolling pin. Judging from the spices on the counter around her, she was making the cinnamon buns that were quite popular among the crowds that showed up. When she worked, she always made sure that there were plenty of cinnamon buns to go around when she left. I've always thought that was due to the fact that she just didn't want to tell me the secret ingredient.

But who could say for sure?

The line moved slowly. André and I stayed quiet. He was on his phone, playing Tetris. Today he let his hair fall around his shoulders. He wore a grey undershirt with a black button up shirt over the top that he had left unbuttoned, and black jeans with his black boots. I don't think he would know how to let loose if he tried, it was always the same style, same clothes, so dark. I wondered what he would do when it got hot out.

"Hey."

The voice was behind me. I turned around and saw Bryan standing there with a little girl. Cute little pigtails fell over her shoulders. She wore shorts and a pullover sweater with a big blue dragon animatedly walking alongside a smaller pink dragon. *Hm, Dragon Tales. Didn't know kids these days watched that.*

"Hey," I said to Bryan and the little girl.

Bryan looked me up and down, taking in my appearance. It was enough to get me to try to cover up a bit. I pulled at the hem of my shirt, my fingers itching to undo the knot. Bryan chuckled.

He stepped closer to me. "You look nice," he spoke softly. His voice was low.

"Thanks," I breathed. After a moment when I was just staring into his green eyes, I cleared my throat. I introduced the two boys on either side of me. André gave him a small smile and turned back to the counter as the line moved up. Bryan just smiled. We all moved up and he introduced me to the little girl at his side. His sister, Anna.

"Hello, Anna." I bent down and held a hand out to her. "It's nice to meet you."

"You too," was all she said. She didn't even shake my hand.

I smiled and straightened again. Turning to stand next to André. We ordered our food and found an empty booth to sit in. When I asked him questions about his past since I didn't know him all that well, he seemed hesitant to comply. He would either shrug or answer with one-word answers.

When we finished, we threw out our garbage.

"I'm just going to walk home," André told me, already heading toward the door. I followed him, asked him to wait for me but he just shook his head. "Janessa? I want to walk, okay?"

"Okay."

It seemed like such a strange request but I granted it, letting him go. His behaviour wasn't as strange as I once would have thought. Now it was just something I could expect from a foster kid. He was distant, untrusting, a little too independent for a fifteen-year-old. He never asked my mom or me for anything and only accepted the most basic of things, like food, a bed, a roof over his head. He hasn't tried to steal anything. Yet. There was still time.

"Janessa?"

I jumped a foot into the air at the sound of someone else's voice from behind me. Turning, I see Bryan clutching his chest and chuckling. "I honestly don't see what's so funny." Ironically, I was laughing too. I swatted at his arm when he didn't stop, even when my laughter started to die down.

"You scare so easily," he commented.

"Your sister seems..." I searched for the right word. She didn't talk to me much when he introduced her to me. He lifted a brow then, waiting. "I mean, she's cute."

He nodded. "She is."

I smiled and silence fell upon us.

"Hey, listen, so I'm free tonight if you, maybe, want to get together again," he said.

I felt my smile fall from my face as I knew what I had to do. After last night, I really wanted to say yes to hanging out. He was really fun and for a while, I had forgotten that I was this weird, shy girl in school with a bad past. He made me forget that for a while and made me feel like I could let loose and just be normal, whatever that meant. But when he asked this, I knew I had to say no. "I just have to finish some leftover homework and then I've got work."

"Where do you work?"

I pointed to the building behind him, lifting my gaze to the bakery's sign. "*A Slice of Heaven.*"

He nodded once, almost seemed disappointed. "Ah. Well, then, maybe I'll see you later."

"Yeah, sure."

Then he was gone.

⋘❦⋙

Around 4:30, I started to get ready for work. I pulled my thick hair into a ponytail and then decided against it, twisting my hair into a bun and securing it with pins.

On my way out of my room, I saw the list that I had started to make. I hadn't added anything new to the five things that I already had on the page. I knew Natalie would have a few ideas, so I folded up the list and tucked it into my purse. Maybe I would jot down a few of her ideas if I liked them.

At work, Natalie and Amy were already there. So was Trevor. He was busy bussing tables, with that ever-present pout on his face. Amy was chatting Natalie's ear off about her new piercing. I saw her pointing to her ear several times, her arms waving around comically. Natalie had the *shoot-me* look. And I would, just to put her out of her misery — if I wouldn't miss her when she was gone.

I sent her an apologetic smile as I walked past. My mom was in the back pulling a pan of cinnamon buns out of the oven, and chatting with Anita.

I put my purse and my sweater on the hook in the back and wash my hands.

"Hey, honey," mom said. "How'd it go with André?"

"Good. I think he has a really good shot, but…" I didn't want to say anything. I'm sure he would think I was trying to interfere in his way of life if I told my mom how worried about him I was.

"But?"

"I don't know. Never mind." Mom looked like she was going to argue and beg me to tell her what was on my mind but then we heard Natalie shout that we were low on cinnamon buns.

I was in the front with Natalie as we worked together to make the sandwiches, especially when it started to get busy and two hands had become more of a necessity.

It wasn't long before we were closing up.

Natalie had left a couple hours before and it was just me and Amy.

"So, basically, it didn't hurt nearly as much as I thought it would," Amy was telling me as we exited the building.

The piercing that she had gotten. She had gone on and on about it while we closed and was continuing to talk my ear off. Luckily though, when we stepped out, I saw Natalie waiting for me.

"Sorry, Amy. I gotta go." I gave her an apologetic look before quickly darting toward Natalie, waving at Amy over my shoulder. "Oh, my god…"

"I know." Natalie nodded. "I swear, that girl loves to hear herself talk." I got into Natalie's car. We had decided that we would go get some ice cream before she gave me a ride home. "But, it did give me an idea."

"What is that?"

"Maybe we should get our cartilages pierced. Oh, come on!" She must have seen the look on my face because she continued. "I'm just saying, it could be a fun thing to do. Besides, my mom would get angry with me if I got another piercing."

"Shouldn't that be a reason *not* to do it?"

Natalie already had a couple piercings. Two on both her ears and a belly button. She usually showed that off more at school than anywhere else. But now she wanted another one? Her cartilage, no less?

"No, because if she's angry with me than she would be paying attention to *me* instead of her stupid fights with dad." If she were a cartoon character, steam would be billowing from her ears. I think she was just angry that her parents were too busy bickering with each other, to bother trying to raise their only child. Her jaw tensed.

I noticed.

She let out a breath. "Besides, I just think it would be fun."

We pulled into the parking lot in front of the ice cream shop. We both got out. I couldn't help but think about the single piercing in both my ears. I had little snowflake earrings dangling from the holes. It was almost boring really. *And* I had decided to get out of my comfy little nook this month, experience something new.

"Alright," I told Natalie as we stood in line.

"Alright, what?" She asked a little distracted. When she turned her gaze from the menu in front of us to my face, she understood. "Oh! Really?" She grinned from ear to ear.

"Why not? Could be fun?" I shrugged, but deep down, I was nervous. I suddenly had knots in my stomach just at the idea of going to get a hole punched out my cartilage. But in a good way.

Natalie and I stayed there for a little while longer just talking and adding things to the list.

The Game

Get a cartilage piercing
Get a tattoo
Say yes to something you would never do
— It also cannot be on this list

But later that night, as she pulled into my driveway, I noticed another car sitting there. A black Honda. I didn't recognize it. It didn't belong to anyone that I knew. But the car didn't give me a good feeling. All the giddiness and happiness I had felt only an hour ago evaporated.

Maybe the car belongs to the neighbour's guests, I thought. As much as I wanted to believe that, I couldn't.

I said my goodbyes to Natalie and got out, making my way to the door. The closer to the building I got, the more anxious I felt. And when I opened the door, I knew I wasn't overreacting.

There in my living room sat the man that was responsible for all my nightmares. The reason some of my fears were so deeply embedded in me. The reason I sometimes felt paralyzed. The reason I was always so jumpy.

Thomas Maxwell.

Or otherwise known as… my father.

❧ *Three* ❧

It has been thirteen years since I last saw Thomas. I was five then, so all my memories of the man were viewed through terrified toddler eyes. But looking at him now, I could see that he hasn't changed a bit.

"Ah, there she is," he said when he saw me standing in the doorway. He was smiling like he was genuinely happy to see me.

I didn't know how I felt seeing him now. I hardly knew him but there were things I wanted to say to him. I wanted to tell him what it had been like to know that he had left me and my mom without even a backwards glance. I wanted to tell him how much mom had struggled to make a good life for us. I wanted him to understand what he'd put us through.

Mom always had a talent for baking and always wanted to open a bakery for herself, but after she and Thomas got married, she'd put her dream on hold. Or she'd let her dream take a backseat to her life with him. Whenever I asked about him, she didn't lie.

So she told me everything.

How he had made sure that she would never be able to follow her dream. When she got pregnant with me at eighteen, she was just graduating and decided to put college off for a year. But then they got married and the next thing she knew, she was a stay at home wife and mother, her dreams crushed by the man that she had vowed to stand by for life. Everything she had was never truly hers. Then, after he left, the house we had lived in was raided; everything, gone.

Even her bank account had been completely wiped clean.

The Game

We had moved in with my mom's younger sister who had just left home as well. Mom tried to find work and even found a mediocre job just to contribute something. I started school and then my aunt got sick, so it was up to my mom. But with one paycheck, it wasn't enough and then we got evicted a few months after. I remember having to move in with my grandmother because we had nowhere else to go. My mom still worked hard. She got a second job and only spent time with me on the weekends. My grandma took me to school and picked me up. A lot of the time it was my grandmother that dealt with my nightmares of my father, which only added to her worries.

Mom and grandma fought constantly which only stressed my aunt out. She had a rare form of cancer called myocardial sarcoma, or heart cancer. They had tried to remove it but it had already spread and chemotherapy didn't help. She died a few months later. Even as a child, a six-year-old, I decided that one day I would become a doctor to help people like my aunt. To be better than my father.

The summer that I turned seven, we moved here, where we met Olivia Liese. She took pity on my mom and gave her a job. My mom did night classes at a community college so she would never be away from me in case I needed her. She had worked so hard to get to where she is now. *I* have worked hard so I'm not like the man in my nightmares. Then he shows up out of nowhere, standing in our living room as though none of that had happened. As though he's not to blame for all that's happened. It's not fair!

I looked over to where mom sat in an armchair. It was just to the right of our three seater sofa. She had a glass of wine in her hand, and she refused to look at me. She knew how I felt about this man and all the trouble he had caused us, on purpose or otherwise.

"Janessa," my father said, reaching toward me. He successfully took hold of my arms. "It's so good to see you again." He pulled me to his chest and hugged me; it did nothing to comfort me.

I was tense in his arms and my neck prickled with fear.

Slowly, I reached up and I put a hand in between us. He didn't fight it, he let me go. "Mom," I called to her. She lifted her head in acknowledgement. "I'm gonna go to bed." I walked around my father to kiss my mom goodnight and headed up the stairs.

I changed into my pjs, a pair of white cotton shorts with little watermelon on them and a pink cami. I let my hair loose, running a brush through it quickly. I took out my contacts and slipped on my big black-rimmed glasses. Then I climbed into bed with my chemistry textbook and notebook and began skimming my notes.

❧❦❧

It was an hour and half of going over my notes when I heard something hit my window. It sounded very small, the *pings* making that all the more obvious. I felt cheesy when my first guess was tiny pebbles. I looked up from my textbook and many notes that I have rewritten and simplified for studying purposes and looked over at my window. It was covered with a see-through, light pink curtain. The moonlight casting a soft glow on my floor.

Ping.

A little annoyed now, I got out of bed and headed toward my window, lifting it to open it. There, in my side yard, was Bryan with his hand curved ever-so-slightly as if he was carefully holding something in his right hand.

"Bryan?" I asked into the night. "What are you doing here?"

"I needed to ask you a question."

"And you couldn't wait until morning?" I wondered.

"Well, I could've." He sounded very hesitant to continue now. "But," he said the word a bit forceful, "I wasn't going to be able to sleep until I knew your answer."

Uh oh, what could he possibly find so important that he had to venture out of his safe and warm home, just to come here in the middle of the night? He had to be crazy. Then, just to avoid hearing his question, I asked one of my own. Something that just dawned on me.

"How'd you know this was my room and not someone else's?"

I think I saw him shrug. "It was the only one with a light on, so I took the chance."

"So, what's your question then?" I asked, moving to sit on the edge of my windowsill.

"Can you come down so I don't have to keep shouting?"

I chuckled. Then agreed to it. "Meet me at the front door." He nodded once. I closed my window and tiptoed down the stairs. Thomas was still there, now fast asleep on the couch. Beside him, though, on the coffee table, I saw a bottle of whiskey, opened and half empty. I could not believe this was happening. I shook my head in anger, at him for being here, at my mom for letting him stay, at myself for not saying anything.

As my foot hit the last step, it creaked slightly under my weight and I froze. I heard Thomas move, grumbling to himself. But he was still fast asleep, thankfully.

I slowly crept outside where Bryan was already leaning against the large post on our porch.

"Hey," I greeted him softly now that I could clearly see him. He looked very comfortable in a pair of grey sweats and a white v-neck tee. His hair was tousled beautifully, one little lock of hair fell in front of his face and I really wanted to do something about it. Somehow, I was able to keep my hands to myself.

"Hey." He smiled, pushing himself off of the post and came toward me, his hand outstretched as he took my hand in his. His hand was just as soft as I remembered from last night. How was it so soft? "So, my question was, will you, Janessa Reynolds," Bryan started, and got down on one knee; my eyes widened like saucers, "be my girlfriend?"

There was a moment where I paused, just one second when it was so quiet, you could hear a pin drop. Then, I burst out laughing.

"What?"

"Nothing." I cleared my throat and took deep breaths. "You want me to be your girlfriend?"

He just nodded, still on his one knee, waiting for me to give him something more than that. An actual answer.

Then looking into his glittering green eyes, and at that moment, I felt nothing. No pressure from someone else. Free, almost weightless.

So, a part of me wasn't surprised when I heard the word slip from my lips, "Sure."

❦

"Don't hate me," Natalie started when I answered my phone the next morning. I barely heard her as I looked over me to the alarm clock. It was 10:42.

"Why would I hate you?"

"I made an appointment at the tattoo parlour a town over." Now I was awake. She did *what*? I sat up as I waited for her stupid pause to end. "For tomorrow."

"*What?*"

I had no idea she wanted to do it so soon. I didn't even know what I wanted to get done.

"About that, I was thinking we could get matching tattoos," she told me.

"Of what?"

She explained to me what she was thinking. She thought we could get our tattoos on our wrists. Her's would say, *She Keeps Me Safe.* And she thought that I might like *She Keeps Me Wild* to be mine. I had to admit that it was cute. But I really would have liked to have more time to think about it and mentally prepare myself. Whatever I would get would be on my body for life.

"Nat?" I waited for her to stop talking before I continued, "Did you ever think that maybe, just maybe, I would have liked to come up with my tattoo myself?"

"Well, sure but I figured that you'd probably delay it so long that we'd never do it."

"Well, sure, I'd be altering my skin forever. I would have liked to have had time to think about it at great length."

"Fine," she conceded, "I'm sorry. I was also thinking that my friend and your friend, Bryan, could come with us. For moral support."

"I thought that we would be each other's support."

"Not if we get them done at the same time with two different artists."

"I see," I mumbled. "Speaking of Bryan."

I filled her in on my decision to date Bryan. She seemed very thrilled at the idea. A little more thrilled than I had thought was necessary but I let it go because there was a sound at my door that got all my attention almost immediately. "Hey, I gotta go, okay?"

"Okay, bye. Talk to you later."

"Yeah, bye."

I threw my phone on my bed and went to my door, pulling it open to find Thomas standing on the other side. He had a smile on his face. "Good morning, sweetie."

Once again, I was frozen in place. Just staring at him. And again, there was so much I wanted to tell him. So much about what he had caused, so much hurt and anger. The words were on the tip of my tongue and I wanted to say it, all of it, but my mouth and my brain refused to work. I wanted him to understand what my mom had been through when he left. But I also wanted him to leave, because he may have caused a lot of discord back then, but she was happy now. She was finally right where she wanted to be and I could just imagine him ruining all of it.

"I made breakfast, want some?" He asked. "Or brunch, since it's almost lunch."

"I have work," was the first thing I had said to him since I saw him again. And the last thing that was spoken between the two of us before I closed the door on him. I let out a breath and looked over at my alarm clock to see that it was indeed 11:15. I had time but he didn't know that.

⋙❦⋘

Thomas was still there the next day. He even offered to drive me to school, which I quickly declined. André and I walked out of the house together but then he got on his bicycle and left just as Natalie pulled up in front of my house.

Usually, the school was a safe haven for me but today, every time I looked up at the clock, I watched its hands move very quickly. Even my heart was racing nervously in my chest and my stomach was all full of knots. Natalie wanted to leave at the beginning of lunch, which would give us a good two hours, at least. The three of them were skipping class but I had a free period after lunch so not all my morals were being compromised.

When the bell signalling lunch rang, I felt like running to my locker and hiding but unfortunately, Natalie had already thought of that. She was waiting there, leaning up against the locker next to mine. Beside her was James Garcia, Bryan's best friend. I couldn't see Bryan. Maybe he was outside already, I thought as I finally got to my locker.

I opened and put my books inside of it.

"And there she is!" I heard someone behind me say before I felt a pair of arms drop over my shoulder. I turned my head slightly to see a grinning Bryan looking back at me.

"Hey…" I singsonged a little awkwardly. I know Natalie knew that I had decided to date him but seeing such affection as this, as he drew me closer to him, I felt a little awkward and shy.

"Alright, we gotta go if we want to make it for our appointment," Natalie said.

I really wanted to say that I didn't want to go today but I didn't have time to. Bryan's hand slid down my arm and he grabbed my hand, dragging me down the hallway. James followed but Natalie took her time to lock my locker the way I like it.

❧ ❦ ☙

When we got to the tattoo parlour fifteen minutes later, I was sitting in the back of the car.

Bryan held my hand the whole time and he sat in the middle of the three seats in the back just so he could put his arm around my shoulders. I spent the whole time with my head on his chest, surrounded by his scent. Which wasn't *so* bad. Because of him, I wasn't so focused on what I was about to do.

The Game

We all went into the building. I gripped Bryan's hand for support, but the way he grinned at me made me think he knew how freaked out I was.

"Wait here," Natalie told me, leaving me by the small lounge. It had three chairs, and a coffee table, magazines and artist portfolios. She and James go up the counter and talked with one of the employees. I sat down while the knot in my stomach grew worse.

"Hey, you okay?"

Bryan sat down beside me, his arm behind me on the chair.

"I'm fine," I grumbled, just watching Natalie and James. I leaned my head back on the chair, hitting his arm, having completely forgotten about it. Immediately, I jerked up and leaned forward on my knees.

He chuckled. "You're cute."

"You know, for a guy that's supposed to know what girls like, you have forgotten that girls don't like to be called cute."

"I have not. Most girls don't, but I get the feeling that you're different." He looked at me, lifting his hand and brushing his fingers along my cheek. It left a trail of warm tingles in its wake. I could feel myself blush, and he chuckled. "Besides, I just really wanna kiss you. Can't stop thinking about it, in fact." He leaned forward as well now.

I felt my cheeks heat up even more just at the thought of his lips touching mine. Mostly because if he were to kiss me, it would be my first kiss. Just as he was my first boyfriend, I have never kissed or been kissed, not even for a dare.

I looked over at him. There was a gleam in his eye, an excitement that scared me just a little. I wanted to slide over but I couldn't without Natalie noticing — now that her stare was pinned to me — and have her questioning me. She would pester me with questions until I told her. It was because of her insistence that I have completely given up trying to surprise her for her birthday or Christmas. Unless it was last minute, she would be able to get it out of me.

So instead, I just turned my gaze from Natalie to Bryan. "You know, I'm not sure you will," I challenged.

"What's that supposed to mean?"

"I mean that I'm surprised you asked me out to begin with and I can't help but think that someone told you to." I looked into his eyes to see if he would lie to me and say that wasn't true. I figured the eyes would be the best bet since they were the window to the soul. But he revealed nothing. "If you were to kiss me, it would be because someone told you when to do it."

The smile on his face grew a little. "Babe," — now my stomach was in knots for a whole other reason, not to mention the sudden attack of butterflies — "you offend me."

I tried to stay cool, keeping my voice steady. "So, you're not denying it?"

He was silent for a minute. Rubbed his chin with his forefinger and thumb. "You really think that I won't kiss you? And if I were to, it'd be because someone told me to?"

"Good to know your ears work," I mumbled mostly to myself.

"One of these days I am going to prove you wrong."

"Yeah, you wanna bet?"

It was another challenge, but not one he was able to accept right away because Natalie and James came back to sit on the other two chairs that were left open. Bryan and I had gotten to the two-person chair.

"It has been paid for and they're just setting up." She turned to me then. "You excited?"

I shrugged. "Not so much excited as nervous."

She smiled.

"Wait, what do you mean it's paid for?"

"I mean, it's my treat."

I balked. "*What?*"

"Oh, come on, relax. If I had let you go up there, you could have told them to not go ahead with it."

"That's not true," I rebuttal. "Fine, but I'm paying for the piercing."

She nodded, accepting it as a win. "Do you want to see the pictures that I gave to them?" She waved her arm around, gesturing at the building we were in.

The Game

"Okay."

She opened her phone and went through her images before she came upon two with the same script. "You said mine was the *She Keeps Me Wild*, right?"

She nodded. "What do you think?"

"It's cute. I liked it," I told her honestly. "But now we have to stay friends because I would not want that to be a sad reminder of a bitter end to a friendship."

They all laughed. I chuckled a little, looking at the pictures.

She Keeps Me Safe
She Keeps Me Wild

A few minutes later, two artists came out and invited us into their stations. Bryan followed me into one and James followed Natalie. The room looked very clean, sterile even. That was a good sign. There was a black dentist-like chair, which I quickly sat in and looked at the artist, who was covered in tattoos.

"What's your name?" I asked when he turned toward me with a swivelly table where he held a vial of paint with the tattoo gun next to it. It had to be attached to the machine behind him, which I'm sure he would do any minute.

"My name's Jared," he told me.

"I'm Janessa. Nice to meet you."

He nodded once in acknowledgement.

"Where do you want it?"

"Right wrist," I told him, lying my arm down on the extended arm next to me.

"Alright," he said and then got to work, laying down a purple stencil of the tattoo on my arm. It actually looked really good, I liked it. And just looking at it, there, on my arm, felt right. "How's that?"

"It's good," I told him and he fired up the gun. "Wait." I breathed, preparing myself for the gun. Then I nodded and he got to work. The needles biting into my skin, leaving a trail of black ink behind. It felt like getting a hundred needles all at once. He wiped away pools of ink which left behind a smudge but also left the tattoo permanently etched into my skin.

There was no backing out now.

The whole first bit, I spent breathing through my nose and holding Bryan's hand tightly. He had taken my hand first when I had sucked in a sharp breath at the beginning and neither of us had bothered to let go.

By the end of the experience, Jared wrapped up my arm and told me to keep it wrapped for a minimum of four hours or overnight. I nodded and took in his recommendations before thanking him and walking out with Bryan behind me.

Four

After school, Bryan took me home. We had decided to do homework together. He thought he really needed help with math so I offered. I don't know why because I am a terrible teacher. But when we walked across the threshold, I saw my father sitting on the couch on the phone, talking about... something in hushed tones. He looked up when he heard me, scowled and waved for us to leave.

He didn't have to tell me twice.

I walked out immediately. Bryan looked confused but had the good graces not to ask about it. The door shut behind us and that is when I released the breath I had started to hold when I saw my father. I really wished I knew why he was here and what he could possibly want.

Bryan and I went to the library. We found an empty table in the far back corner where most people didn't usually venture. I sat down but was too absorbed in my curiosities with Thomas that I didn't pull out my books right away. Bryan did, however, and was baffled when I didn't.

"Hey, you want to talk about it?"

I shook my head. I wouldn't even know where to begin and what parts I could leave out, so I didn't show how damaged I really was. "No, I'm good." I took my books out then.

I helped Bryan with the questions he had trouble with and somehow made it sound easier than it was, and helped him to understand it in a way his teacher apparently couldn't.

A couple hours later, I had completed a decent amount of homework that I felt somewhat accomplished.

"Hey, so listen," Bryan started, waiting for me to look up at him. "There's a carnival in town. I was wondering if you wanted to come with me."

"Why?" I asked.

"I want to hang out with you and get to know you." He stepped closer. "I want to know what makes you tick. Your fears," — *That one was easy, my father,* I thought — "your ambitions, your *pleasure* points," he said the last one in a low voice. I felt myself blush, I was having a little trouble breathing and it only then dawned on me that he had gotten closer. His hand was on the small of my back and he had pulled me against him.

I had been so focused on what he was saying that I hadn't even felt his big hand on my body. I took a deep breath and put a hand on his chest, pushing him backwards slightly. He lifted a brow.

"Personal bubble," I explained.

"Well, I am about to pop it," he said, stepping forward again and cornering me against the wall.

I laughed. "I'd like to see you try," I told him, pushing him back again and starting to pack up my books.

He just smiled. "So, what do you say? Me and you, the carnival?"

I wanted to say no again but then I looked at him. He had a cute little pout on his face.

"Please?"

"Okay, fine, but only because you're cute."

He put a hand on his chest, feigning a heartache. "I'm not cute. I am sexy."

And cocky, I thought.

"Any girl would be lucky to have my full attention."

"Is that why all the girls run when they see you?" I asked.

"Feisty." Pause. "That's hot. I like it." He was grinning now. "Well, now you have to go with me because you just hurt my feelings," he joked.

I laughed humourlessly. "I already said I would go. But first, I need to go home."

"Right."

Bryan took me home.

When I walked inside, I went to the bathroom and took off the bandage around my tattoo and took out the aftercare kit. There was a little card with information on the proper aftercare instructions. I followed it exactly.

Then I wore something comfortable and something I knew that Bryan would approve of. A jean skirt above a pair of black tights cut off at the knees, a black button-front cropped cami, and a loose grey cardigan to let my new tattoo breath. I grabbed a pair of sandals that I've only worn a couple of times. I drop them off at the door before heading into the kitchen.

"Hey," I greet my mom, "where's Thomas?"

"He went out. And he would not appreciate you calling him anything but 'dad'."

"Well, I am not going to call him 'dad' because he's not my dad. He gave up that right a *long* time ago."

Mom pulled out dishes from the cupboard and added silverware to the pile. "Well, you could at least talk to him."

"I did, yesterday."

"You said three words," she said, going to the table and setting the plates down. "Three words does not a conversation make." Then she looked at me. "Your dad told me about it."

"Mom?" I started, going to lean up against the doorframe. "Why are you so okay with him being here?"

"I'm not." She shook her head.

"Then why-"

I was interrupted by the doorbell as it rang, signalling Bryan's arrival. André bounded down the stairs, pulling the door open. "Oh, it's you." I could hear André's disappointment from here. Who could he be expecting?

I look back to mom. "I can stay in tonight if you want."

"No, honey," she quickly said. "No, go. Have fun. But be careful."

I gave a small hesitant nod, went over to her and kissed her cheek. "Okay, bye." I hurried to the stairs and slipped on my shoes, buckling them on the side.

"All I am saying is I'll kill you if you hurt my sister," André was saying to Bryan.

I rolled my eyes at his faux protection. "André, leave Bryan alone." I hooked my purse onto my shoulder and pushed past him, out the door. "Let's go, Bryan."

❦

"You know, I've never actually been to a carnival before," I admitted, as we pulled into a parking space near the carnival's entrance.

"Really?" He looked at me in disbelief. "Well, allow me to be your guide."

I got out of the car and he followed my lead. Once I got close to him, he took my hand and led me through the throng of people to the entrance. He pulled out cash for our entrance fee, even denied my offer to pay for it. He bought a whole roll of coupons.

"Geez, how long are we staying?" I asked.

He laughed. "Come on." He wrapped an arm around my shoulders.

There was an assortment of vendors selling different types of food, funnel cakes, candy apples, fried pickles, etcetera. There were tons of games with stuffed animals as prizes. It was all very cheesy, but as I took it all in — the fatty food smells, the sweet cotton candy, the loud chatter of everyone enjoying the festivities and the vendors, and the excitement that left a buzz in the air — I was truly happy.

Bryan and I stopped at the beanbag toss and slapped down a couple coupons. Enough to buy a few rounds. He let me go first, which only left him disappointed because I landed the shot with perfect precision.

He scowled. "Okay, that was beginner's luck."

"Was it really?" I asked rhetorically as he stepped up to take his shot. And missed.

"Definitely. It was definitely beginner's luck."

I took the next shot and it landed just on the edge of the hole. "Maybe," I conceded.

"So, where did you learn to throw like that?" He stepped up.

"Math," I answered just as he threw his bag. The answer startled him so much that the bean bag landed on the ground a few feet in front of the target. I laughed. "Aren't you supposed to be good at this?"

"In my defence, these beanbags are tiny."

"Right," I sarcastically agreed, "I'm sure that's the problem."

"Were you serious about math teaching you to throw?"

"No, I was kidding." I tossed, another in. "When I was growing up, my mom did the whole tossing-a-ball-in-the-backyard thing. When she had time."

It hadn't happened often but when she was able to set aside some free time with me, we would go back there and we would just spend a couple hours throwing a baseball back and forth. I cherished those little moments with my mom.

"I noticed that you don't talk about your dad much," he commented, picking up a beanbag and taking a go at it. "Why?"

I just looked at him and wondered how much he would be able to handle. As I looked at him, I realized I didn't want to scare him away. I licked my lips. So I decided to answer his question as honestly as possible. "Uh, well, my parents' marriage fell apart when I was a kid. And that was when he just up and left. Gone. One day he just packed his bags and left. That's it."

"That's awful." The way he said it sounded so genuine like he truly believed that it was awful that I had grown up without a father but then he just smiled. "You know, in a crazy way, you're pretty lucky."

Involuntarily, I scoffed. Was he serious?

"What?"

"Nothing." I shook my head and threw another bean bag in. Score! To change the subject, I said, "I just realized that I am *really* good at this."

"You just realized that?"

He took another shot, and this was his first good throw as he finally got it in the target.

"Maybe, we should do something you're good at," I suggested.

He nodded, throwing an arm around my shoulders and pulling me through the crowd. "Eating. I bet you can't eat as many corn dogs as me."

"Ooh," I sounded really excited, and then, "yeah, probably not."

"Come on, you haven't even tried."

"I have tried corn dogs. I am not a fan," I told him.

"Well, that is about to change."

He sounded so sure. I had to admit that I found his confidence attractive. I gripped his hand as he walked with determination to the stand selling the corn dogs.

He ordered a few and I found us a table. It was then that my phone beeped with a message. He was still in line, waiting for his order so I thought I had time. I checked my phone quickly.

NAT: Hey, you home?

Swiftly, I typed a message letting her know that I was not at home, that I was with Bryan. I asked her if something was wrong. There was this nagging feeling in the pit of my stomach that worried me. What if something had happened with her parents and she needed me? What if-

"I got us four corn dogs," Bryan said, sitting down beside me, balancing two of the little trays on his forearms. Carefully, he set them down.

My phone beeped again.

NAT: Nothings wrong.

She didn't say any more than that.

"You okay?"

"Yeah," I answered Bryan. "Natalie just texted me and it had me worried and now she's just being cryptic. It's nothing." To prove that I meant it, I put my phone on silent and dropped it into my purse.

"Okay."

I slid one of the trays toward me and watched as Bryan eagerly dug in. He bit into the corn dog just as I raised mine to my lips. I bit into it and sure enough, it tasted exactly as the frozen store bought corn dogs that I've had in the past. There was a small hint of it being homemade but it was so small that it was barely there.

Suddenly, two people dropped down beside me. "Hey, guys."

It was Natalie and James.

"So, I see you're both on a date," James commented with a grin.

I glanced at Bryan and saw him roll his eyes. The action looked weird when it was done by a him. "Dude, what are you doing?"

"Oh, nothing. We just have a bet about whether or not this," James gestured between me and Bryan, "was real."

Natalie was watching us carefully and smiled when she made eye contact with me. I smiled back. "Well, it is real." I leaned closer to her. "I'm offended you'd think otherwise."

She raised her hands in surrender. "I just know you very well."

"Yeah," I said slowly. "You do. So you also know that I could never lie to you."

The four of us talked for a bit. Bryan even gave up two of his corn dogs just so Natalie and James had something to snack on. Once again, I couldn't believe that people thought this guy was such an awful person. I've seen the effects on the girls he's dated, but I also know him a little better now. It all didn't add up. He was so nice and caring and sweet and gentle.

How could this amazing guy be the big bad boy that everyone loved to hate?

It was a little later when Natalie and James got up and left, bidding us goodbye. I think I managed to make Natalie believe a little that my relationship with Bryan was real. Especially when I had slid closer to him and I relaxed in his arms when he wrapped an arm around my shoulder. I saw a little smile spread across her face so I know that in a small way, I had won.

"Can I ask you something?"

I looked at Bryan, nodded.

"Why's Natalie so protective of you?"

I answered with a question of my own. "Why do you think she's so protective?"

He shrugged. "Just the way she sat so close to you. She looked like she was ready to pounce if I said anything inappropriate. I don't know."

"Let's just say that I have not had an easy childhood and she knows about it." Getting into specifics would mean I would have to tell him about the abuse that my mom and I endured with Thomas. I didn't want him to suddenly look at me like I was this damaged thing that he could no longer be around, or treat me like a freaking China doll.

"I get it," he said, which shocked me. I hadn't said much and yet he claims to get the situation. "I mean, I get where she is coming from. My sister hasn't had an easy childhood either and I'm very protective of her."

The air around us held a tinge of sadness and I didn't like it. I came out with him because he had begged to give me a good time and that meant smiles! Laughter. Not depressing frowns.

I looked around us until I saw a photo booth. "Come on." I pulled at his arm until he followed me and I led him toward it, as he had done to me the whole night.

"This is cheesy," he commented.

"Oh shut up. Get in," I instructed, pulling back the red curtain.

Bryan got inside, but not without some hesitation. He pulled me along with him by the waist and slipped in a dollar. I was sitting on his one leg, his arm never let go of my waist.

"Okay, ready for take one?" He asked.

We posed for each picture. He made sure I stayed on his lap, his arms tightening whenever I tried to move to the seat beside him. We made silly faces, serious faces, I told him a joke to make him laugh. I guffawed at his laughter. We went twice, one strip for him and one strip for me. He gave me the second one, the one where our happiness was a lot more obvious.

I had gotten comfortable on his lap, even turned slightly toward him and hugged him around the neck. There was a shot where I was kissing his cheek and if you looked closely, I swear he was blushing. Probably just my imagination, but for now I was going to take it.

"These look..." I trailed off looking for the right word.

"Amazing. We are definitely photogenic."

"Photogenic?" I asked in disbelief. Was he serious? "You've got your tongue out and your eyes crossed for this one." I pointed to my strip, picture two. "Not very photogenic if you ask me." Lie! But I wanted to see if I could deflate his ego a bit.

"Oh really. You're just jealous or vengeful, I don't know which," he said and pointed to picture number one on his strip.

My hair had been pulled in front of my face and except for the fact that my hair was dry, I looked like the Grudge.

I laughed.

We played a few more games before he took me home.

❧ Five ❧

Bryan met me at my locker the next day. He was scrolling through his phone when I saw him from down the hall. He hadn't noticed me yet but I had to stop and look. He looked amazing in a pair of grey shorts, flip-flops and a blue button-up, of which he had left the top few unbuttoned, exposing a small part of his chest.

At that moment, I couldn't believe that he was actually my boyfriend. I couldn't believe that he had *asked* me to be his girlfriend, considering how plain I was.

I had decided to dress up today a little. Short shorts, a blue button front crop cami, a light cardigan and flip-flops. I even took a few minutes to apply makeup and style to my usually boring hair. I guess a part of me didn't want him to think he had made a mistake when he had asked me to go out with him.

"Hey," he greeted when I got closer.

"Hey," I said simply. I bunched the ends of my cardigan sleeves in my hands and tried to open my locker quickly.

"You okay?" He asked. He touched the small of my back and I jumped. That only deepened his concerned expression.

"Yeah, I'm fine, why?"

"I don't know," he shrugged, "probably nothing."

I tried my combination a few times before it finally unlatched and I pulled the lock free. Swinging my locker open, I grabbed my math textbook; I quickly dropped it into the crook of my elbow.

"Hey, wanna get out of here at lunch?"

"And go where?"

"I don't know, wherever you want." He dropped an arm around my shoulders, guiding me the wrong way to my class but I let him. I had time. "Just get away from here."

"Okay," I agreed. "How about McDonald's?"

"It's a date." He grinned. He kissed my cheek, which made me blush, and then he ran off with a wave in my direction.

❦

"I remember this one time, Ness and I went to a bar. I had just gotten us fake IDs-"

"It was once and I haven't used it since," I interrupted Natalie's storytelling. James and Bryan chuckled.

We were sitting in a booth. Bryan and I sat together, our legs touching, his arm around my shoulders, my head on his chest, especially now that we've finished eating our burgers. Natalie and James were sitting as far from each other as the booth would allow, but James just couldn't keep his eyes off her. Whether she was talking or not. They had decided to tag along for some weird reason, so our 'date' had become a date with a third and fourth wheel.

"Anyway, Janessa was taking shots, a lot of them. And then she went out to the dancefloor, and she looked like she was having seizures." Natalie laughed, so did the boys.

Bryan looked at me and his eyes were questioning me now. And my dancing skills, which, by the way, are fantastic.

"Natalie, that was you," I told her sharply.

This happened a few months ago when Natalie had gotten us the fake IDs. It had been just a few weeks before her eighteenth birthday and I had been hesitant about it because I was afraid that we would get caught. But we hadn't. It was the only relief of the night. We went into the *Late Night Club* just a few towns over and she headed for the bar. I followed her, just to make sure she didn't do anything stupid. Unfortunately, I failed because apparently, alcohol makes her stronger.

She had a few shots, then a few more before she took off toward the dance floor where she had seen a few guys earlier. As she had said, I, well, *she* had looked like she was having seizures. I think it had something to do with the many bodies that were pressed up against her because, I guess she had started to get warm, so she started taking off her jacket. I was just thankful that I had gotten to her before she'd gotten her shirt over her head.

Then we left. I drove her back to my house, where my mom was heavily concerned about her. Natalie had drank a lot of water and then passed out on the couch. I had a lot of explaining to do, starting with the fake IDs, which my mom had taken and cut up.

Somehow our roles had gotten reversed in her version.

"You just think that was me."

"No, that was... That was you? Wasn't it?" Now she was confused, trying to dig through her brain for the information that she was missing.

"Nope. Not me. You know I would never drink alcohol."

I remembered putting *try alcohol* on my list, maybe that would be the one thing that I wasn't going to complete.

"One day you will," Natalie said it like it was a promise. "Bryan, you have to help me get her drunk."

To my dismay, Bryan was all too eager to help her.

I just stared at him open-mouthed.

"Sorry, babe, but I kinda want to see what you're like when you're drunk," he told me.

"I do not approve," I told him, but he didn't care. He just chuckled and brought his lips closer to me, kisses my temple, then grinned. I felt myself blush, as I lowered my gaze and stared at the leftover fries in front of me from beneath my lashes.

"Oh!" Natalie said, loudly. "Janessa, what do you want for your birthday?" I glared at her for bringing that up now, in front of the guys. She took it as a sign that I was confused as to why she was asking me, because she continued, "'Cause you know how I am. I need to buy gifts months in advance."

That was true. She always asked months in advance about my birth or Christmas. She always said that she needed that time to pick out the perfect present, but I think she's just hoping that I'll have forgotten by then.

I opened my mouth to say something but then we were interrupted by a melodious voice. "Bryan!" We all turned to see Megan Lee and her two best friends, Amber and Lynn, that were always trailing behind her. Megan looked beautiful as ever, her golden locks that fell perfectly over her shoulders. On her arm was her expensive-looking purse. She looked at everyone at the table. "Hm, since when do you let strays hang out with you?"

It wasn't hard to figure out who she was talking about. Stray? Really? I started to look for a way out of the situation, not because I couldn't fight back, but more because I didn't want to. I had known that being with Bryan would mean having to deal with all this drama but that didn't mean I had to stoop to her level.

"Good to see you too, Megan." I tried to smile but it just came out all wrong.

The fact was, I didn't like Megan. I didn't like that she was one of the girls that Bryan had been with. I didn't like that when she's around, I feel like there's no contest; that Bryan should be with her and not me. I didn't like the way she smiles at me like she knows something that I don't. Like she knows how to break me.

I'm not the kind of person to hate people without getting to know them first, but Megan was different.

And that's what I hated the most; my hatred for her.

"Oh, I never said it was good to see you," she replied coolly. She even had the audacity to slide in beside Bryan and wrap her arm around his.

To say that I felt powerless was an understatement. I just watched Bryan, waiting to see what he would do, as Megan leaned closer to him. She whispered something in his ear and laughed while he smiled back; it looked forced.

Grumbling to myself, I nibbled on some of the fries that sat in front of me. Natalie took notice but she only smiled sympathetically.

"Janessa?" I heard Megan say, which shocked me. I figured she would continue her *stray* joke. "I'm having a party this Friday, after the game. You should definitely come." She was trying to be nice but the smile she had on her face was definitely fake, though I seemed to be the only one to notice.

Hesitantly, I accepted her invite, but only because I thought it would be the end of her presence at our table. It wasn't.

⋘☙⋙

The only good part about today was my classes. It was the only place where I felt like I belonged. Where I didn't even have to try too hard. Why did I think that dating Bryan was a good idea? That was just the thing, I hadn't been thinking. I had been listening to that stupid list that I created only a few days ago. And Natalie. That's who and what I had been listening to.

But still, when he and I were alone, I really felt whole. Almost. I don't know, I just know that with him, I didn't have to try. We had fun and it was effortless. But surrounded by other people from his world, like Megan, I felt like a fish out of water.

After I accepted Megan's invite, Natalie had been excited and talking about it nonstop. Obviously, she knew that I'd invite her to come with me. I was not about to go alone. I needed someone there that would make me feel included, not just a tag along.

Bryan said he'd talk to Megan about her behaviour, not that I asked him to, or even mentioned it on the drive back to school, but he promised nonetheless. Maybe he could tell that it bothered me. Or maybe all his practice had paid off and he knew how to put his girlfriend first. I don't know which it was but I was touched that he would do that.

He dropped me off at home after school. He killed his engine and we just sat for a minute.

"You don't have to go to the party if you don't want to," he told me.

"Well, if I am being honest, I don't." I noticed his face fall. Had he been hoping that I would want to go? "But I'm sure your friends will be there and if you want to introduce me to them there, and only if you want to, I'll go."

His face lit up. "Awe, babe." He squeezed my hand affectionately, which he had been holding the whole ride over, holding my hand above the console between the two of us. "You really don't have to go, if you're not comfortable going."

"There's still time for me to back out," I told him with a smile.

"That's true," he said. He brought his free hand up to my face and he ran his thumb across my cheek. My stomach wound up in knots and the butterflies swarming furiously whenever he touched me, or when he leaned in to kiss my cheek. Or when he looked at me like I was the only girl in the world... Okay, that *had* to be a practiced look.

He dropped his hand. "Give me your phone."

"What?"

He had said it so suddenly that I was startled back to the present after getting lost in his eyes.

"Give me your phone, so I can give you my number."

"Right." I shook my head clear. Digging through my bag, I came up with my iPhone and handed it to him. "There's no password."

He unlocked my phone and created a contact for himself, even sent himself a text from my phone. I heard the chime from his pocket as the message was received. Then he handed my phone back.

"There," he said, smiling.

I smiled too. "I should go. I'll see you tomorrow."

He nodded but wasn't looking at me anymore. He had dug his phone out of his pocket and he was busy typing a message.

I got out of his car and headed up the walkway to the house. As I entered the building, my own phone dinged with a message.

BABE: Miss me yet?

I couldn't help chuckling at his message. I also wasn't surprised that he saved his contact the way that he did. It definitely had a Bryan touch to it. I was just typing back when I heard someone from the couch call to me.

"Can you get me another beer, honey?" Thomas asked.

He was sitting on the couch with his feet up on the coffee table. His smelly socks still on, stinking up the vicinity where he sat. Mom was not going to like that when she finds out.

"And a sandwich." He pointed at me as if to make it known that he was talking to *me* and not someone else. He barely looked at me as he continued, "Daddy has a meeting tonight."

André was sitting with him in the armchair to his right. If Thomas was really so incapable of making his own meal, why hadn't he asked André to do it? I knew for a fact that he was a whiz in the kitchen. I hit **SEND** on my message and couldn't help rolling my eyes, as I trudged into the kitchen.

I actually hoped his meeting would go well because, the sooner he left, the better. For everyone.

I slapped down four pieces of bread, may as well make myself one too. I made the sandwiches and even searched the fridge for a bottle of beer. There had to be one, or maybe he imagined it. I wouldn't be surprised. I mean, how had he survived without a wife for so long if he can't make himself a freaking sandwich? I found a bottle near the back of the fridge, it sat with a couple others and I grabbed it.

With his prepared sandwich and his beer in hand, I go back to the living room and hand it to him. He looks at me long enough to accept the meal and then looks back at the television screen. What? No 'thank you'? I wanted to ask. I am not his slave. Even if he seemed to think I was.

In the kitchen, I sat down at the island and pull out my books to start on my homework. My phone *dinged* then and saw a message from Bryan.

BABE: I am definitely up for a movie tonight. Pick you up at 8?

I looked at the clock on the wall behind me. That would give me a few hours to get as much done as possible, not to mention make dinner. I'll probably stay up late again tonight finishing off the rest of my homework, but oh well, I'll be out living.

ME: It's a date.

I turned my phone off and for the next little bit, I worked on my chemistry homework. But when I heard movement from behind me, I turned to see Thomas slipping on his shoes. As he was heading through the door, I remembered mom telling me to have a conversation with him. Say more than three words to him.

So I slid off the chair and ran out into the hall to catch him before he slipped out the door. "Th- Dad?" I said.

He turned around and looked annoyed. Very irritated, in fact. "What?"

"Mom told me to have a conversation with you," I said. I watched his face and all I saw was impatience. "You know, she wanted me to talk to you."

"Well, now's not a good time," he said. He smiled a tight-lipped smile. "But how about later?"

"Sure". And then he was gone.

Well, I tried. I had to get credit for that.

I went back into the kitchen and worked on my homework for a few hours until the door opened. It was a little after six when mom slipped in through the back door with a few grocery bags. She started to put them away when she really saw me and smiled.

"Hey, honey. How was school?"

"Just great," I told her. And for the most part, that was true. School had been great, except for my little encounter with the school's queen bee. You'd think that was the head cheerleader — Natalie — but it wasn't. The queen bee was Megan. She wasn't really apart of a clique. She just existed as the most desired girl in the whole school. "How was work?"

"It was good. But," she stopped to look at me, "I had this thought that the three of us could have a night in, *tonight*, as a family."

Three? Night in? Family? Me, mom, and Thomas? That sounded like a recipe for disaster.

"Well, Thomas isn't even at home, so that won't work," I told her.

"*I* meant you, me and André. I really think that he's going to be sticking around so we should make him feel as welcome as possible," she told me. She sounded really sure.

"Fine," I said. Then something she had said stabbed me with anxiety. "Wait, tonight?"

"Yeah, unless you have other plans," mom said.

I wanted to tell her about my plans but I didn't want her to feel like I abandoning her. It was kind of last minute, Bryan was going to be here in a couple of hours to get me. Would he be mad if I cancelled so soon after making plans with him? I hoped not. I forced a smile and shook my head, "Nope, no plans here."

"Great."

Then I turned my phone on. I quickly typed a message to Bryan:

ME: Hey, I am so sorry about this but I'm afraid I have to cancel.

I left it at that and went to help mom with dinner.

❧☙

Later that night, I bounded down the stairs in my pjs where André and mom were already cozy on the three seater. I took the armchair and waited as mom pressed the play button on the remote. It was the first movie night that mom and I had in a while and I loved it. I missed having this time with her. But with André taking up the spot next to her, the spot I usually had, made it feel a lot more crowded than it was. I felt like the third wheel.

I felt left out.

I tried not to dwell on the emotions as I held my own bowl of popcorn, much smaller than the one that mom and André were holding and just watched the movie.

André had never seen the movie — *The Day After Tomorrow* — so I heard a lot of whispers from mom as she was explaining bits and pieces of it to him.

Despite the third wheel feeling, it was a surprisingly good evening and I went to bed completely relaxed and ready to finish the rest of my chemistry questions. I kept glancing at my phone. Bryan had responded hours ago but I couldn't help but look at my screen to see if he just wanted to talk, about anything really.

I sighed. This was why I turned off my phone earlier.

So that's what I did again. With my phone off, I was able to finish my homework sufficiently and fell asleep feeling accomplished.

❦ Six ❧

"Where do you think you're going?" I heard Thomas ask from the dining room table. He had a few layouts on the table, one of which he used to cover up another. Next to his layouts was a glass of some sort of dark beverage, *whiskey?* I was surprised to find him somewhere else in the house that didn't have the three seater.

I dropped my overnight bag down by the door with my backpack, heading into the kitchen. I debated pretending I hadn't heard him, but with his booming voice, it didn't seem logical. I grabbed the water jug from the fridge and poured myself a glass.

"I'm spending the night at a friend's," I told him. *Not that it's any of your business,* I added mentally, a little bitter. I brought the glass to my lips and took a sip.

"But it's a school night," he said, like that actually changed my plans.

Natalie and I have had sleepovers on school nights so often since we had met that it no longer affected me. Even mom trusted me to get to school on time with a couple dollars in my pocket for lunch. If it was a cause for alarm, she wouldn't be so okay with it.

"Your point?" I muttered as I brought the cup to my lips again.

"My point is that it's a school night. You can't spend the night at your friend's." He left the dining room table and made his way toward me, stopping at the island. "If today was Friday, then we would be having a very different conversation."

I just looked at him. Who the hell did he think he was? He'd spent thirteen years doing God knows what and now he thinks he can just come back, and uproot the way we live our lives? I definitely wanted to say something to him. He couldn't possibly think I would just stay home tonight because *he* said so, did he? I watched him carefully as I said, "You don't get to tell me what to do. You are not my dad."

He looked taken aback. Definitely just as surprised as I was that I had found enough courage to say that. Then his eyes hardened and his voice went cold as he walked around the island toward me. He grabbed my arms tight, his fingers digging into my upper arms. I could smell the alcohol on his breath as he spoke, "I think now's as good a time as any to teach you to show me some respect."

I clenched my eyes shut when he raised one of his hands to slap me, but then we heard a shrill voice shout, "Thomas. You are one phone call away from spending the night in jail." Thomas looked back at mom, who held her phone out in front of her, her thumb poised to hit a button. "I suggest you let her go."

With the looming threat of the police hanging in the air between them, Thomas did let me go. But not before growling, "This is not over," when mom turned her back.

He went back to his plans, but he never stopped watching me.

I tried to be strong as I finished my drink. I quickly chugged it and then turned the glass upside down in the sink. I felt a tear slide down my cheek when I got to the front door. I sat on the stairs as I waited for Natalie to come, swiping at the evil tears that betrayed me. My whole body shook as I wrapped my arms around my body, trying to hold myself together.

❧❧❧

"It was so scary," I told Natalie as we entered the convenience store on the block. "He grabbed me so tight, it hurt."

"Oh, sweetie," Natalie soothed, giving me a side hug. "I'm sorry. Are you okay?"

"Yeah, I'm fine," I told her. "He just kind of gives me the creeps. Not to mention this cold, evil chill down my back, now when I think about it."

Natalie led me down the candy aisle and slapped a package of Twizzlers into my arms. "From all you've told me about the man, he is evil."

I nodded.

"Do you know why he's here?" She looked at me, already I was shaking my head. "Do you know what he's planning?"

I held up a hand to stop her sleuthing; not because we could be overheard — we couldn't. The place was completely empty, we couldn't even see an employee who would help us. I just assumed they were in the back. I stopped her because I knew what she would do. She would start going in deeper into why he was here, what he wanted, who was involved and I didn't want to know that information.

I just wanted him gone.

That's exactly what I told her.

"Fine."

We finished collecting the rest of our desired sugar-filled treats and just as we headed toward the cash register, I realized that Bryan was there. Not in line with a buddy, but rather he was behind the counter with a red polyester shirt with the store's logo on the front. Over his left breast, he also had his name pinned to his shirt. He smiled when we got closer.

"Hey, guys," he greeted us both. He didn't take his eyes off me.

"Hey, Bryan," Natalie responded while I just smiled and gave him a small wave. I dropped the snacks on the counter and watched as he rung us through.

"What are you guys up to tonight?"

"Sleepover," I answered. He was my boyfriend, I should at least say something while we were in each other's presence.

"On a school night?"

Ugh, he sounded just like Thomas. "You got a problem with that?" I clipped. I sounded bitter. I couldn't help but feel like he was telling me what he thought I should do, just the way Thomas thought he could just waltz back into my life and start ordering me around. Now I was glaring at him.

"Nope." He popped the 'p'. "I've got no problem with it. It just doesn't seem like you."

"Then that just goes to show how little you know about me."

"I just mean that with your good girl persona and always doing your homework and handing it in on time..." He trailed off a little. "I just wouldn't have thought you would be the kind of girl to have a sleepover during the middle of the week. That's all."

That had better be all, I thought, but I just smiled kindly. "Oh, right. Got it."

Bryan bagged our choices and handed it over, which Natalie accepted. "I'll see you later?"

By his gaze, which was pinned solely on me, I knew he was talking to me and completely leaving Natalie out. "Yeah."

❧❦☙

For the next few hours, I worked toward completing my homework. Long enough for Natalie to finish her own and order pizza, which was our only option for a meal. Her parents had gone out an hour ago and neither of them gave a time that they would return. And their cupboards and fridge held very little options. Plus we were just too lazy to get crafty.

"Alright, dinner is served," Natalie called.

She was in the kitchen and from my spot on the floor in the living room, I could hear the clinking of plates.

"How many do you want?"

"Two to start," I told her as I finished off the last remaining question. Then I closed my books and tucked them into my bag just as she returned. She handed me a plate with two slices of Hawaiian and plopped down on the couch, already indulging in her meal.

"Can I ask you something?"

"What's up?"

"Is Bryan treating you right?"

I looked at her and wondered where this concern was coming from. I guess I knew that it was always there, being my best friend and having my back and all, but after the last couple days when she had suggested that Bryan be the only guy I date, I had to wonder.

"I don't know," was all I said. What else could I say? He and I had only been together for a couple of days, been on two dates, learned things about each other that you wouldn't be able to learn in the halls of a school, but it's only been four days. "I think so, yeah."

She nodded. She took another bite of her pizza, already down to the crust. Then she set her plate down on the couch along with the crust. She came over to me and knelt in front of me, taking my hands in hers. "I love you. You are my best friend in the world." Her voice shook a little. "I just want you to be happy."

"I know that, Nat," I told her. I was confused where this behaviour was suddenly coming from. "I love you too."

We finished our dinner, talking about prom. She mostly tried to pressure me into going but I was dead set on staying at home. I still had to finish writing my valedictorian speech and practicing it was going to take time. I tried to start it, but couldn't find a good angle so I quit for a day. Then a week and now it's almost time for it to be ready. As long as I set aside some time this weekend for my speech, I should be okay.

Natalie was so giddy about prom that she wanted to show me her dress. Again. I was there when she had bought it but she was just so excited that she couldn't help running up the stairs to her bedroom and coming down with the long silk creation in her hands. The neckline was modest, off the shoulder, and the back dipped down to her tailbone. The sleeves were long and it was a beautiful pale blue. She was definitely going to be the belle of the ball.

She held the dress up to her frame and gave a little twirl.

"Isn't it beautiful?"

I nodded. It really was. But I was just glad that she was smiling.

"You know, it's not too late to get you a dress too," she said again. That had become her catchphrase the last few weeks whenever the topic arose.

"So I've heard," I mocked. "But seriously, I don't want to go."

"It's prom, the most important night of a young girl's life."

I have heard this all before. It's always the same conversation with her when the idea of prom comes up. And the same thing happens. I say I don't want to, she begs a little —as she's doing now, her hands folded together and a pout on her face — and then when I don't give in, she's a grump the rest of the conversation. I think she's convinced it'll change my mind.

"I'm sorry, Nat. I'm not going and that's final, please?"

"Fine," she grumbles, turning and bringing her dress upstairs again. She waits until she's in my presence again to add, "But I won't have any fun without you."

"That's the idea," I joke.

And the mood is immediately brightened.

A little while later, we're in the kitchen assembling homemade banana splits and making a mess of syrup, sprinkles and banana peels as we do. We keep saying that we'll clean it up later but after finishing them and plopping down on the couch, we can't seem to find the energy to go and do it.

I am sitting on the couch with the lower half of my body hanging off and the other half resting a little awkwardly on the back of the couch. Natalie's body is curled in on itself while she takes up most of the couch with her lean frame.

"What do we do now?" She asked.

"Well, we could clean up the mess."

She tilted her head back to see it. She wasn't in the best position to do so but I didn't say anything. "Eh," she said, shrugging, "it's too far away. Besides, my parents won't notice it."

"Have I ever told you that you are the laziest person that I have ever met?"

"Yes," she nodded. "I believe you've mentioned it on one occasion or another."

I sighed. "Fine, you pick a movie and I'll clean our mess." I pulled myself into a sitting position as she jumped up and headed toward their movie shelf. I rolled my eyes and headed into the kitchen and began to tackle the work.

We were still awake at the end of the movie, lying lazily on the couch as the credits began to roll. We listened to the end song.

"Hey, Nat?"

I looked over at her. She looked up, opening her droopy eyes to gaze at me.

"Do you like James?"

Throughout the whole movie, I couldn't stop wondering if that's why the two of them were hanging out so much lately. It appeared that when she wasn't with me, or at school, or work, she was out with him. Was there something going on that she hadn't thought to tell me about?

"I have no idea what you're talking about," she grumbled, dropping her head down on the armrest. Readjusting until she was comfortable, but looked the opposite.

"I just mean that lately you've been hanging out with him a lot and I was just wondering if there was a reason for that."

"Yeah, he's my…" She trailed off, looking up at the ceiling as if she would find the answer there. If she had to think this long about it, was it possible that I was right? That she liked him and didn't know where he stood so she couldn't properly label his position in her life?

"He's your what?" I urged.

"Friend?"

"Are you asking or telling me?"

"He's just more of an acquaintance," she said, sounding surer of herself. "We were friends once and then we weren't and now we're just seeing if there's even a friendly spark left."

"A friendly spark, or a romantic one?"

She snapped her gaze to me from the ceiling.

I chuckled. "I'm just saying that I want you to be happy. I want you to try to be happy and maybe be open to love again."

Last year had to have been the longest year of my life. As much as I had been glad that she had found someone that made her happy, I had missed my best friend.

There was a boy, Christopher. He had been pursuing Natalie the entire summer before our eleventh year and she finally caved in the first week after the start of classes. I had been supportive and even tried to be more outgoing because eventually, that seemed to be the only way I would be able to see her. But the spotlight had been too much then, so I backed out and made every excuse in the book when I was invited out with her and Chris.

In school, however, I was never far behind.

We still hung out, but it started to thin the longer their relationship continued until we didn't hang out at all. Chris acted like I was a bug beneath his feet and never gave me the time of day. He never spoke a word to me, in one way or another, if Natalie was around. But as much as I hated him, he made her laugh.

Until he started talking to his ex, who I had seen on occasion but never met. Not that he cheated — to my knowledge — but he ended it just a few weeks before last summer, throwing away all the plans they had made.

I hadn't heard about it until I had pulled into my driveway after a particularly hard day. It was pouring rain, so much that my wipers had been on high speed and even then, it barely did what it needed to allow a clear view. But she was there. Standing on my walkway, looking up at the sky while the rain poured down on her face. I realized later that she was trying to cover up tears.

She swore off guys then, until now. I hope.

I took Natalie's hands in mine. "I don't know what James did in the past to deserve your mistrust, but I'm sure he's changed. And I think that you both would be a lot happier if you gave him the benefit of the doubt."

"Out of the two of us, you always were the smart one," she said, caving.

"I know, so you should listen to me."

She laughed.

Simultaneously, we checked our phone to see how late it was. 10:23 pm. So we went upstairs. I took the floor while she claimed her bed, throwing a pillow my way. We cleaned our tattoos and went to sleep. Even in the dark, I could see the outline of the words that had been embedded in my skin. I ran my fingers along it, feeling it's slightly bumpy texture.

With the words in my head, *She Keeps Me Wild*, I look at Natalie and wonder how I got so lucky to have a best friend quite like her. She was the sister I never had. She was the wild to my tame. I don't know what I would do without her.

Feeling completely blessed, happy and blissful, I fell asleep. Slowly, but surely.

❦

The next day, Bryan met me at my locker again, his phone in hand. I paused a little ways away, just to admire him for a moment. He looked gorgeous in a grey v-neck long sleeved shirt, his sleeves rolled up to his elbows. He wore jeans today with a pair of Nikes.

Just then my phone dinged with a message.

BABE: Didn't your mama ever teach you that staring is rude?

I couldn't help the grin that stretched across my face as my cheeks burst into flames at having been caught. Then Bryan came up to me, putting his hands on my waist and bringing his lips closer to touch my earlobe, ever so slightly. A shiver ran down my spine and he chuckled.

"You look beautiful, by the way," he told me.

His hot breath fanned my ear and caused another pleasurable shiver to run down my spine, which I now just accepted. He was going to elicit these kinds of reactions from me, I was just going to have to get used to it.

I threw my arms around his neck, drawing myself in closer to him. He was tall, so tall that I had to stretch up on my toes just to rest my head on his shoulder. He smelled really good. Bryan wound his arms around my waist and held me to him.

Suddenly, out of nowhere, without even consulting my brain, my mouth said, "Let's skip."

Seven

I felt Bryan's body tense in surprise. "What?"

"Let's skip." This time, I'd had enough time to think about the consequences, but I didn't care. There was a thrill in making such a reckless decision and in just a few minutes, I would understand what it felt to go through with it.

He bumped up my chin with his forefinger so that he could look at me dead on. "And do what?"

I thought back to my list, to all the things I wanted to accomplish in the next month. There were so many things but only one seemed just right at this moment. "Let's go to the movies. I haven't been in a long time."

And so we went to the movies.

In our little town of Cauville — which consists of three thousand people — had a movie theatre, but it was real small and didn't open until after noon. Bryan and I had to drive a town over until we found a theatre that was open this early in the morning, and was playing the movies we wanted to see.

He picked one and I picked another, that way it was fair.

We tried to see if we could beat the other into paying for the movies, both bank cards poised and ready. But each time, he would shout something insane or point behind us, and make me look away. I can't tell you why I fell for it, but the lit-up look on Bryan's face when the machine scanned his card instead of mine was worth a moment of stupidity.

The first was the new Marvel movie, which he only picked because he thought I wouldn't enjoy it. I grumbled and complained about the cheesiness of his choice through all the previews and then the movie started.

For the entire two hours of the movie, my mood about it absolutely changed. The more I enjoyed it, the more he enjoyed it himself. I caught him watching me on several occasions, just when *I'd* been hoping to catch a peek at him.

By the end of the two hours, I was gushing about it more than he expected. He tried to get an opinion in before I interrupted him, but it was never a full sentence, I had loved it so much.

Then we picked the next movie, which would be starting in an hour so we decided to head out toward the mall just next to the theatre.

"What do you want to eat?" He asked. He had his hands in his pockets, watching me intently.

"I want a burger," I told him. I pulled his hand out of his pocket and directed him toward the A&W counter.

"You're a girl after my own heart," he said, his voice low. "You like Marvel movies and when you go out to eat, you actually *eat*."

I just smiled.

"I should have started dating you a long time ago."

My heart squeezed. Curious, I turned to him and asked, "Do you think we would have lasted?" I thought about all the girls he'd dated. If he had started dating me a long time ago, *would I just have been another girl among many? Would he even care? Does he now?*

Bryan cupped my face in his hands. "Yeah, I think we would have," he said. "If you keep surprising me the way you have been."

"Oh, I surprise you?"

"Definitely." He smiled, his lips closing the distance between the two of us, inch by inch. And then I was rescued.

"What can I get for you guys?"

I heard Bryan grumble angrily to the lady, under his breath, before I stepped up to her. I ordered a teen burger, with onion rings on the side and a root beer. Bryan ordered a double Mozza burger, onion rings and a Coke. As we were walking away he made a distasteful cocaine reference.

The Game

I rolled my eyes. Then checked the time. It was lunchtime, Natalie would be heading to the cafeteria and looking for me. Only she doesn't know that I won't be there, so I shot her a quick text. Then she'd know not to wait up for me. I knew she'd wonder why and her immediate response confirmed it. I couldn't lie to her just as she couldn't lie to me, so I didn't.

As I did, I felt butterflies and nerves and guilt. And not because I was here with Bryan — which I was strangely calm about — but more because this was the first time that I've ever skipped class, let alone a whole day before. I have — had — a perfect attendance record. The fact that I was with Bryan was not going to look good to my mom and, now Thomas. (Now that he was around, pretending to be my father, I had a feeling he'd blow a gasket if he found out).

It's not like either of my parents would clap me on the back and congratulate me on finally being a teenager. No. They were going to kill me.

"Oh, god, I feel sick," I mumbled.

"Don't worry, we'll get some food into you and everything will be fine," Bryan promised.

"How can you be sure?"

"Because," he smiled, carrying our tray of food to a booth and sitting down, "I've done this a thousand times."

I followed him, sitting across from him. "Yeah, well, my parents aren't as easy going as yours. My mom will be pissed. And Thom— my *father* will beat me to death."

He chuckled; he thought I was joking. "It'll be fine." Bryan reached across the table and took my hand in his. "You have no idea how many times I've heard a girl—"

I groaned. *Why did he feel the need to mention his earlier conquests?*

"—say that about their parents, but it's never actually as bad as they think it'll be," he continued, completely oblivious. He bit into his burger, a bit of mustard spilling out of the corner of his mouth. "I'm sure it'll be fine."

He seriously thought he was comforting me, and a small part of me accepted this comfort, but now all I could think about was my mom. And how mad she was going to be. If we could just keep Thomas from finding out, then I'll *truly* be fine. I still remembered how he'd grabbed me yesterday and fear ran down my spine.

We finished our meal and then we headed out to watch the second movie.

After, we were going to go back to school, but then we decided against it and just drove around town.

We started talking about the future. Not as though we were still going be together then, but rather what we both planned to be. Where we saw ourselves in the next few years. I had already guessed his answer just from the skills that he showed on the football field; but I'd never have guessed that he thought he wouldn't ever get married.

It felt weird to be talking about such things with him so soon after officially meeting him but, *what can I say?* I was intrigued.

I talked about my surgical dreams and he was surprised, to say the least. Apparently, something about me did not scream 'scrubs', but rather 'pantsuits' for a boring accounting job or a lawyering one. I couldn't help but laugh at his assumption.

He dropped me off at home at the end of the school day.

Thomas was sitting out front, his elbows on his knees. He looked like he was waiting for someone. I seriously hoped that it wasn't me. I don't know if I could take any more encounters with him. I seriously debated asking Bryan to drive to the next street over and then I'd just hop fences to get in through the back. But asking that would mean telling him why and I wasn't ready to open up that much just yet.

So I thanked Bryan for the ride and for spending the day with me. I was about to get out of his car when he pulled me back, so the door shut softly behind me. Then he leaned closer, he put his forehead to mine and, and just for a moment, we just sat there, breathing in and out. I licked my lips and brought my hand up to touch his cheek.

He just laughed. "I'll see you later."

"You know, you actually had me believing that you were going to kiss me."

The Game

"Did you want me to?" There was a twinkle in his eye that had me blushing a deep scarlet. He chuckled again, amused. "You did. I can tell."

"I'm leaving now," I said, but he pulled me back when I tried to leave again. "Okay, you have got to stop doing that before you—"

Then his lips were on mine. His hand up against my cheek in a soft caress as he kissed me.

Too soon, the kiss was over and I was left feeling flushed. Bryan held my hand and I let that be my excuse to stay a while longer. There was a rough knock on the passenger side window and I turned to see Thomas glowering at me.

"Who's that?"

"No one important," I told him and a part of me wished Thomas would hear. I wanted him to know exactly how I felt about him, what I told people about him; but audibly saying anything was terrifying. "I gotta go. I'll see you later." I left him with a kiss on his cheek, so *so* close to his mouth and then got out of the car.

Thomas had gone back to sitting on the porch — *thank god!* I refused to make eye contact as I stepped around him and went to open the door. *Was that it? Did someone lock him out? Did he need me to open the door for him?* Nah, I told myself, slightly shaking my head. *It wasn't possible.*

"You know, there are two sides to every story," Thomas suddenly spoke, my hand on the knob.

I already knew that. But I wasn't sure what he was talking about. I paused anyway and turned to look at him. My first real, and willing eye contact today. "So?"

"Don't you want to hear mine?"

I really wanted to ask him why he thought his story would hold any interest for me. But instead, I bit my tongue and stayed silent. I didn't want to hear his story because who knew how much of it would be the truth? I was willing to bet that it'd be more fib than non-fiction if I stuck around to listen.

"We met in high school," he began his story anyway. "We fell in love. I loved your mother more than anything. But then she got pregnant with you and just threw her dreams out the window. She put aside everything just to stay at home and raise you-"

Was he giving me the stink-eye?

I held up a hand immediately with a quick, "Okay, okay, *stop*," which he first ignored but eventually gave into. I didn't believe a word he was saying right now. "You really think that I'm gonna believe that *I'm* the reason mom didn't get what she wanted right after high school?"

"She must have been feeding you lies if you believe otherwise."

"Lies?" I asked, disbelieving. This man had started this story by telling me that he had loved my mother. So why the *hell* would he go to such lengths to *try* and twist mom's story. But I was there and whether I liked it or not, I remembered a lot more about it than I wanted to. A little too much. "If anyone is spouting lies here, it's *you*."

Then I went inside and headed toward my bedroom, where I remained until it was time to head to work.

☙❦❧

"Can you explain this?" My mom asked when I headed to the back of the shop. She played a voicemail recording from her phone that, very clearly, told my mom every class I had missed. I just looked at the scowl on her face. "What were you *thinking*?"

"I... I..." I realized then that I didn't have an answer for her. Not even to explain my actions, because how could I? I had made an impulsive choice and skipped a whole day of learning just to spend it with my boyfriend. How was I supposed to explain that without making him look bad? Even when I tried, it all just came out wrong.

"Was it *his* idea to skip the *whole* day?"

I knew she'd jump to that conclusion. "Mom, no. Weren't you listening?" I tied the apron around my waist and moved to wash my hands. "It wasn't Bryan. It was me. He was just as surprised as you are. It was just a spontaneous decision."

"Janessa, honey, you *need* to go to school."

"Mom, it was one day," I insisted.

"You are grounded, young lady," she said, pulling that punishment card out for the first time in… well, ever. She had never needed to punish me before. "You will go to school, you will go to work, and you will come home. If you made plans to go somewhere with your boyfriend, don't bother. You won't be going. You'll be strictly supervised tomorrow *and* during the weekend."

She was angry and fuming. She didn't even wait to hear my acknowledgement before she turned around and headed back to her baking.

I just stood there for a minute, basking in my first punishment; it felt rotten. But then I thought about today and how amazing it'd been to spend it with Bryan, away from everyone at school, and to just relax; it made all this worth it. Well, almost, since it robbed me of my weekend.

Dang, there was a party Bryan wanted me to go to with him tomorrow night. I guess I'll have to cancel.

"How mad was your mom?" Natalie asked when I made it to the front where Trixie, another girl that worked here, was wiping down any exposed surface she could find.

"Really angry," I answered. I clocked myself in. "I mean, it was one day. *One* day. It's not like it was gonna ruin all my hard work. But it cost me my weekend anyway."

"No!" Natalie cried. "But the party tomorrow, we were going to go together. The first party you actually said *yes* to."

"I know. I'm sorry, Nat. But hey, maybe James will go with you," I sang, teasingly. I nudged her shoulder and she rolled her eyes as she caught my drift. "Oh, come on, don't tell me you haven't thought about what I said yesterday."

"Maybe I *have* thought about it," she admitted, bashfully. "But to be honest, I don't know. There's just a lot going on right now with my parents and your dad— father," she corrected when I glared at her, "being back."

"Why would Thomas be a factor?" I asked. Just then, the bell above the door jingled. I looked over and saw Bryan coming in with

James. "Ooh, ooh." I gently tapped Natalie's hand, eagerly. "Now's your chance to ask him."

"Actually, I have to go to the back and get—"

"Nope," I interrupted. "Ask him, come on," I continued in a whispered tone as they came closer.

Bryan just smiled as he looked at me. "Hey."

"Hey." I smiled. I realized then that it was time to face the music. "Bryan, about the party tomorrow night…"

"Did you change your mind?" He looked both disappointed and resigned. Like he knew I might back out.

"Sort of," I admitted. "My mom grounded me because of today. So, I can't go, but that doesn't mean you shouldn't."

He pouted that cute little pout that he does sometimes. "Then I guess we'll have to make the time that we have at school great."

I couldn't help smiling. I was so thankful that he was as willing to accept my punishment as I was. I didn't want to piss off my mom any more than I already had but I also didn't want to have to give Bryan up. "I gotta warn you, today doesn't paint a very good picture of you to my mom."

"*Please*, have you met me?" He gave me an '*I can't believe you thought that*' look. "I can change her opinion just like that," he said, snapping his finger.

"I bet," I agreed with a grin.

Then I looked over to Natalie, really hoping that she had gone through with asking James out. If anyone deserved to find someone special, it was her. The two of them seemed to be talking about something happy and I could only assume that he'd agreed to go out with her.

How could he not? She was amazing! The best person in the world.

Then we started to get a lineup and Bryan and James were forced to leave.

Later that night when I was alone, the door opened and in walked Megan. I was still in the process of cleaning tables and putting up chairs when she did. She walked over to me, gloating;

like she'd won some big prize or something. The grin on her face was very unnerving.

"What?" I snapped. She had been waiting for me to say something and since we were closed in *almost* every sense of the word, I didn't have to be nice. Not to *her*.

"Nothing, just a little birdie told me that you weren't coming to my party," she said, almost sounding sad about it. "I was really looking forward to it."

I couldn't keep the half-scoff, half-laugh from leaving my mouth and it startled her. Then I just outright laughed. "Just cut the crap. You and I both know that you hate me and, frankly, I hate you too. So don't go spouting that bullshit."

"Fine." Her sweet face turned into one of a priss, spoiled child. And an angry one at that. Her eyes were cold, calculating and angry. "You're going to break up with Bryan tomorrow. And you're going to do as I say."

"Or what?"

She didn't reply, but the look on her face said that she knew something. Something I didn't know she knew and she was going to use it against me if I didn't do as she said. But what could she possibly know? "Now, why would I give up my leverage?"

Then she turned on her heel and left the building, laughing. Laughing as if she had won some sort of battle that I hadn't even realized we were fighting.

Well, if she wanted a battle, I'd give her one.

❧ Eight ❧

That night when I arrived home, everyone was seated in the living room. André and mom were sitting on the three seater and Thomas was nowhere to be seen. They both looked so anxious that I *felt* anxious. Was this really because I had skipped a day of school? If it was, this was an overreaction, right? An intervention? Or maybe it was Thomas.

Did something happen to him?

Was he gone?

I couldn't help the hopeful feeling I got from both possibilities. I refused to let the smile play across my face as I walked into the living room and put my purse down against the wall. "What's going on, mom?"

She turned to look at me. "Honey, please, have a seat." She gestured toward the armchair. "We need to talk."

I did as I was asked and sat down. I felt really uncomfortable under their scrutiny. But I was curious, so I asked, "Is this because of what happened today?"

"You mean you skipping school to be with your boyfriend?" André smirked. At the same time, mom said, "No." She glared at André and lightly smacked his shoulder.

"This *does* have something to do with you though," she continued, slowly turning her gaze to me. "And your relationship with André."

What relationship? I barely had one. He was just another boy, another kid in my house, but he would be gone soon, so I didn't see the need to create anything. Especially not something that he wasn't looking forward to reciprocating. "Okay..." I said, dragging the word out. "What about us?"

"Well, first, I need to tell you a story."

And she did.

She told me a story about something that had happened thirteen years ago. Something I had successfully blocked out of my mind. We used to be a family of four; two parents, a little girl and a baby boy. And when my father left, he took the little boy with him.

A couple of years later, she started fostering kids as a way to make up for abandoning her baby boy to a monster.

Here, my mom interrupted her story. "And honey, I am *so* sorry for all the things you had to put up with over the years."

Then she explained to me that she had found the boy that was supposed to be my biological brother and when my gaze shifted to André, he turned away. Almost embarrassed, or ashamed, or fearful. Fearful that I might push him away and find him disgraceful. I could see it on his face and I didn't have to be a mind reader to understand that feeling. That fear.

If mom was right about him being my brother *and* if she was right about him being raised by Thomas... I couldn't imagine *what* André had been through. But I could understand that, whatever it was, it made him distrusting.

I may have pushed a lot of Thomas related things out of my head but there was a reason why Natalie Liese was my only friend. There was a reason why she was the only one, outside of my family, that knew about my past and all my fears. If I was so scared to allow someone into my life for fear that they would judge me, then I could only imagine how André must feel. It would make sense why making friends was never on the agenda for him.

"Honey, please say something," mom said, worried.

I didn't know what to say. I couldn't stop looking at the boy in front of me and thinking of all the horrible things he must have had to overcome to get to this point in his life. I thought about all the things that Thomas had to have put this kid through and I began to see him in a whole new light. André used to just be this annoying kid that followed me and Natalie around for absolutely no reason and refused to make friends. But now? Now he was a boy that had overcome a lot of things.

I found a new admiration him. I don't know if I was ready to share my mom but I did know one thing, something inside of me changed. It was like flipping a switch. I was willing to accept that he was my brother. I could see some similarities in his face now that I looked. The angular shape of his cheekbones and the chestnut shine to his long hair.

"Honey?"

André still wasn't looking at me and mom was watching me intently, worried when I wouldn't speak. I got up to ease both their worries and sat in the last remaining seat next to André. Now he looked up just as I wrapped my arms around his head and drew him closer. Almost hesitantly, he returned the hug with his arms around my waist.

"Welcome home," I whispered to him.

His grip on my body tightened and I heard — and felt — him exhale when a small gust of warm air hit my arm. I looked at mom over his shoulder and she was smiling. I think she was just happy to be with both of her kids again.

Then she got up and walked out of the room, leaving André and me to our own devices.

"Alright, I'm going to go change," I told him, slightly lifting my shirt off my body and grimaced at the smell of it. Definitely smelled like the bakery and not the good parts of it. "I'll be back and then we can do something."

He nodded, smiling. "Sounds good."

Those were the first words to have left his mouth since mom started talking. I smiled, got to my feet and headed out of the room. I stopped at the doorway and looked back at him. One thought startled me then; I had a brother. And he made a whole lot more sense now that I was in on the secret too. His protectiveness of me to Bryan didn't seem like an act anymore.

I came back down once I had changed and found André still in the same spot as when I'd left, this time though he was eating a sandwich. "Hey," I called to him and jolted him out of a thought. "What do you want to do?"

He shrugged. "We could watch a movie. Play a game. Just talk."

I nodded and sat down on the couch again. I pulled my legs up under me and looked at him. "Alright."

So that's what we did.

We talked. Mostly about our past, catching up on the things that the other had missed. We were both hesitant to talk about it. He didn't want me to feel bad for not having been there.

He wasn't loved much, especially not by Thomas, who had spent most of André's young life beating on him. Thomas was always working and when he wasn't, he was making André wish he was dead. He couldn't take the abuse anymore so one day after he confided in a teacher about his home situation, child services came along and took him away from Thomas.

It was a very brave thing for André to have done and I was proud as I listened to my brother.

I didn't want to tell him what it had been like to live without Thomas because, although mom and I had our trials, what he had been through was worse. No kid should have ever have gone through that, especially not alone. I told him anyway because he begged. He said it was only fair for me to share my story since he shared his.

By the time I finished, Thomas returned.

André and I — awkwardly — decided to go to bed. We ran up the stairs past Thomas and we didn't look back. Even so, I could feel his eyes on me the whole time.

の❦よ

My lungs burned.

It was like I was being deprived of air. It was also the thing that woke me up and made me realize that the reason I was deprived of air was that I was trying to breathe through fabric.

Suffocating or not, it was obvious. Someone was smothering my face with a pillow! I flailed and struggled futilely. My one hand hit on my attacker did nothing to dissuade them. Not even a measly grunt of pain, not that I would have heard through the pillow anyway. More desperate now as spots danced in my vision, I kicked my legs. It was also futile.

Just then the pillow was ripped from my head and I bolted into a sitting position, gulping in a large lung full of air. I was wheezing terribly when my attacker sat down beside me.

The first thing I noticed was the smell of alcohol on his breath. Not cheap beer but rather, mom's expensive scotch. When I met his bleary stare, it was none other than Thomas.

"Listen to me, and listen good, if you breathe a word of this to anyone, show disrespect to me, and I will make sure it sticks." There was no remorse in his tone as he just glared at me. The streetlights from out my window cast a glow across my bedroom and highlighted Thomas' not-so-handsome face. "Do you understand me?"

"Yes," I croaked, gripping my throat as I sucked air into my lungs.

He threw my pillow at me and then he just left the room.

I looked at my alarm clock to see that it was shortly after three in the morning. I wasn't going to be able to sleep now, not with almost having been murdered.

I knew he would do it too. I could feel it in my bones and, if that wasn't enough, I had a memory to cherish as well. If I did anything against his wishes, he would *make it stick*. I didn't know which was worse; saying something and dying at his hands, or letting a would-be murderer roam free in our home by staying quiet.

I debated for a minute about going to the police but, even if they came and took him away, how long before he came back and tried again?

I felt tears burn their way down my cheeks. I sniffed and wiped them away. Only, the more I wiped my face, the more tears materialized.

Eventually, I cried myself to sleep… only to be woken by my alarm clock the next morning.

That morning, I was lazy getting ready for school. I pulled on a pair of skinny jeans, a plain white camisole, a mismatching pair of socks and an oversized hoodie that I practically swam in. I didn't bother with my contacts and just slipped on my glasses before heading to the bathroom to run a brush through my hair. I pulled my thick hair up into a messy bun at the top of my head and wrapped two elastics around the mass for good measure.

I finished up the rest of my morning routine before heading down to the kitchen where mom had left a plate of omelettes for breakfast.

"Good morning," mom greeted me, as did Thomas and André.

Collectively, I returned the greeting with a bored tone. I grabbed a plate of omelettes and wolfed a couple down.

I went to the front door, and slipped on my red converse and slung my bag over my shoulder just as Thomas came forward. I already felt myself shrinking back against the wall. Realizing too late that I had just allowed him to box me into a no-exit corner.

"Remember what we talked about?" he asked in a hushed tone so mom and André couldn't hear from the other room.

I just nodded, — it was all I could muster. A cold shiver ran down my spine as he smiled down at me.

Terrified and utterly alone, I went to school. Thomas let me. He'd walked away and allowed me to leave, laughing.

I hated rain and snow; really anything that fell from the sky. And today, it was raining. Not heavily but there was no guarantee that it wouldn't get worse by the end of the day. I flinched when I heard the door open. Then mom and André were behind me.

Mom held out her hand to me and at first, I thought she was asking for my car keys. How was I supposed to take André and I to school if I didn't have a car? We didn't live close enough to walk. There was a *reason* we'd gotten the car in the first place.

But then she said, "Cellphone," and cleared it up. I wanted to protest, especially today, which had begun terribly. But I didn't have any energy in me to resist, so I dug through my backpack and handed it over. "Good. Now, remember, *straight* home."

I nodded once to show her I understood and remembered.

"Also, tonight, we're having a family dinner and I would really like for you to be there."

She said it as if I had a choice when she *knew* I didn't. I had absolutely no choice. But I nodded anyway, agreeing.

"Great. Have a nice day, kids."

Mom all but shoved André and me off the porch. I pulled my hood up over my head to somewhat protect myself against the rain as I ran to my car with André on my tail.

§

"So, basically, we're *actually* siblings." I told Natalie all about last night and the new information that had been brought to light. She couldn't stop staring at me, her mouth agape.

I couldn't figure out why but I always wanted to have a sibling. I'd just hoped that it'd be a sister, but a brother would do.

"Oh- ma-Gawd!" she squealed. "That is amazing. I mean, I know it's André and he's kind of annoying but I am *so* happy for you guys. I am *so* thrilled you guys have been reunited."

"That was a little over the top," I commented. "But thank you. I just hope I don't screw this big sister thing up. I mean, how do you be a big sister when you've never had to be one before?"

I closed my locker door; the sound resonating in the hallway, and I realized I may have slammed it too hard.

"I don't know, but I'm sure you'll figure it out," she said. We started heading to math class. "And you've got a lot of catching up to do. You've missed so many years to be his big sister and now you're going to be leaving in two short months, not to mention moving three *hours* away."

She was right. I had to claim my place as André's sister before I left. Becoming a surgeon was going to be hard enough without adding a long lost brother to the mix.

I also told Natalie about my little visit from Megan last night.

"That son of a—" She shouted, already heading toward the cafeteria. But I yanked her arm back to stop her.

"Just stop. Obviously, I'm not gonna do what she wants but I'm *also* not going to egg her on," I told her. I looked her square in the face so she would know I was serious. It was hard enough not strangling that girl when she was next to me; I didn't need my best friend to make it harder. "Please?"

"Fine," she conceded reluctantly. "I won't say anything *unless* I see her."

"No!" I hissed. "Not at all."

"I'm not making any promises," she said, crossing her arms stubbornly. Just then, the warning bell rang.

As I turned into my classroom, I hoped that Natalie wouldn't do anything stupid; like try and talk to Megan.

I took my seat as a few classmates and friends of classmates trickled into the room. I admired the risk they took so that they could talk to their friends for a few extra minutes. I smiled a little at them as I pulled out my books. My textbook on my desk and my notebook on top of my textbook.

I was still pretty annoyed at Megan and not up to pointless conversation with my classmates. I even went so far as to put my head on my books and my hood over my head. Anything to make people avoid talking to me. Which worked, for *most* people.

Abruptly, my hood was ripped from my head and then Megan screeched, "Did you do it?" in my ear.

"Please, Megan, I am *not* in the mood." I cringed away from her voice.

"I don't care. Did you do it?"

"I haven't seen him yet," I told her. She just stared at me; oblivious to my reasoning.

"Give me your phone, I'll do it."

I shook my head. She was crazy if she thought I was giving her my phone. (I forgot at that moment, that I didn't have it). "No."

She actually looked surprised. "Excuse me?"

"I am not giving you my phone so you can break up with *my* boyfriend *for* me. That's not happening." I pulled my hood back over my head and put my head back on my desk. "So leave. Go to your own class."

I couldn't tell if she left or not because I'd closed my eyes but she must have. When the bell rang and the teacher called the class to order, I looked up and Megan was gone.

ও৯ Nine ৫৬

"There you are," *I heard* from behind me before a pair of arms wrapped themselves around my body. His lips brushed my ear and I shivered. A *good* shiver. "I've been texting you all morning, why haven't you been responding?"

"Because as a secondary punishment to skipping school all day, my mom took my phone away this morning," I told him. "I don't know *when* or *if* I'm getting it back." I turned my head to look at him. Bryan's arms were holding me tight so I couldn't turn in his arms if I wanted.

"How are we supposed to talk to each other now?" he whined.

"Oh, well, there's this thing, it's called face to face."

"Haha," he laughed sarcastically.

"Or, you know, we could always resort to old-fashioned note passing," I said when he finally let me go enough so I could turn. I stroked his face gently with my fingertips.

"Okay, okay, I get it." A small smile graced his already handsome face. "I just missed you this morning."

I scoffed. "You would not have liked me this morning," I said. He frowned, confused. I added, "I didn't sleep much so I was in a bad mood."

"I'm sure I could have fixed that," he said as he leaned close to nuzzle my neck. For a second I forgot that we were in public and laughed as it tickled me. I could feel him laugh against my skin, the sound of it a low hum in my ear. He lifted his head to look at me. He was smiling and his green eyes seemed to be smiling too as they twinkled. "See?"

"I was in a good mood alre-"

Bryan put a finger to my lips to stop me from finishing my sentence. "Can't you just let me have this?"

"Fine," I surrender and turned back to my locker, long enough to lock it and then sling my backpack over my shoulder. "Let's go to lunch, I'm starving."

He wrapped an arm around my neck and drew me in closer to him. A few people stopped to stare but I was too focused on the sound of Bryan's voice as he told me about the game tonight. He was so anxious and nervous. It was the last game of the season. I tried to help him stay calm and not overthink the whole thing but it didn't work.

"Maybe if you came to the game," he suggested.

"I wish I could. But I'm grounded, remember? And we have this family dinner tonight that I'm scared enough about without adding an angry mother to the mix," I blurted without realizing. Bryan just looked at me and nudged me, good-naturedly.

"That's what you're worried about?" He asked. His brows rose, interrogating me. "A dinner?"

It wasn't the dinner I was worried about; it was Thomas. I wanted to tell him this but just looking at his handsome face, made me hold back. I just smiled a shy smile. "Yeah, I guess. It's stupid when you compare it your worries."

We got in line and Bryan picked up a tray and took my outstretched hand when I tried to pick one up myself. "We'll just share," he said close to my ear. He gently pressed his lips to mine when I tried to protest. I lightly shoved him and rolled my eyes but otherwise relented. I picked what I wanted and Bryan put it on his tray as we slowly slid along behind a small line up of people.

"You know," Bryan started after a moment of silence, waiting for me to meet his gaze, "you can tell me if something's bothering you."

"I know," I said quickly and smiled.

"Because, as it turns out, your mom called mine and invited us to dinner at your place tonight; the one you mentioned," Bryan told me. I was confused, she'd said *family* dinner. "But I won't be able to make it until after the game."

I was going to have to have a talk with my mom. *Why did she tell me it was family if she had invited my boyfriend's family too?*

"Janessa?" I felt someone nudge my shoulder and I looked up at him. "Did you hear me?"

Hear him? *Of course* I heard him; he said he was coming to dinner tonight. "What about the game?"

He rolled his eyes. "So you *didn't* hear me," he muttered under his breath. He probably hadn't meant for me to overhear. "I won't be able to make it until after the game."

"Oh, okay. That's fine, I won't be able to come to the game anyway, so we're even," I said, glumly. I couldn't believe that I was missing my boyfriend's last game. I briefly debated sneaking out of the house to watch it. But I quickly abolished that idea. As much as I wanted to be there for Bryan and Natalie — who was going to cheer for the last time with the squad, — I just didn't want to risk my mother's wrath.

Bryan paid for our lunch and then we headed toward my table. He didn't even try to steer me toward his friends like I'd expected him to. James, Evan, and Reggie sat across from Lynn, Amber and Megan. Megan glared daggers at me but I refused to let her scare me. I looked away and kept walking.

Being a perfect gentleman, Bryan pulled out my chair before pulling out his own. He even let me have the first pick on the tray, though it had already been divided earlier. The more I saw this side of Bryan, the more confused I became about all the awful things that people said about him, boys and girls alike. I'm sure the girls had their own versions to tell, but so did I. And he was just too nice for all the rumours about him.

When I asked him what everyone had against him, he just said, "Just jealous, I guess. I mean, I'm the quarterback. I'm popular. I get all the best girls." He bumped my shoulder with his and I blushed.

Bryan sat so close to me.

I was sitting with my right leg pulled up onto my seat. Bryan's arm rested on the back of my chair, his fingers lightly grazing my bare arm.

I had taken my hoodie off earlier and left it in my locker. His fingers on my arm felt really nice.

Bryan grinned, looking at me as he took a bite of the crust off his pizza. (It was Friday, so the cafe served pizza.) Everyone's favourite day and, a lot of the time, there was none leftover for me. And if there was, it was already cold by the time I ate it.

"Don't take this the wrong way, but what's with you and Megan?" I asked, dipping my spoon into my yogurt.

"Are you jealous?" He waggled his eyebrows and I wanted to smack him. He just laughed.

"I said, 'don't take this wrong way', by that I meant I'm not jealous so don't think that," I insisted as he finally sobered up.

"Well, nothing's going on between Megan and me," he said.

"She seems awfully possessive of you."

Bryan got this concerned look that crossed his face. "Is she bothering you?"

Yes! I wanted to say because, frankly, I didn't want to deal with her. But just thinking it made me feel nauseous. "Nothing I can't handle," was all I said instead.

"I can talk to her." He leaned toward me, our faces just a couple inches apart.

"Didn't you already do that?"

"I can try again," he said, closing the distance between us and... kissing my cheek. I was slightly disappointed.

"It's fine, don't worry about it."

Then, André, Natalie and James came over, taking up the remaining three seats around the circular table.

"Bryan, Megan wanted me to ask if you had gotten your tux yet," James said as he sat down.

Tux? The only thing I could think of that Bryan would need a tux for was prom. And if Megan was asking, that meant... "You're going to prom with Megan?" I couldn't keep the disbelief or jealousy out of my voice. Sure I wasn't going and I wouldn't even if he asked me, but still! To know that he was going with *Megan*, hurt. I guess I'd just expected him to ask someone else, or go stag.

Bryan glared at James before he turned back to me. "Yes, I'm going to the prom with Megan. But only because I'd asked her months ago." Even with that explanation, it still hurt that it was *Megan* that he was going with. It'd sting less if he was going with someone else, someone other than Megan. "What do you want me to do? Tell her I can't go with her?"

I wanted to tell him yes, that's exactly what I wanted him to do but instead, "I don't care. Do whatever you want," were the words that came out of my mouth. Then I turned to the others at the table. "Excuse me."

⋘ ❦ ⋙

I went to the bathroom again. With the same hope that splashing water on my face would somehow make me feel better. But this time, Megan followed me in. The door banged against the wall and she walked around me, her posse standing guard outside; I could hear them chatting to each other. Megan stood in front of a mirror and dug through her purse until she raised a tube of lip gloss and leaned toward the mirror to reapply.

She looked at my reflection and smiled.

I rolled my eyes and went to grab a paper towel to dry my face.

"So this is where you come when you get into a fight with that boy toy of yours." She laughed.

I wanted to smack that stupid grin off her face but couldn't find the strength or the will to do so. I was just so mentally exhausted and physically drained. I hadn't slept very long and the fact I had been smothered by a pillow in the middle of the night, had something to do with it. I did *not* want to have to deal with this today.

"I thought we'd come to an understanding. You were going to break up with him. I have been *more* than patient with you," she said. She sounded almost nice.

Then she turned towards me, her perfectly manicured hand on the edge of the sink.

"What could you possibly blackmail me with that would make me even *consider* listening to you?"

"That's not what you should be worried about," she told me, stepping forward. She stood right in front of me, lifted her manicured finger and pinched my chin when I didn't meet her gaze. She lifted my chin and I glared at her. "You *should* be worried about what I'm going to do to you if you *don't*." She dropped her hand and smiled a grand smile. "Anyway, ta-ta for now!" Her voice changed its pitch as if on command as she took on a whole new persona.

Then she sidestepped me and practically skipped away.

I turned back to my reflection. I could *not* believe I was dealing with *this* today. Megan had to have known that sending James over would lead to this; me finding out about their prom date. She just had to.

Images of Bryan and Megan walking into the gym looking amazing filled my head and once again I turned the tap. I held my hand under the steady stream until it turned red with cold. Then I cupped my hands and dipped my face into the water. I heard one of the stall doors open but I didn't bother looking up.

"Word of advice; one girl to another," she said.

I dried my face and resisted the urge to glare at her. She was about my height, brown hair with blonde highlights and brown eyes. There was something about her that was so familiar... but I couldn't figure out why.

"Her bark is much worse than her bite," the girl smiled and washed her hands, dried them and stepped back in front of one of the two free mirrors. She ran her fingers through her locks before turning back to me.

"Thanks," I muttered.

"I'm Melissa, by the way," she said, her hand outstretched.

I shook it, once; nicely. "Janessa."

"It's nice to meet you." She smiled. It was genuine like she could start laughing at any moment. There wasn't that underlying evil to it like there was with Thomas and Megan. It was real. "I like you," Melissa said suddenly. "You seem nice."

I didn't know what else to do, so I just smiled.

"See you around." She patted my arm and left, taking that warm smile with her.

And I really hoped I would see her around.

❦

I didn't see Bryan at all for the rest of the day. Which was weird since I didn't know which places to avoid. I saw Natalie a few times in passing, and Melissa more frequently than I could have hoped for. Turns out we were in the same Chemistry class; I didn't notice until today.

I thought that that's why she'd been so familiar before but then she told me about her twin brother. When she said his name, it finally dawned on me that Chemistry wasn't the only reason she was so familiar... She was Melissa Cooke, Reggie Cooke's twin sister. AKA the twin of my boyfriend's friend. Great.

I tried not to hold it against her and, the more we chatted, the easier it became. She was nice and even invited me to sit with her at lunch if I ever wanted to. I told her I might take her up on that.

Before I knew it, the day was over and I trudged to my locker.

I noticed a sticky note was stuck to the inside of my door. It said:

J -
She's just a friend, you're the one I want to be with.
- B

Though the note was sweet, I couldn't help but wonder how he got into my locker. *Oh well. I'm sure I could ask him at that stupid family dinner.*

A couple hours later, I descended the stairs in a jean skirt and blouse. I'd blow-dried my hair for the occasion. And I was still unsure about whether I looked cute or not. Unfortunately, mom wouldn't let me stand in front of my mirror any longer, debating.

So, here I went to suffer through the dinner of my nightmares.

From my vantage point, I saw Bryan's little sister, Anna. I remembered her from the other day. She held the hand of an older woman, who spoke to a tall blonde wearing a pantsuit and looked like she always had something to say. I'd never met either of them, but had occasionally seen them around town.

From where I stood, I saw my mom entertaining Olivia. They seemed to be in a heated discussion about something. When my mom glanced my way, I knew it *had* to be about me.

"Ready to get this over with?" André asked.

I jumped, startled. I had barely seen him since we got home. He'd gotten a snack from the kitchen and disappeared into his room until now. He had his hair tucked up into an annoying man bun and he looked barely presentable in a pair of black shorts and a black dress shirt. I turned back to the crowd until I found Thomas at the bar, and nodded. "Yeah. The sooner, the better."

André nodded in agreement and then we both walked over to where our mom was.

"And there they are," she exclaimed happily. She came over and wrapped an arm around the two of us, drawing us towards her. Mrs. Liese just watched us with a smile on her face.

She reached over, took my hand and squeezed, before turning to my brother. "Your mother says your return has been a long time coming."

André blushed and looked at me, maybe begging me for help with his eyes but I just chuckled and shrugged. There wasn't much you could say to Olivia but give her answers you knew she wanted to hear. It also happened to be a lesson you had to learn the hard way.

I grabbed a glass of punch and headed out into the living room to mingle with the other woman since there was no one else my age. Bryan and James were both on the football team and Natalie was on the cheerleading squad. Neither of them would be here until later tonight.

Anna tugged on her mom's sleeve until her mother groaned, gave up and went into the kitchen with her. The tall blonde came up to me then.

"You must be Janessa. Your mother speaks very highly of you," she said. "I'm Mrs. Garcia, James' mom."

I smiled and shook her hand. "Nice to meet you."

"I'm so sorry," she suddenly said. She even looked it, that sad apologetic look on her face concerned me; what she said next only made it worse. "James tells me you're dating Bryan."

It wasn't the first time I'd been approached and talked to about this *particular* decision in my life, but it was the first time that someone else's parent did it. Sure, James' mom probably had insight into Bryan's home life or whatever. She probably even knew Bryan better than all the other kids at school, but I couldn't help the annoyance I felt.

"Yeah, I am," I answered, trying with all my might not to roll my eyes. I didn't want her to think that I was raised to be rude in uncomfortable situations. I wasn't sure if she had picked up on how bitter this conversation was, but *I* sure had.

"You poor thing," she said as if dating Bryan was this enormous tragedy that was going to derail my life. She even took my hand in hers sympathetically. "I just want you to know that everything's gonna be okay. You don't have to do anything you don't want to."

I couldn't help hear that sentence as an innuendo. Was she seriously thinking that Bryan was going to manipulate me into having sex with him? Was that what she was thinking? I think my confusion showed because she became ever more sympathetic then before. Her lip jutted out in a small pout as she drew me into an awkward hug. Or maybe that was just *my* perception of it.

"I'm sorry, but I'm not sure what you're getting at."

She jerked back to look at my face. "Oh, honey, do you not know all the awful things he's done to his girlfriends?" I took a slight step backwards and just looked at her, hoping she wouldn't need a response to continue. She didn't. "Oh, honey, you don't *actually* think you're special," — she paused, frowning — "do you?"

"Excuse me?"

I could *not* believe that someone would just say something like that to me. She seemed puzzled by my reaction. Maybe she thought that I should have clued in by now; that Bryan wasn't sincere in anything he said or did. That everything he'd told me was a lie. And maybe she was right, maybe I was being *way* too naive by trusting Bryan so completely.

I was so confused. *What* was going on?

I took a deep breath — inhale, exhale — and said, softly, "Excuse me," and left the room.

ᴥ Ten ᴥ

A couple of hours later, I found myself on my back porch curled up with a book on the patio sofa. I was stuck between reading and sneaking glances at the strip of photos of Bryan and myself, the ones that we had taken at the carnival. I'd begun to use it as a bookmark so that it would always be with me. But now, I just looked at it and instead of remembering the good times that it used to represent, I couldn't help but wonder how this boy could be so horribly perceived by the outside world.

I went back to my book when the screen door opened and someone stepped out.

"Hey, here you are."

Taking a moment to look up, I saw Bryan sit down beside me, lift my legs and then set them on his lap. I assumed the game had gone well because he was smiling from ear to ear.

"What are you doing out here all by yourself?" He asked. "Shouldn't you be in there, with the rest of the party?"

"No, because *they're* who I'm trying to avoid," I grumbled, getting back to my book. Plus, the back porch was the furthest I could go without getting into trouble.

"Are you still mad about Megan?" He asked.

I wasn't anymore, but now that he just oh-so-casually mentioned her name, I was. I glared at him to show him just how mad it made me. Especially when it was added to all the things I'd been told in the past week by acquaintances I barely knew.

He reached over, took the book from my hand — his finger holding my place — and he set it down beside him. I really hoped he wouldn't remove his finger, I couldn't remember the page I was on. But he didn't. Instead, he brought up his hands so that he could gesture with them as he spoke. "I already told you, she's just a friend, okay?" He said it softly, watching my face. "You're the one I want to be with."

I got a fluttery feeling when he said it.

"It's not just that," I said, trying to ignore how I felt.

"Then what is it?"

"You." He frowned, confused. Like he didn't know what people said about him. I continued, "Everyone. Everyone keeps telling me that you're bad for me; that you're just using me. That I'll regret being with you if I don't do the smart thing and run away in the opposite direction."

"I see."

"Do you?" I asked. He just nodded. "Can you prove them wrong?" I watched his face. "Can you tell me right now that they're all wrong; that you're not who they say you are?"

He paused. He actually paused. Took a moment and looked away from me, long enough for my heart to fall a little in my chest.

"No, I can't."

My heart plummeted. Right into my gut. They were *right*? I know I wanted a doomed relationship but I thought we'd last a little longer than a week.

"You can't?" I repeated, more for myself. "You can't..."

"I can't prove them wrong because they're right. I *am* a player." He watched me, *waited* for me to react and for a minute, I was just frozen by his confession. I pulled my feet away from him and planted them on the porch. I gripped the edge of the sofa and focussed on my breathing; in, out, repeat.

Everyone had been right and I was the stupid little girl that ignored their warnings.

"Janessa..." He said softly. His voice floated over to me like a caress. "Let me get this out." I felt him move closer and then he reached out and touched my arm, his touch so soft against my skin.

For a split second, one tiny second, I stayed like that, letting his touch warm me.

And then I came to my senses. I jumped up. "Don't touch me." I moved around the wicker table and sat down on the single armchair next to the sofa and stared out into the night. Anywhere but at his face which looked so hurt. If I looked at him now, I might let him talk. I might even let him convince me. And I couldn't let myself do that.

"Janessa, please listen to me."

"Why should I?" I snapped. "So you can tell me more lies? Lies that I'll believe because I'm an idiot."

"You're not an idiot," he denied quietly. Almost as if he was afraid to speak.

"Oh really?" I glared at him. And he stared at me, a pleading look in his eyes. "Then what am I?" I continued. "If I'm not an idiot than what am I?"

"You're the girl I want to be with; the girl that I'm falling for."

His sentence hung in the air between us; it was silent. You could hear a pin drop, it was so quiet. I choked on a laugh. "Are you serious? You really think I'm going to believe you? Now?"

"Ask me anything, I'll tell you anything you want to know."

"Why should I trust anything you say to me now?"

"You... shouldn't."

He was serious, the look on his face said so. But what I couldn't figure out was why he want to tell me everything when he was just playing me. When all he'd intended to get out of this, was my heart so he could shatter it to pieces? That's what I didn't get. The look on Bryan's face begged me to give him a chance to explain himself and the situation that we were both in.

So I asked him why he played with girls' hearts.

He explained that it had once been a game that he played with Reggie and Evan but they both met their current girlfriends through it and had quit. James never played. He thought that it was demeaning and would eventually demoralize each player.

I silently agreed.

Basically, the gist of it was that each player had to date a girl for about a month — longer if that's what it took — and then find a way to make the girl break it off. Bryan would lie, cheat, humiliate and play the horrible boyfriend, just to get the desired end result. He explained the power he felt, knowing the amount of pain he could cause and taking pleasure in it.

The whole while that he spoke, he watched my face. I wasn't one-hundred-percent sure that he couldn't tell how completely disgusted I felt just hearing what he did to those girls. The things he had planned for me. The more he talked, the stupider I felt.

I had fallen for it all. The intense look in his eyes that had made me feel things I never thought I would feel. His touch that was so soft, that I yearned for it, even now.

The way he'd talked to me, looked at me, made me feel like I was the only one he was thinking about; the only one he was paying attention to.

I felt sick. I grabbed my stomach; the uncomfortable desire to upchuck was overwhelming.

And suddenly, I realized he had stopped talking and was waiting for me to say something. I didn't know what he expected. A thanks for being honest? For once?

Did he want me to say that I believed him? That I believed that we were different together? Different than all those others he'd been with? That I was willing to forgive him if he just dropped his stupid game and chose a real, committed relationship with me?

I looked at him and I saw his impatience and anxiety.

He rubbed his hands together — almost like a nervous tick — as he watched my face. Watched me think about what he'd said.

"Now," my voice came out hoarse and dehydrated. I just didn't want to get up to slake my thirst. I licked my lips, swallowed and started again. "Now I know why all those girls hate you. You're awful. How could you do that to them?"

"I know," he said, nodding in agreement. He lowered his head to the floor and ran his fingers through his already dishevelled hair.

"Why did you tell me all that? You could have just lied your way through it." *It's what you're good at,* I thought bitterly.

"You're right." He bobbed his head. "Lying is one of the things I do pretty well." Then he lifted his gaze from the floor to me. "I told you all this because being with you this past week; I finally understand Evan and Reggie's relationships. *Why* they stopped playing."

I stared at him. Was he joking? He couldn't possibly think that I would just flat out believe him after he admitted that he was an expert liar? Did he? Before I could ask about it further, the screen door opened and Natalie popped her head out.

"Hey. Dinner's ready." She stepped out. "Your mom wanted me to come get you." She looked at me and then Bryan. Immediately, she picked up on the tension between us. "Everything okay?"

Before I had time to back out, I nodded. "Yup, everything's fine." Then I turned to Bryan, "Right, *babe?*"

I don't think he believed that I was okay with *anything* that he'd said but he smiled anyway, nodded, and got up just as I did.

There was a fold out table that had been propped up in the living room. The couch, armchair and coffee table had been moved against the wall to make room. Must have happened when I'd ducked out.

Bryan's hands grazed mine, almost like he was testing how far he could go. I still wasn't okay with everything I'd learned and I knew for a fact that I didn't want him to touch me.

I didn't know if I was going to feel like that indefinitely, but for tonight, I snatched my hand back and crossed my arms in front of my chest.

I sat at the head of the fold-out table with Bryan, Natalie, James, Anna, Carter — James' older brother — and André. I was in the perfect position to keep an eye on Thomas. If he made a move towards me, I wanted to know before it happened. It was the only way to protect myself.

Every now and then, I met Bryan's gaze and I realized that when it came to guarding myself and my heart, I was useless.

Since Anna was just seven, we all tried to keep the conversation appropriate and PG. Most of us, at least. Carter, James' older brother, kept making crude comments about James and Natalie's 'long time coming' relationship. And he wasn't lazy with his sexual innuendos. Each time I caught James glaring at his brother. Anna sat next to Bryan and she'd look up at him, confused, whenever something was said that wasn't meant for her young ears.

When he'd first told me that he had a seven-year-old sister, I'd assumed he was good with kids. And watching them now, it was quite obvious that I'd been right. Whenever he looked at her, his love and adoration was palpable. There was a moment when he leaned toward her and whispered something in her ear and she laughed. But it was his resulting grin that touched me. Then, suddenly, he met my gaze. In that moment before he lowered his gaze to his plate, something had flashed in his eyes.

The others at the table kept up the conversation really well. Our table was definitely louder than the adults'. It looked like James and Carter's parents were the only ones making an effort to keep up the discussion. Even Natalie's parents were quiet, sitting as far from each other as they could get.

After dinner, I started clearing the table. Anything to separate myself from everyone else in the room. I wasn't sure what to say to them or even how to contribute to the conversations so I didn't even try. I set the dishes to the side of the sink, I would get to it in a minute.

But just as I turned around, I collided with somebody. One upward glance confirmed my suspicions; it was Thomas.

He nodded toward the back porch. "Come with me."

Numbly, I did as I was told. I stumbled out to the back porch.

"I need you to do something for me," he said, his voice gruff, "punk."

Punk? The nickname itself tickled an old memory. It was his old nickname for me. Whenever he got angry with me as a child — didn't matter what I did — he'd call me 'punk'. In the same harsh tone he was using now.

What could I possibly have done now?

Thomas threw down a wad of legal documents that were stapled together by a corner and pointed to it. "Sign it."

I just stared, at him and the document. What was it? What would I be signing over to him? What did he want?

"Now!" He shouted. I flinched.

I saw people in the kitchen window, they looked out, confused by the sudden shout. Thomas smiled and waved nonchalantly. He waited a beat for everyone to turn their attention somewhere else and when they did, he turned back to me. There was a darkness in his eyes and I realized that the cold, hard edge to his voice was still there.

"Sign on the dotted lines!" He hissed angrily through his teeth, enough not to alert anyone but enough to terrify me.

I sat in the armchair and pulled the document toward me. I looked it over and realized that it looked very familiar. It was a document that stated that, on my eighteenth birthday, I had the choice to take over my grandfather's company.

Before he died, he'd had a very established and very well-off company that he'd inherited to his daughters. Until his oldest relinquished her claim and his youngest died of cancer. After that, he'd changed his will to include his grandchildren, myself and André — though I hadn't known he was included in it until last night.

Before I'd signed this last August, I had a say in what happened to the company until I gave it away to my grandfather's remaining grandchild — André — to inherit on his eighteenth birthday. Currently, it was in the hands of a fine young lady that knew what she was doing — unlike me — and had been appointed by my grandfather herself.

I had always known what I wanted to do and running a company wasn't it. And I trusted my grandfather enough to have appointed someone he knew would be capable of continuing his legacy.

I looked up at Thomas. He was holding out a pen for me. I reached for it but didn't move to sign it.

"Sign it!"

"I…" My voice came out small, sad and pathetic. It was barely audible. I cleared my throat. "I can't."

"What do you mean you can't?" He bellowed. He didn't bother to disguise his anger anymore. He took a threatening step toward me. "Just sign the damn thing!"

"I can't. I don't legally own these shares anymore!" I said loudly, but it still sounded so weak.

There was a momentary pause before he started laughing. I think he figured out what happened. And why.

I hoped that he would just leave it at that but he didn't. He slapped me hard across the face. Enough to make me bite the inside of my cheek. The rusty taste of blood filled my mouth as I lifted my hand to my face. My hand was shaking like crazy and my cheek stung. When my quivering hand finally made contact with my face, I felt dead inside. So I just sat there, cradling my face and staring out into nothingness.

I was sitting on the porch, my knees pulled up to my chest and my one hand still cupping my cheek when Bryan stepped out and came over to me.

"What happened?"

I really wanted to tell him. I wanted to tell someone. I wanted to confide in *someone* but then the memory of last night came back to me. Thomas' threat. My lungs being deprived of air. I was still scared, and shaking in my bare feet but I could try to chalk that up to the sudden chilly breeze.

"Janessa?" Bryan knelt down beside and put an arm around my shoulders, drawing me toward him.

I wanted to flinch away, be fearful of another man-slash-boy's touch but his touch was too comforting to deny. Soft. I almost felt safe in his arms. Like I could tell him the big bad truth and I would be okay, there would be no repercussions. But telling Bryan gave him power over me that I just wasn't willing to hand over so easily. I didn't even know if I could trust him anymore.

I lowered my hand to swipe at my eyes and nose, but didn't move fast enough to hide my cheek. I'm sure it was as red as a tomato; it certainly felt inflamed.

"Janessa? Talk to me."

I wanted to say something, but then I realized that my mouth had a small pool of blood waiting to be swallowed or spit out. I didn't want to swallow it — it as gross enough just being in my mouth — so I got to my feet to go spit on the lawn. It was the closest spot I could spit without too many people asking questions. When I was done, I turned to see Bryan standing a few feet behind me.

I wanted to be mad at him. I wanted to hate him. I wanted to distrust him but I couldn't find the strength to. So I closed the distance and let him wrap me in his arms; then I sobbed into his chest. I soaked his shirt in tears.

But he didn't protest. Instead, he just held me to him and once again, I felt safe. I felt protected. It was so hard to hate him and be mad at him and not trust him when he made me feel like this. He held me to him and at some point, I could swear I felt his lips on my hair and then I felt a small spark of something ignite within from the crown of my head to the tips of my toes.

I don't know how long we stood like that but eventually, he walked me back inside and asked if I thought I was going to be okay tonight. I nodded, saying yes, but deep down I didn't think I could. I just kept replaying last night in my head and remembering the pillow over my face.

No, I *didn't* think I was going to be okay tonight.

But I wasn't going to let Bryan stay over just because I felt safer when he was around. I couldn't put him in harm's way. I couldn't risk it, so I lied.

"Yeah, I'll be fine."

And then he left.

❧ Eleven ❧

That night, I went into my room and peeled out of my skirt and blouse, and changing into my cotton pyjama shorts and my pink cami. Then I shoved my chair under the doorknob and just watched it anxiously, going over scenarios in which Thomas could still come in. When I felt a little bit safer, I backed onto my bed and pulled out my notebook where I had begun my valedictorian speech.

What was there to say?

I'd jotted down some ideas about knowing yourself and following your heart. Plus a couple ideas about learning from your mistakes. I liked my ideas, but I didn't know how to put them into my speech.

Words had never been a problem for me. I was good at words. Give me an essay topic and I'd had more than enough to say. Essays were nothing.

But this speech was different. This speech would have an impact. This speech mattered. And I was stuck.

Below were my starter attempts but they were cliché enough to be in a movie. And probably were.

My cheek still hurt. It distracted me from my frustration and, unfortunately, my speech. I needed to finish this.

I wanted to be original. But I had a feeling that I wasn't going to be. All the best ideas had been taken. Everything's been done.

Why is this so hard? It shouldn't be. I'm good with words!

I was hard at work when I heard the sounds of shouting from downstairs, there were also sounds of dishes being thrown. Pots and pans. Mom's favourite pots and pans. It had to be mom and Thomas.

Mom was once again fighting in my defence and I hated the thought. What if she got hurt? What if I lost her?

I wanted to creep down the stairs so badly but just the idea of opening my door scared me. Even knowing where Thomas was, I didn't feel safe.

Just then there was a small knock at my door. I moved my chair and tucked it under my desk again. "Come in."

André came in slowly and I opened my arms for him, which he gladly accepted. I held him against my body and murmured the usual — 'it's going to be okay,' 'it's going to be fine' — into his hair. I felt him nod against my ear, but I barely believed my sweet nothings. How could *he*?

I didn't know how much longer he would be staying. Thomas could still do a lot more damage. He could even take André again. My arms tightened around my brother. I was *not* going to let him be taken again.

At some point, we fell asleep in my bed, despite the noise and ruckus that my mom and Thomas made downstairs. The next thing I knew, there was shrill sound going off just next to me. My alarm. I reached over André to shut it off and then rubbed the sleep from my eyes. I slowly became more aware of my surroundings, which meant that I became very aware that Thomas had moved my chair from under my desk to the right side of my bed, just so he could sit and watch me sleep. Or was he really after André. He did come back into our lives shortly after André did.

Then Thomas held out a phone for me. It wasn't mine so I know he hadn't snuck it out of mom's purse. It was still an iPhone, white, blue waterproof otterbox. Before I had a chance to ask about it, he was already talking. "Keep this on you at all times. Don't let your mother take it from you. I am going to use it to get in contact with you."

"I could just throw it away," I mumbled.

"If you do," he said, looking toward the pillow. His translation was not lost on me. If I got rid of it, he would *make it stick*. "Bad things happen when you defy me. Do you understand?"

Bad things also happened when we listened and did as he asked, but I wasn't going to mention that. I'm sure he would *make it stick* just for that. I nodded to answer his question.

"Good." Then he got to his feet and walked out the door. I immediately grabbed the chair and tucked it under the door handle again, which was stupid because he had already gotten in.

I felt like a puppet and he was my master. He pulled the string any which way he wanted and there wasn't anything I could do to go my own way. He would always pull me back. In my despair, I fell to my knees and just let the tears fall down my face. But when a salty tear hit my cheek, I flinched slightly at the contact. I wiped the tears away, careful not to irritate my cheek further.

Then the cellphone in my hand dinged with a message. I rolled my eyes at the contact that he had chosen for himself: DADDY. He was crazy if he thought I wouldn't change it.

DADDY: I am leaving now. Be sure to keep me updated on everything that happens with your mother and André. If your mother starts dating anyone, I want to know about it!

I didn't respond. I didn't think that's the way that this worked. He just wanted updates into my mom's life. He actually thought he had the right to know. Just knowing that he could contact me any time he pleased, made the idea of throwing this stupid phone away all that much more appealing.

But then another message came through.

DADDY: This phone has a tracker. It has to be on you at all times.

Great. A tracker.

That caused the tears to fall even faster. I felt completely trapped in a corner with nowhere to go. He had me trapped. I couldn't throw away this phone or he would make good on his threat and kill me. But if I kept this phone on me at all times, then he would always know where I was. But there was one thing he couldn't control. What I did to this phone.

I went into his contact, tears still streaming down my face, and I edited it. I changed **DADDY** to **THOMAS**. His number was the only number that existed on this phone. I didn't even know what would happen if I tried adding a new contact, like Bryan's. I needed to talk to him. Especially after all that he had told me last night about *the game*.

If Thomas really was leaving as he'd said, then he wouldn't mind if I confided in someone about this whole thing, right? Natalie... She was my best friend. I couldn't lie to her. And she already knew about Thomas and his abusive antics. The pieces would click in her mind if I told her about what happened right before he had slapped me, hard, across the face. I looked at my alarm clock, it was still early in the morning.

6:47 am.

I was way too vigilant at this point to even think about going back to bed. So I crept downstairs, slowly. I peered over the banister and sure enough, the living room was completely empty and devoid of a human presence. He really was gone. The thought crept into my mind but I couldn't just blindly accept that, so I kept searching. I checked the kitchen — which looked like it had been cleaned up but I still spotted some dents that couldn't be so easily cleaned. I checked the dining room, living room; even checked the basement — which was rarely used as is — and sure enough, he was gone.

If it weren't for the phone in my hand or the fact that I caught sight of the bruise across my cheek in every reflective surface I passed, I would have said that it had all just been a nightmare. The phone was proof, the bruise was proof, he had been here. And now he was out there.

I was no longer hungry but I tried to choke a pop tart down anyway. Just to say that I had eaten something.

Then I grabbed my notebook from upstairs and started making another attempt at my speech. I sat on one of the bar stools tucked under the island, keeping a close eye on the front and back door.

They were the only entrances and if he came back, I'd know about it, immediately.

Hours ticked by while I sat in that kitchen. Finally, mom and André came down.

André looked rested but slightly confused and embarrassed — probably because he woke up in his sister's bed. He rubbed his eyes clear of sleep and yawned as he took a seat next to me.

Mom, on the other hand, looked like she hadn't slept at all. There was a hospital bandage on her forehead and I had no problem guessing the cause. When I asked how many stitches it needed, she inhaled sharply and let out a breath. "Eight," she said, and then she turned away from me.

I just hoped that was the only injury she'd gotten.

Mom started on breakfast, André sat at the dining room table, and I took notice of the clock on the stove. It was ticking closer to eleven, which meant I needed to leave.

❧

A couple hours into my shift, things started to slow down a bit, so Natalie and I got a moment to talk. She asked me about what happened last night and I told her as much as I was willing to say. I didn't say that Bryan and I had talked or that he had explained everything to me. I wasn't sure if I was just being naive to believe him. He could have bluffed his way through the entire conversation. He could've lied and made it sound like the truth.

I hated that I couldn't tell the difference.

I could tell that there was something on Natalie's mind, but I had to get all this out so I wouldn't interrupt her. When I was done, I blew out a breath, relieved.

"I feel so much better. It feels so good to have that off my chest," I told her as I wiped down a table and she followed me, taking her 'break'. "You okay?"

She nodded, even forced a smile. But I had been her friend long enough to know when she was faking or forcing something. So I straightened my stance and waited for her to tell me. I was not going to move from this spot until I knew everything. "Yeah, I'm fine. It's just that, my parents sat me down last night and..." She trailed off.

I could see that she was starting to tear up. Whatever her parents told her last night broke her heart. Finally, it dawned on me. "It's going to be official?" I asked. "They're really splitting up?"

She took a seat at the table I was cleaning and nodded. "Yeah, they are. They're gonna wait till after graduation to sign the papers." Natalie adjusted the sugar packets at the table and shifted the little promotion display about our new summertime cupcake. "They just wanted to give me a heads up."

"Oh, sweetie..." I sympathized. "How about you come over tonight? And we'll have a sleepover. We can talk," I smiled when she did, "or we could *not* talk if that's more appealing."

"It's okay," she smiled. I knew that look on her face; she was thankful and appreciative. Sure, she had known that her parents' marriage was over a long time ago but to know that it was really happening; it was life-changing.

I smiled as I took her hand.

"But thank you. I mean, I knew this was coming for a long time. They were always fighting and he was always out with other women. I knew this was coming, mom knew it too. But, I don't know. I guess I was still hoping that they could work it out. A small, stupid part of me thought they could fall in love again and want to be married to each other."

She slid the sugar packets case back and forth from one hand to the other. When I saw Amy giving me a look, I got up and continued to wipe down tables. Natalie returned the sugar packets and followed me.

"Maybe this is better," she said almost inaudibly as a customer walked past us to the counter. "Maybe them being divorced is for the better. Maybe they'll finally be able to be happy.

"But it's going to be weird, you know? Going between houses just so I can spend time with both of them. It'll be strange to live in two different houses."

I nodded as I listened.

I knew for a fact that it was better for my parents to be apart. But I didn't think there was any amount of space between the two of them that would make me feel even the slightest bit safe. Thomas could be on Uranus and I would still worry that he would be able to find my mother. Or that he would still be able to pull my strings, threatening me to do his bidding.

But Natalie's parents were different.

Her dad would never physically hurt her or her mom, no matter how angry he got. In that way, she was lucky. She never had to worry about her safety but the fights were just as terrible. Especially when it's your parents fighting; shouting at the top of their lungs because they've reached their limit. And the worst part is not being able to do anything about it.

I understood better than anyone what that was like.

"Are you sure you don't want to come over tonight?" I asked when I finished wiping down the last table.

"No, it's okay." She shook her head slightly and smiled. "Besides, I have a date with James tonight." She blushed a little.

I clapped a hand over my mouth to keep the squeal inside. I had to admit that I was a little surprised that they were still going out. Megan's party had been last night, after the game, they were supposed to have gone to it but changed their minds. She had already been hesitant to ask him to that party, so *excuse me* if I was surprised. Good surprised, but still.

"Who asked who?"

"He asked me." She turned and walked back into the backroom, but not before I saw the eye roll she was trying to hide. "But I think I'm going to cancel. He'd asked before this whole thing with my parents went down and now I just want to be alone."

Once the door closed behind us, I took her hand, "Natalie, honey." I waited for her to slowly turn to me. "You'll torment yourself all night if you stay cooped up in that house with your parents. Besides, you deserve a night of fun."

She gave me a look that said she was unsure about what she wanted.

"Come on, Nat, you know I'm right. You know you need this."

I walked out at seven that night.

Bryan was leaning up against his car, waiting. I don't know if he was waiting for me but, by the way, he immediately pushed off his car and walked toward me, I figured he *had* been. He wore shorts, a black tee, and flip-flops. His hands were in his pockets as he stopped in front of me. "Can we talk?"

"I can't, I need to get home."

I wanted to talk to him. I needed to know where we were going to go from here. Did we fake it as we had last night? Did I trust him? Could I? There were too many questions in my head, but it was going to have to wait.

"Can I give you a ride?"

"I drove myself today," I told him, already digging through my purse to look for my car keys. I walked in front of his car to mine and unlocked it.

"I'll meet you at your house, please?"

"Fine."

At my house, I walked inside and dumped my purse on the couch and dropped my keys right next to it. "Mom?" I looked around. The house appeared to be empty until I heard sounds coming from downstairs. I opened the door and shouted, "Mom!"

"What?" She asked as she moved to stand at the bottom step and looked up at me. "What's the matter?"

"Nothing," I told her. "Never mind." I closed the door behind me and headed upstairs to change into my pyjamas. I even put on a sweater in case I needed it. Then I headed back downstairs and outside. Bryan was already there, sitting on the porch steps and he turned when he heard me.

He gave me a once over, and then did a double take. I was already starting to feel self-conscious about it now. I pulled my sweater around my body tighter and joined him on the steps.

"What do you want?"

"I wanted to check in with you last night. I even texted you," he said. "Then I remembered that your mom had your phone..." He looked at me. I think he only did that so that I would be able to see the intensity in his eyes and the sincerity on his face as he spoke. All of which he could easily fake, as I'd learned last night. "I was worried about how I'd left you. Are you okay?"

"I'm fine," I said quickly. I tried to keep my lip from quivering but he really seemed like he cared. He just seemed so genuine. I just wasn't sure what was real anymore or if anything that left his mouth was the truth.

I think he mistook the quiver in my voice because he wrapped an arm around my shoulders and pulled me toward him, comfortingly. Once again, I couldn't help feeling safe in his arms. Protected. Almost.

Then he asked something that I hadn't expected, but should have known was coming. He looked at me. "Are *we* okay?"

The way he asked the question, I thought he wanted us to be okay. I wanted us to be okay too, but I also wanted to be able to trust my boyfriend. I wanted to be able to trust him to tell me the truth, to mean what he said, to touch me because he wanted to and not because it was necessary to win some stupid game.

"Ness," he said, with such emotion that I almost thought he was going to cry. He took my hand. "Please give me another chance. Let me at least try to make it up to you."

"Okay." I nodded. "I'll give you another chance. But no more lies. There has to be complete honesty between us."

I shouldn't have been surprised by how quickly he agreed. Inwardly, I kicked myself for already doubting him. I told him I would give him another chance and that was exactly what I planned to do.

❧ Twelve ❧

I made dinner that night. Mom and André were in the basement the whole day. I can't say that I wasn't curious about what they were up to. I even tried to take a peek but they ushered me out every time. I figured that it was a surprise for me. But that was ridiculous!

I put my entire focus on making a late dinner, just simple pasta. While the water boiled, I put some more work into my speech. I think I'm making progress but I'll have my mom go over it when I'm done.

I set the table and gathered the others. Mom asked how work was and I told her it was fine. I left out the part about Natalie's parents. I was sure mom would pick up the phone right away and give Olivia a call.

Over the years Olivia had become to my mom what Natalie was to me. If this was Natalie and I'd just found out that she and her husband were getting a divorce, I wouldn't hesitate. I would be there for her. I knew my mom wouldn't like that I was keeping this from her but I was also pretty sure that Olivia would want to tell my mom herself.

I asked her and André about their day. They had spent the whole time cleaning out the basement; going through the junk that we had down there and throwing it away. I was curious about what they were throwing out. If I remembered correctly, the only things mom and I'd put down there were things that had belonged to Thomas from grandpa's office.

After high school, Thomas had gone to work with my grandpa but after he got fired for something illegal — that was all the information I got — grandpa had gotten Thomas escorted out without allowing him to take his stuff. So my mom cleared out his office and kept everything. I think she thought it could give her a clue into what went wrong in their marriage. From how she'd described her relationship with him before the 'I do's, he had been the sweetest, most caring guy that she had ever dated. They'd been best friends. But, though that was all true, he'd been very secretive.

Everything my mom had of his that hadn't already been taken by Thomas when he first left, was in the basement. Was she clearing it all out? Maybe she was finally getting him out of her life for good. But why wouldn't she let me help her? I couldn't understand why André was allowed down there, but *I* wasn't.

Though that bothered me, I tried not to dwell on it.

I cleared the table and did the dishes. Then I headed to my bedroom to finish working on my speech. I was hard at work when the phone that Thomas gave me rang. It was the theme song to Jaws. I was frozen in place, turned toward my bed to stare at the phone as it rang and rang. Then it cut off. And the sudden silence that filled the room was almost deafeningly. So much so that when the sound of feet running up the stairs startled me enough that I jumped onto my bed.

I tucked the phone under my pillow, waiting for someone to open the door but no one did. Not mom or André. The hallway turned silent and then I heard the muffled sound of a ding from under my pillow. I looked at it.

THOMAS: When I call, you answer.

What could he possibly want to know, he'd just left this morning. Not a lot had changed since he did. I quickly responded, sending an apology and then put the phone on silent. I didn't want mom hearing it and adding more time to my punishment. I covered the phone with a few sheets of paper as I went back to work on my speech.

It was a few hours later when I heard the sound of pebbles hitting my window and for a second I thought Thomas had come back. Making good on his promise to *make it stick* because I didn't answer his call. But then where would he be if I wasn't around to feed him lies... I had already decided that I was *not* going to risk my mom's safety by giving him facts. So I would try to lie my way through every conversation that we were going to have.

Another pebble hit the window and I searched my room for some weapon, anything to give me even the smallest upper hand. I picked up a high heeled shoe from the back of my closet, praying to God that I wouldn't need to use it.

Then I moved over to the window and looked down.

It wasn't Thomas. It was Bryan, pulling another romantic gesture. I dropped my shoe on the floor. Just as I opened the window, Bryan threw another pebble and it hit me in the forehead. I had to commend him on his aim, but it shot a small stab through my skull. It didn't last long, I was just momentarily dazed.

I looked out my window again and this time, I saw Bryan climbing the fence between my house and my neighbors'. On their side of the fence was a tree and one of its branches almost touched my window. I figured him wanted to climb their tree so that he didn't have to shout up at me. When I saw him doing just that, I anxiously bit my nails.

"Bryan," I stage whispered. "What are you doing here?"

Now he was grabbing ahold of the branch that was hanging over the fence. He put a finger to his mouth, the universal sign that said '*shut up*'.

"Be careful," I said in the same volume as before. I looked over at my door to make sure that mom was not coming down the hall toward me. I was grounded, I was not allowed to have company without any supervision. Having Bryan over like this was a serious no-no. I could get into even more trouble.

I was about to protest when Bryan slid himself through my window.

My mouth was open to say something, to get him to leave but I froze when I saw the black eye that he was sporting. "Bryan..." I whispered. Slowly, I moved toward him and raised my hand to touch his face. He hissed softly when my thumb made contact with his bruise. "What happened?"

"Walked into a pole?" He joked.

It was *not* from a pole; that much I knew. I gave him a look that said so. His face fell. Much like his attempt at lightening the mood. "I'll be right back," I told him, "stay away from the door. I don't want my mom seeing you."

Mom was in the kitchen. She was pouring herself a cup of her fancy scotch, which was considerably emptier than usual. Thomas had definitely had more than his fair share. I opened the freezer and grabbed what little of the frozen vegetables we had — since we didn't have an ice pack — and went back to my room.

She stopped me before I'd made it very far though. "Where do you think you're going with that?"

"My cheek is acting up," I lied over my shoulder.

"Okay, but bring that back down when you're done with it."

I nodded and all-but sprinted up the stairs. I closed my bedroom door behind me. "Here," I told Bryan, handing the pack to him. He accepted it gratefully and touched it to his eye, hissing when the cold made contact. Bryan was nestled into a corner, his head leaning against my window sill and his legs pulled up slightly to make hollow triangles with my floor. "Want to tell me what happened?"

"Will you tell me what happened with your cheek?" He gave me a look that told me he already knew.

I sighed. "Bryan, did you get into a fight with someone?" He looked away, looking quite amused. "Is this who you are? Getting into fights with random people off the street?"

"Oh, now you're judging me?"

"Hardly; I'm asking you a question. I want to know what's going on. Is this something I should expect from you from now on? You sneaking into my bedroom with a black eye that you got from God knows who?"

"I'll tell you if you tell me what happened to your cheek."

I sat quietly. I wanted to tell him. Just like last night. I wanted to have someone to confide in but Thomas made that hard to do. I couldn't tell anyone if I wanted to live. Plus, if that phone he'd given me had a tracker, then it could also have a mic, couldn't it?

He could be listening in on any conversations I had. He could make sure I didn't break his trust. A trust he'd forced me to keep when he threatened me.

With that breathing down my neck, I lied to Bryan. "I walked into a tree.?"

But he caught my lie just as easily as I'd caught his.

"What happened to being completely honest with each other?"

"You lied first," I pointed out, "I know you didn't walk into a pole."

"And I know you didn't walk into a tree," he said; a small, barely-there smile graced his features. He lowered the frozen vegetables and looked back up at me through his eyelashes. "That guy, Thomas; he did it, didn't he?"

I looked away, feeling ashamed. Mostly ashamed of the fact that there even *was* a connection between Thomas and me. Slowly, I nodded.

Bryan set the vegetables down and moved toward me. He pinned my legs on either side of his waist and pulled me onto his lap. "My dad gave me the black eye," he admitted. I looked up at him, startled by his confession. "He got a little too drunk tonight, frustrated with a case and lashed out when I tried to take the bottle away. He'd had way past his limit. I should have known better."

I hushed him, putting my hands on either side of his face. "It's not your fault." Before he could say anything, I pressed my lips to his and snuggled closer to him. He tried to help. He pulled me tighter against him. I kissed him and he kissed me back.

Did it matter that he could be using his relationship with his father to create a connection with me? Partly. Was he lying about it? No, I didn't think he was. This wasn't something people talked about, much less lied about.

I didn't care that this connection could be a part of his game. As much as that thought nagged me, I didn't believe that our connection was fake. It could be, but I didn't believe it.

I broke the kiss when my head started to swim. We were breathing heavily but we were also smiling. Just like that, everything was back to the way it had been before last night. Only, now it was better because I knew the truth.

Bryan looked at me, green eyes versus brown and his thumb brushed across my bruised cheek. I closed my eyes and let myself just *feel*. I loved the way it felt when he touched me and held me; like close wasn't close enough.

I wrapped my arms around his neck and then rested my head on his shoulder. We sat like that for a while, with our eyes closed and our bodies pressed against each other.

It was a little while later when I untangled myself from him and stood up. I thought I heard someone coming up the stairs and didn't want them peeking into my room. But it was just André. I heard his bedroom door close and figured he was going to bed.

I closed my door, tucked my chair underneath the handle and turned back to Bryan. He just watched me carefully, a little worried himself. I noticed by the way his shoulders tensed in the moonlight. I sat beside him and he put a hand on my bare knee. His touch sending tingles throughout my entire body.

"Don't worry," I told Bryan. "Thomas is gone. He left this morning. I'm just being cautious because technically, I'm not allowed to have company."

"I should leave then. I don't want to get you into trouble." Bryan stroked my cheek with his free hand.

I couldn't help but look at the growing bruise under his eye. I felt scared and angry. Scared for him, his sister, his mom. And, most of all, angry at his father. But underneath it all, I felt relief. Because now I'd found someone that understood the abuse that I was going through with Thomas. It's great talking to Natalie about it and just having someone to vent to, but she doesn't understand the way Bryan does.

And that makes a difference.

"Are you worried about your sister?"

Bryan shook his head quickly. "No, she was asleep when I left. I don't think my dad would go into her room."

I slid closer to him and wrapped my arms around his neck. He buried his head into my shoulder. "And your mom?"

"She's got her hiding places. She should be fine."

My neck felt wet and I pulled back to look at him. He was crying. Hastily, he wiped away tears but it was too late; I'd already seen them.

"I'm sorry," he said, "it's just such a relief to get to talk to someone who understands."

I nodded, knowing exactly what he meant. "It's okay to cry." My voice came out in a whisper. He nodded, and this time he didn't fight it. I suddenly wanted to cry too. I had never seen a guy cry before; it was almost like seeing my mom cry. Her sobbing was contagious. "You can stay here tonight. You just have to leave early so my mom doesn't see you."

He nodded again.

Getting to my feet, I went and brought back the box of Kleenex I had on my desk. He accepted them gratefully.

"Can I ask you something?" I asked, sitting beside him. Bryan set the Kleenex down next to him on his other side, then he lifted my legs to either side of his body and lifted me onto his lap.

"Shoot."

"It's about Megan," I said.

His brows lifted, curious. "Okay...?"

His hands moved under my shirt. Bryan's touch brought a shiver down my spine. I tried to ignore how it felt as I asked my question. "I already know that you guys are going to prom together, but is there anything else going on between the two of you?"

"Is she bugging you?" I bit my lip and refused to say anything else until he gave me a real answer. But he took my silence as the answer to his. "I knew it. Why didn't you say anything?"

"Because I can take care of myself," I snapped. He still hadn't answered *my* question and his silence gave me the impression that there was something between them. I tried to get off his lap but Bryan held tightly, refusing to let me go. His eyes begged me to let it go. "Just answer my question; is there something going on between the two of you?"

"No."

I lifted a brow skeptically. He definitely wasn't telling the whole truth.

He must've read my face because, finally, he sighed and said, "A few months ago, she asked me if I wanted to get back together and I told her no." I had a sinking feeling... Like, the kind of feeling where you knew you weren't going to like the end of a story. "She'd looked so sad, so I told her that I'd consider it *if* my next girlfriend," he paused to gesture at me. "You know, if you and I didn't work out."

I let this new information sink in. I still didn't like it but I just had to find a way to beat her at her own game.

We sat there talking for a little while longer, in hushed tones.

When it started to get later, I brought the not-so-frozen vegetables back into the freezer. Then we went to bed. It was a struggle at first, trying to find a comfortable position. I even tried to snuggle up on the floor but he wouldn't let me and held me close to his chest. He fell asleep quickly.

The next morning, my alarm went off at around 8:00. Bryan groaned awake as I hit the snooze. I sat up in bed, which earned me another groan from Bryan.

"Where are you going?" He grumbled. "You're not doing that stupid I-just-woke-up-like-this thing, are you?"

"No." I laughed through a grand yawn. I wasn't normally a morning person, but today I was. I moved over to my desk and angled my notebook toward what little sunlight filtered into the room. I sat down on my floor; my chair was still tucked underneath the doorknob. "But I *need* to finish this."

"What is it?"

Now he was intrigued enough to at least half sit up and look at me. I laughed when I glanced over at him. Without my pillow hiding his bed head, his shaggy hair stood up in every direction.

"It's my valedictorian speech."

"I'm not even surprised that you're giving the speech this year," he said, flopping back down on my bed. I laughed under my breath as he slowly started to drift off to sleep again.

I worked on my speech for another hour, after which I sat down on the bed. The mattress dipped under my weight. I shook Bryan's shoulder. He grumbled and rolled over, which only made me shake his shoulder harder. "Bryan, wake up. It's time for you to go."

"Just five more minutes," I heard him grumble.

"Babe, I already gave you an hour. Come on, time to wake up." It was such a shame to wake him up; he looked so peaceful and almost childlike when he slept.

"Fine," he said, letting a huge yawn rip through him, "I'm awake."

"I can see that," I said.

He finally crawled out of my bed and went to my door. I got anxious because I didn't know if anyone else was awake. It seemed like a huge gamble to let him walk out the front door. So I pulled him back and looked into the hall. It was clear.

"You know," Bryan started, whispering in my ear, "this is the first time that I've ever slept in a girl's bed without having sex with her first." He chuckled but I didn't find it nearly as amusing as he did.

"Come on."

I walked ahead of him down the stairs and then let him quietly slip through the front door. The middle floor was completely empty, or at least, it had been from my vantage point.

But when I went into the kitchen to get breakfast, I almost jumped out of my skin. There was André; sitting at the table eating breakfast. The smile on his face told me exactly what he was thinking. He caught me. And, I was absolutely sure that he would *not* hesitate to out me.

It had definitely been a gamble to bring Bryan down this way. And I was definitely not much of a gambler.

❧ Thirteen ❧

"So you wanna tell mom or should I?" André asked, scooping cereal into his mouth. His eyes gleamed with a mischievous sparkle.

"You know," I glared at him, grabbing a bowl from the cupboard, "I was just thinking that I'd keep it from her for as long as I could." I poured myself a bowl of cereal. "I know I should tell mom, deal with the consequences, but…" I wasn't even sure how to finish that sentence. There wasn't really an alternative to it. I should just tell mom, live with the repercussions.

"So…" André dragged out the single syllable, "you wanna tell mom or should I?" He asked the question as if he hadn't heard me.

I glared at him. "Shut up. I'll tell her."

I sat down beside him, scooped Froot Loops out of my bowl and shoved it in my mouth.

I looked over at André as he ate and smiled. I don't know what it's like for other people with siblings, but after being apart for so many years, it was so nice to have a breakfast buddy, someone that I could share a big six-person table with.

Mom had gotten it a few years ago when she thought we'd have company on a regular basis. But that didn't happen and we just decided to keep the table. In the mornings, when she was already at work, the empty space was kind of lonely.

The other foster kids weren't morning people, *at all*, so they never woke up early enough to eat with me.

It was kinda nice to have someone to share a breakfast table with. Even if he was hogging two chairs.

The Game

André sat with his back to one chair, his feet perched on another one next to him and a bowl of cereal balancing on his lap. He looked so relaxed and so at home, that I almost couldn't be mad about it. *Almost.*

"Put your feet down." I smacked his shoulder.

He rolled his eyes and, in a huff, pulled his feet back and set them on the floor. He finished his breakfast, slurping as loudly as he had last weekend when we'd had breakfast together before we went out to drop off his résumés.

"You know, I never did get a chance to ask about the job offers." I waited for him to look up. He took his time. Was he really that tired?

"Have you gotten any?"

"Not yet," he said, shrugging like it wasn't a big deal.

"Well, if I didn't have to work today, I could take you around for another go at it," I said, punctuating that fact with a pitiful punch in the air. "You know, *really* get your name out there."

"How hard is it to get my name out there?" I was about to answer when I realized that he was being rhetorical. "I mean." He got up and brought his bowl to the sink. "André Maxwell. It's not really a name that you'd forget."

I can't believe I'd never bothered to ask his last name. I mean, now it all sort of made sense; now that I knew we shared the same mother... and father. Had I known that he shared Thomas' last name, I would've thought it was a coincidence.

One of the first things mom had done when Thomas was out of our lives for good — or so we'd thought — was changed our last names. She'd taken back her maiden name and cleansed her life of Thomas.

"About that," I mused. "What do you think about getting that changed?"

"To what?"

"Reynolds," I said, matter-of-fact. "It's mom's maiden name. She took it back after dad," — the word was like salt in my mouth — "left. It's mine too. It could be yours if you wanted it to be."

He looked at me thoughtfully, leaning against the island. "Well, I've never thought about it."

"It was probably never an option for you before."

He nodded. "Maybe. I'll think about it."

Then he left the room and I finished my breakfast.

At work, I briefly saw mom. Told her about the idea of, maybe, changing André's last name if he decides it's something that he wants to do. She seemed thrilled by the idea.

"Yeah," she'd said, "if that's something he wants to do, I'm all for it." She'd seemed so happy that I hesitated to tell her about Bryan. "But, sweetie," mom reached out and touched my arm, "we're not gonna force this on him, right?"

"Of course not," I agreed.

Then I went back to work.

It was a long eight hours. I kept expecting Bryan to walk through the bakery doors but he didn't and I didn't know why I expected him to. It's not like he *had* to come visit me at work; it was just a silly expectation. But when he didn't, it was kind of a letdown. And even worse was when Megan came in with her posse. I tried to keep busy so that I wasn't forced to talk to her.

Amy saw her and grinned, ready to serve and I thanked the Heavens that Amy took the fall. But Megan didn't bother being civil with the poor girl. She had the audacity to ask for someone else because Amy hadn't washed her hands earlier. Which I knew for a fact wasn't true; Amy may love to hear herself talk (and because of that she was annoying), but she is a stickler for rules.

Amy was stunned and looked to me for help. I sighed and was about to step forward and take her place when Natalie beat me to it.

She put a hand out in front of me and mouthed the words, "I got this." She plastered on her typical customer service smile, and walked over to Megan.

"Sorry, Natalie," Megan smiled. "But I want Janessa."

"Oh," Natalie said, "I'm sorry, but the oven in the back is making this weird sound and Janessa's the only one that knows how to fix it." Then she turned to me. "Right?"

"Right," I said slowly, backing out of the room.

Everything Natalie had told Megan was a lie because the truth was, I barely knew how to fix a sink, let alone the oven.

In the back, Trevor was cleaning dishes and Anita was busy *cleaning* the oven. They both looked over at me. They were probably wondering what I was doing back there.

By the end of my shift, I was tired and just ready to go to sleep. When I got home, André was on the couch, watching a show and mom was sitting at the dining room table. She looked as though she were waiting for someone. When I got to the table and asked her what was up, it dawned on me that André could have snitched.

Mom was calm as she gestured to the chair in front of me. "Sit." She sent André away and turned to me. I could see the disappointment on her face.

I didn't know how to start, but I tried. "Um, so, I assume you know."

"Know what?" Mom urged. She wanted me to say it.

I took a deep breath. "Bryan came over and stayed the night."

"Yes, I know." I felt like I'd let her down; the thought made me sick to my stomach. "You know how I know?"

"André's a snitch?"

Mom didn't have patience for my jokes. So she continued to talk as if I hadn't spoken at all. She kept her voice calm, which was scarier than if she'd shouted. "André told me. And though I am very angry about that, I am a little more concerned that something happened last night."

I knew what she was getting at but I really didn't want to believe that she thought I'd do that with her sleeping across the hall. "Oh... well, Bryan got beat up and he just needed to go somewhere he felt safe. I got him the..." I trailed off when I saw mom's look. She didn't care why Bryan came over. It hurt that she thought... "Mom, you don't *actually* think I would do that, do you?"

"What else am I supposed to think?" She looked at me pointedly. "You got a tattoo, you're skipping school, and it all started when Bryan became your boyfriend."

"Don't you think that's a bit of a leap, to just assume that Bryan had anything to do with those things?" I asked. I'd already told her Bryan had nothing to do with Thursday. It was all me. I'd already told her this. "And the tattoo would have happened with or without him. It was my idea *and* Natalie's. We were planning on doing it together."

"Regardless, you can't be alone with this boy."

"Mom—"

"You want to be ungrounded?"

"Yes."

"You want your phone back?"

"Yes."

"Then things are going to have to change." She finished her drink. "You are going to have a strict curfew. The conditions of your grounding will remain, but I *will* allow you to go out. I will ask where you're going, who you're going out with, and you can't ever be alone with your boyfriend. Is that understood?"

Understood? I may as well still be grounded. Sure, she gave a bit of leeway in the fact that I could now leave the house. And even have company without supervision (unless that company was Bryan). It should feel like a win, but I felt even more constricted than before.

"Nessa, do you understand?"

I nodded. "Yes."

"Good." Mom got up and went to her purse and came back with my phone. "Now, curfew on a school night will be 9:30. Sharp. And 10:30 on the weekend." Mom held my phone out to me but before I was able to grab it, she snatched it back. "*Don't* test me. I will tighten the leash if you even *think* about breaking your curfew."

"Understood." I sighed.

She handed over my phone. I took it and headed upstairs before I checked it. There were several messages from Natalie and Bryan, and there was a group chat that looked like it had just been created a couple days ago… and hadn't been used in just as long.

Natalie started it with a simple 'hey', and the boys added to it with their own 'hey's.

Since I had a two hours before my curfew, I opened the group chat and sent a message.

ME: Hey. Anyone feel like hanging out at my place tonight?

I took my time taking a shower and went back to my bedroom, slipping on a pair of shorts, a plain white tee, and a jean vest. I checked my phone to see if I'd gotten any responses. Then my phone beeped with quick messages from each one of them saying they were in.

I pulled my hair up into a messy bun and waited for my friends.

᪥ ℰ ᪥

Ten minutes later, Natalie, James and I were in my backyard, lying on a couple blankets. I was trying not to be a clingy girlfriend but I kept checking my phone every few minutes. The longer Bryan took to show up, the more worried I became.

"Would you relax, Ness?" Natalie said from the other side of James.

When we first put the blankets down, James opted to be in between the two of us, claiming that if he didn't, *he'd* feel like the third wheel. But now I did, especially with Natalie lying on top of James to get to me. Not that he seemed to mind. To take my mind off their intimate show, I thought about Bryan and when he was going to get here. He'd said he would come.

"He'll be here," she insisted when I checked my phone for the umpteenth time. "In fact, there he is."

I tilted my head back to see that Bryan was coming around the corner, walking toward me. Natalie murmured in surprise about the bruise under his eye. I ignored it and jumped up to meet him halfway. Bryan was wearing his red polyester uniform, which explained a lot. I threw my arms around his neck — as if I hadn't seen him in days — and he scooped me up, wrapping his arms around my waist and lifted me off the ground slightly.

"How's your eye?" I asked. He set me back down but kept his hands on my waist. I touched his black eye and he watched me while I did.

"I'm fine." He smiled, pressing his forehead against mine. "How's your cheek?"

"Eh." I shrugged. "A little makeup and I'm good as new."

He reached up and stroked it, looking a little sad. "I'm sorry this happened to you. If I'd known what your home life was like, or your past, I never would have picked you," he whispered.

He sounded so sincere, so unlike the boy on Friday that had explained the game.

"Why does *that* matter?"

"Because I've been through it. It's my life," he said, pausing to take a deep breath. "And now when I look at you, I see someone that's been hurt so much already. Which is why I stopped playing. And why I agreed to be completely honest with you. You deserved to be loved, and I want to try."

My heart was in my throat, I was so touched.. Happiness flowed like adrenaline through my veins.

"I just hope you can forgive me for lumping you in with those other girls."

I nodded and kissed him. He kissed me back; his lips turned up into a smile against my lips. "Yeah, I forgive you."

"Hey, guys!" We heard from behind us. "As cute as you are, how about we play Truth or Dare?"

And that's how I found myself, tuning my guitar after being dared to play a song. I'd stuffed it into the back of my closet and I hadn't played in years. Not since my grandpa died. They'd wanted me to play at his wake — a soft little melody in the background — but as heartbroken as I was, I broke down and haven't played since.

"Gah, I'm so rusty," I told them, shaking out my hand. I wasn't used to playing anymore. How was I going to play a song? "Just warning you, I may be bad."

They didn't seem to care one bit. They just wanted to see if I would follow through with the dare or chicken out.

"Give me a song," I asked.

They all started throwing song titles at me.

"Whoa, one at a time."

"Do *Genie in a Bottle*. You would *not* stop playing it when you first learned it," Natalie suggested. "There's *no way* you forgot how to play it."

"Okay."

So that's what I played. She was right. Once I really got into the rhythm, it was obvious that the chords to Christina Aguilera's "Genie in a Bottle" were branded into my brain. And then I was singing along.

When I looked up, I blinked at their reactions.

Natalie was beaming from ear to ear — she hadn't heard me sing or play my guitar in three years. I think there was also a hint of pride in her eyes (probably because she was the one that came up with the dare that set this chain of events in motion).

James gave me a look that made me think he was surprised that I didn't sound like a dying walrus. Which was offensive since I *knew* I could sing.

Though Bryan was also smiling, I couldn't figure out what he was thinking. Or feeling. Even his eyes were unreadable. Was he disappointed?

I tried not to let the dread of that thought stop me from finishing the song.

If you wanna be with me
I can make your wish come true
Just come and set me free, baby
And I'll be with you

"There you have it," I said, setting the guitar behind me.

"I didn't know you could sing *and* play the guitar," James said. Though the statement was clearly meant for me, James looked at Natalie, glaring in her direction.

"Yeah, well, when I was younger I took singing, guitar, and dance lessons."

I moved back toward Bryan and leaned against his chest; his arms curled around me and held me to him.

We played a few more rounds. Then I checked my phone and saw that it was just a couple minutes to my curfew. "I think we should call it a night." I got to my feet. The others all looked like they wanted to protest; like they wanted to keep playing. "If you guys want to hang out with me again, get up."

"Or what?"

"Or I'll probably get grounded again."

That got them moving.

I scooped up the blankets and held the guitar to me as I walked up to the back porch. James and Natalie shouted their goodbyes before disappearing around the house. Bryan followed me up. "Look, I just wanted you to know that my parents asked me to invite you and your family over for a barbeque this week."

"Okay," I said, stepping into the house just as the clock on the stove hit 9:30. I let out a breath and turned to look at him. "I'll talk to my mom about it, okay?"

"Okay."

I kissed him goodnight and he left.

✣ Fourteen ✣

I mentioned the barbeque to mom at the breakfast table but she just said she would think about it. She ended the conversation then. When I walked out of the house, I saw Bryan parked on the curb, leaning against his car.

"Morning," he said, giving me a quick kiss, which André responded to with a groan.

"Just get in the car," I snapped, opening it for him.

He didn't go easily. It was pretty obvious that André didn't like Bryan. The series of groans and glares, and insistence that he'd rather walk accentuated that perfectly.

"André, *please* get in the car. You got me into trouble once, do you really want to do it again?" I asked. If he turned around and made good on his threat to walk, I would be left alone with Bryan and I really didn't want to lose my freedom. "You owe me."

Though I could tell that he didn't agree with my point, he opened the back door and got in. I apologized to Bryan and then we were on our way.

At school, mom couldn't really keep us from being alone. Once, Megan walked by but she didn't even bother looking at me, which was strange. Usually, she made sure to give me a nasty look but today, nothing.

When I commented on it, Bryan just said that he had a conversation with her and she wasn't happy about it. He also mentioned that he'd promised to do something for her. The minute those words left his mouth, I got nervous. What had he promised in order to make sure she stopped bugging me?

Unfortunately, Melissa spotted me from down the hall right then and bounded towards me, singing my name to get my attention. She stopped with a final hop right in front of me. "Hey," she said to Bryan in a flat tone, then she looked at me. "Are you ready for our final Chemistry test? Well, before exams?"

I just looked at her like she was crazy or as if she'd grown two heads. If we had a test today, I would know about it.

"We don't *have* a test today..." I said, slowly, really confused.

"Yeah, we do," she nodded her head. "He wrote it on the board."

Now it came back to me. The little warning on the board about our test today. *Today!* And I had completely forgotten about it. Granted, a lot was going on on Friday, but still. How could I forget?

"We have Chemistry at the end of the day, right?"

She nodded.

"Okay," I told her, "I'll see you later."

"'Kay." And she went bounding down the hall again in the same fashion as before.

In Math class, we had a review for our final math test tomorrow. So I studied as efficiently as I could. I wanted to use my free period to cram for Chem.

In English, I had final presentations. It was a breeze. I'd already done mine so I was able to sit back and discreetly study behind one of my textbooks.

At lunch, I had my Chemistry book open in front of me and I was going over a chapter when Bryan plopped down in the chair beside me.

"Don't talk to me," I hissed. "I need to study."

"Whoa," he said, amused. "I've never seen this side of you before." He leaned forward to kiss my cheek.

I jerked back, whipping my head in his direction. "Don't do that. It's very distracting." I turned back to my work, trying to simplify my notes quickly while also being thorough. I chomped on an apple slice.

"How about I help?"

"Studying is a solitary activity," I said without looking up.

"I know that," he whispered, and I realized he had leaned closer again, "but I can quiz you."

"If there's time."

For the rest of lunch, I munched on my lunch and rewrote my notes. But there was no time to be quizzed. I packed up my books and headed to the library with a quick goodbye to Bryan over my shoulder.

I found a quiet spot in the back of the library and pulled out my simplified notes and began going through them. A part of me started wishing that Bryan was here so he could quiz me. Having a study partner had it's appeal right about now.

I don't know how but my wish was granted and Bryan once again plopped down right next to me.

"Don't you have class right now?"

He nodded. "Yeah, but it's just review. So I thought it was more important to help my freaked out girlfriend with her own studying." He held out his hand for my notes and I gladly handed them to him.

I smiled at him as he quizzed me.

By Chemistry, I hoped I'd retained enough information to pass with an A, at least. I sped through the questions; the answers flowing from me as easily as if Bryan was sitting in front of me asking me the questions himself. I got stuck on a couple questions but I eventually got them.

I wasn't the first to finish, but I also wasn't the last. The whole time I felt dread in the pit of my stomach. I really hoped that I wasn't going to fail. I couldn't fail. I needed to get an A, at the *very* least. I remembered Bryan telling me to text him and let him know how I did, or how I felt I did.

I looked around the room in search of the teacher but he hadn't moved; he was sitting at his desk, reading. On the other side of the room. I reached down into my purse and slowly — and carefully — pulled out my phone. Then I shot Bryan a text: **I'm so gonna fail. Shoot me now.** I put my phone on silent and put it back into my purse. Then I sat there, quiet and innocent.

Suddenly, the bell rang and I was home free. Sorta.

I went out to the parking lot to meet Bryan. I didn't have to work today but mom did and wouldn't be home for a few hours. I thought about inviting him in. I wouldn't be alone, André would be... around. I felt guilty just thinking about it. Just to be safe, I should probably invite a few other people. So I shot out a few texts. One to James — I had finally programmed his number into my phone — and then another to Melissa — whose number I got today — with the same message: **Wanna come over to my house and do some studying/reviewing?**

Melissa was the first to text back with an eager response. I sent her my address and told her I would see her later.

At my house, we all got cozy in the living room with our textbooks and notebooks out in front of us. Bryan next to me, his hand on my ankle and his thumb brushing the inside of my legs. Melissa sat on my other side, apparently wanting to put distance between her and Bryan; as much as she could at least. I had to wonder what their deal was. He was her brother's friend, how could these two have a feud?

I gasped and they both looked over at me. I can't believe I didn't realize it sooner: they'd dated! I wasn't about to tell them my suspicion so I told them I was gonna get some snacks. I jumped up and went to the kitchen, filling a plate with cookies. But the whole time, I couldn't help but wonder if that was why she was so mad at him. Did they date? Did he break her heart?

I guess when it took me longer to get our snacks, Bryan came out to check on me.

"Hey, you okay?"

"Did you date Melissa?" I blurted out the question without thinking. Like an unpleasant bit of word vomit.

"Melissa? No." He shook his head. "No, Reggie made it very clear, when we started to play, that family members were off limits. So, no, I never dated Melissa."

That was a relief at least. I let out a breath. "Then why does she hate you?"

"I didn't realize she did," he said. He sounded like he meant it. "She's always acted that way toward me, from the moment I met her."

"I see." I turned to the fridge, and got out the water jug of juice and filled a glass for myself. "Did you want milk?"

"I got it." I stepped aside and he got out the milk. He poured himself a cup, plus another one.

"How do you know Melissa likes her cookies with milk?"

"Reggie." He kissed my cheek, grinning. He whispered in my ear, "You're hot when you're jealous."

⋙ ✿ ⋘

Mom, André and I pulled up in front of Bryan's house. This was my first time being here and my sense of dread had never been higher. Knowing what I knew about his dad, I wasn't surprised.

Their house was cute.

It was the typical dream house, minus the little picket white fence. André shuffled glumly to the door. Even on his phone, he looked like a little kid who'd lost his favourite balloon. At the door, we stood awkwardly on the porch until I knocked. My mom was busy carrying a dessert tray and Andre was busy pouting.

We waited for a beat before Bryan swung open the door. He looked amazing in a pair of jeans, bare feet, and a dark blue button-up shirt with the sleeves rolled up. He invited us into the house and gave us a little tour of the bottom floor. He left the kitchen for last; his mother was there, prepping wieners and burger patties.

"Hello, you guys. I am so glad you could make it." She smiled in greeting. Then she gave me a hug as if we'd known each other for years.

My mom held out her dessert. "Uh, where...?"

"Oh, thank you. That's very generous of you," Bryan's mom said before she asked Bryan to show her where she could set it down out back. Bryan left and took André with him. I was about to follow when his mother stopped me. "Ah, Janessa, I was hoping to have a moment alone with you."

"Sure, Mrs. O'Donald." I followed her example and sat down at the kitchen table. She grabbed the single cup that occupied the surface.

"Please, call me Cheryl. Mrs. O'Donald is my mother-in-law." She smiled. She sat with her back erect. But she looked exhausted despite her prim posture. I wondered how much time and effort she must have put into the barbecue. "Anyway, Bryan tells me you're planning to go to school and become a surgeon."

"Yes."

"That's good. It's good to have a plan for your life. I'm so happy for you." Cheryl patted my arm and took a sip of water. She smiled. "I wish Bryan knew what he wanted to do."

That confused me. I thought he already did. I told her what he'd told me and she looked like she wanted to laugh. That confused me more.

"Oh, honey, I meant a *serious* plan for his life. Like yours."

"Well, thank you." *I think*. Being a pro football player seemed like a serious plan for someone's life if that's what they really wanted to do.

We talked a bit more and then walked out into the backyard. Mr. O'Donald waved me over this time and I really hoped he wouldn't give me the same talk his wife had. But at the same time, as I made my way over to Mr. O'Donald, I looked around for Bryan. He watched me with concern, completely ignoring my brother.

André looked very serious, and I could only imagine the things that he was saying to Bryan. I'm sure it was all in an effort to protect me.

"Hello," I said when I got closer to Bryan's father.

"Hello dear." He paused a moment, looking uncomfortable. "So, um, I've noticed that you have great sway over my son."

Oh boy, I already had a feeling that this would *not* end well.

"Perhaps you could talk to him about getting serious about his future. It's closer than he thinks it is, you know." He waved a set of tongs in my direction and I stayed back, trying not to get hit with them.

"Of course, sir."

"Obedient and respectful," he said. "I like that in a woman." He closed the barbecue and set the tongs aside before he stepped up to me. I took a step away, intending to get as far away from him as possible without being rude. I had a horrible feeling in the pit of my stomach, and even if it was wrong, I wanted to be sure I was safe. Quickly, he had me cornered between him and the house, a hand planted firmly next to my head. "Though, the headstrong ones are the most fun to break."

"I'm sorry, sir?"

"You know, your father and I have many of the same beliefs.

"A woman's place is in the kitchen. They're meant to stay home. Take care of the house and kids." He grinned and already, I smelt alcohol on his breath. Why were the fathers in our lives — mine and Bryan's — always drinking? "If you want to be with my son, you'll have to give up your fantasy of being a surgeon."

"With all due respect, sir," my voice croaked but I continued on, "isn't that a bit outdated?" *Not to mention, sexist.*

"Maybe for someone as selfish and greedy as *you*."

"Dad?" I turned to see Bryan standing behind me but, mostly, my eyes were on his dad. "Could I have a moment with Janessa?"

His dad shrugged and went back to working the grill.

"You're shaking," Bryan said, rubbing my arms with his hands. He led me away from his dad. Then pulled me into his arms and held me against him. I hadn't even noticed I was shaking until he mentioned it, but sure enough, I was. Out of fear, no doubt. "I'm so sorry about that. My dad can be a real ass sometimes."

"Sometimes?" I looked up at him, touching my fingertips to his black eye.

He laughed. "Touché." He gently touched his lips to my forehead. "I promise, you don't have to be alone with him again. Just stick next to me, okay?"

I nodded. "Thanks."

We stuck by each other for a while but at some point, we got separated. Anna found me then and sat me down on the lawn. She thought it was important that she talk to me. Anna wanted to know if I loved him. It was a little early for me to know. She looked for her brother when I said that.

"He hasn't had it easy. I know that people say mean things about him, but he's a good person. He's just had a hard time," she told me.

It was the first time that someone said even one little positive thing about him; something I saw in him too. It was nice to find someone who knew the Bryan that I knew, the Bryan that didn't come out very often.

"But," I said pointedly, "I do care about your brother a lot. I can tell you that for sure."

She stared at me, scrutinizing. Then she let up and said, "Good enough."

Then she got up and ran to her mother who had just finished making her a burger, bypassing Bryan on the way. He held two paper plates, each with a finished burger in the centre. He sat down with me and handed me one. "What did she want?"

"She just wanted to talk to me for a minute." He looked really curious but I wouldn't budge. "If I thought you should know, I would tell you. I promise." He reluctantly gave up trying to figure it out. "What did you put on this?"

"The works..." His eyebrows quirked up, and I could see the question etched into his features; like, 'isn't it obvious?'

"Pickles?" I quizzed.

"Yup."

"Ketchup?"

"Yup."

"Mustard?"

"Yup."

"Gross..." My face contorted in disgust as I lifted the top bun to peek below at the yellow stain that made me gag.

Mustard had always been my least favourite condiment and there was a lot of it on my burger. There was about twice as much mustard as ketchup. He watched me as I slapped the top bun back down and took a hesitant bite. I gagged at the mustard taste. There was so much of it that I couldn't even enjoy the rest of the burger. Bryan laughed at my look of pure disgust.

"That's *not* funny." I slapped Bryan in retaliation.

"It was pretty funny," he said, going back to eating his burger. He made it look so easy!

I went back to eating my burger too, but each bite took a solid two minutes to down.

"If you hate mustard that much, you don't have to eat it," he told me.

"Well, who's going to finish it if I don't? You?"

He raised his hands in surrender and left it at that, but laughed every time I took a bite and gagged.

By the last few bites, it had grown on me a bit so I didn't gag quite as much.

A few minutes later, I froze in my spot on the ground. On the other side of the backyard, was Thomas. He came out of the house followed by Bryan's dad. Bryan took my hand, and instantly I felt a little better. A small fraction, anyway. Thomas seemed to be looking around for someone and I got the feeling it was *me*.

He was looking for me and I had nowhere to hide.

And then he met my stare and smiled. He *had* to know that his presence made me uncomfortable.

"I thought you said he left," Bryan asked.

"He did," I said "He did leave, but apparently he's back now. And here. What is he doing *here*?" I asked the question more to myself than to Bryan. He shrugged anyway.

If I'd been looking at him instead of Thomas, I'd have seen his look of concern. But I was busy waiting for Thomas to walk over to me and threaten me again.

But he never did. And for the rest of the evening, a single question bounced around my head; *Why not?*

⚜ Fifteen ⚜

An hour later, I was standing at the condiments table with mom and André, they both looked ready to leave.

Bryan's parents had cornered me for a second time in the last hour so they could talk to me some more. I assumed they liked me because they kept smiling and nodding and patting my arm. Well, at least his mom liked me. His father, on the other hand, seemed annoyed that I was a modern day woman. He probably hoped it was just a phase; that it was something I would grow out of soon.

I wanted to tell him he was wrong, that I was going to stay strong and independent, but then I'd catch sight of Thomas and change my mind. It was just easier to nod and pretend I was okay with everything Bryan's dad said then to contradict him.

When I finally escaped and found Bryan, he pulled me close. I wrapped my arms around his waist and snuggled close. He kissed the crown of my head and rubbed my back.

"Your dad has very outdated beliefs," I commented sadly.

"Try being raised by him. It's hard to branch out when he's always shoving the 16th century down your throat," Bryan said, resting his cheek against my head. He was just that tall.

"How does your dad know Thomas?" I asked.

"I don't know," he said. He sounded as confused as I felt. Had his dad never even mentioned Thomas? His dad made it sound like they were old friends. "What makes you think they know each other?"

So I told him what his dad had said when he first cornered me: 'your father and I have many of the same beliefs'. Now we were both confused and I had to wonder if Bryan's dad was involved in whatever stuff Thomas was into when he first came back. I'm sure the police would be *very* interested to hear about it.

Suddenly we heard a scream from within. The high pitched screech of a small child. Bryan immediately let me go (albeit a little harsher than necessary). It stunned me for a minute but then I followed him into the house.

"Anna!" Bryan called out. I followed; a sinking feeling in my stomach that grew with each running step we took.

Our moms, as well as Andre, followed behind us.

We burst through a door and realized it was a little girl's room. Pink walls, a baby blue carpet, and violet bedding. And there, on the floor next to the bed, lay Anna. The blood streaming from a cut on her head was in stark contrast to the colors of her bedroom. Next to her, shushing her, was her father. The man that was supposed to love and protect her.

I glared at him and if looks could kill... I knew he was capable of hurting his children — he'd done it to Bryan — but Anna? *Seriously?*

I remembered him smelling like alcohol all throughout the night but he didn't seem drunk.

I hurried out of the room and down the hall to the kitchen in search of paper towels. When I came back, I pressed it to her wound.

Anna sat up when I got there. She held her hand against her cut, the blood seeped through her fingers. Somehow, Bryan had gotten his dad out of the room. And he accepted my help with Anna's injury.

"The police and an ambulance are on its way," my mom said.

I barely heard her. My head was swimming and my stomach was protesting.

It was one of the reasons that being a cardiothoracic surgeon would be so hard for me — *large* amounts of blood made me nauseous. That was something I needed to work on between now and med school.

Anna started to shiver then and her mom brought her a sweater. Her mom tugged her little arms through the sleeves.

Then my mom tugged on my arm and we went downstairs to wait in the living room. I looked around for Bryan's dad — wanting to know what the *hell* he was thinking; wanting to demand an explanation — but he was gone. Or, at least he wasn't on the first floor.

Thomas was gone too.

I was shaking. I couldn't figure out if it was because I was scared or because I was angry.

I was angry at Bryan's dad for being abusive. I was afraid of my own father, the man who wouldn't hesitate to kill me if I even so much as took a step across his very carefully drawn line. I was angry that this was their life, and that it was mine too.

A few minutes later there was a knock at the front door. A police officer came in and started asking us what happened. The paramedics headed upstairs to get Anna. Bryan led the way downstairs with Anna in his arms. She had a new, clean bandage wrapped around her head and she peered around like she'd just woken up from a nap. Mom, André, Cheryl and I told the police everything we knew and they left shortly after the paramedics did.

With a quick glance in the direction of Cheryl — who sat on the couch looking so pained and lost — I ran out the front and asked what hospital they were taking her to. I told mom where I was going and that I probably wouldn't make it back by curfew. She looked like wanted to protest but one look at Cheryl told her what I had already guessed. Cheryl needed to be with her daughter right now and she was in no condition to drive herself.

At the hospital, they refused to let us through the doors to see Anna until I mentioned that Cheryl was Anna's mother.

We saw Bryan pacing angrily in front of a room that I assumed was Anna's. He glared down at the floor. His arms were wrapped tightly around his chest as if to hold himself together or to keep himself in check. I wasn't sure which one.

When he heard us coming, he took one look at his mother and his gaze hardened.

"What the hell are you doing here?" He asked her. Before she could answer, he rounded on me. "What the hell is *she* doing *here*?"

"I'm here to see Anna," was the first thing that Cheryl had said since we left the house. She'd been so quiet on the drive over that I'd started to get concerned.

"Yeah, well, I don't want you here." His tone was acid and his words were venom. He really hated his mother; blamed her even. But... she didn't have anything to do with it.

I needed to get him away from her; maybe I could talk some sense into him.

"Okay, Bryan, let's take a walk." I grabbed onto his arms and started to drag him down the hallway, but he pulled his arm back. "Come *on*, Bryan. Let's *go*." I didn't want him talking to his mom, as angry as he was.

Bryan and I walked, but the silence did *not* last long. "Why the *hell* did you bring *her*?" He snapped.

I flinched at his tone of voice and sucked in a breath. I sighed. "Bryan, just stop it already."

"Just answer the damn question!" He yelled. "Why. The *hell*. Did you. Bring her?"

I flinched again, but he didn't notice or didn't care. Either way, I was starting to get angry with him. "I brought her because she looked like a wreck when the ambulance left. You didn't see her. *I* did.

"*That's* why I brought her. I brought her because she needed to be here. And her daughter, whether you'll admit it or not, *her daughter wants* her here." I tried to be sharp and clear so he'd understand. But he was too angry and too worried to empathize. "I know how frustrating this situation can be but—"

"How could you?" He interrupted, pinning a hard, cold stare on me. "Your dad left you when you were a kid. You don't understand what it's been like for Anna and me to have lived like that every day, every year; afraid to move, to *breathe*, to do *anything* that would set him off.

"What's your five years compared with my 18?" he sneered.

I felt like I was wearing my heart on my sleeve.

It hurt to know that he felt this way — that my past, no matter how short-lived, was insignificant to him. And I was angry at myself for letting him hurt me. I should've guarded my heart, I should've known...

I felt like crying.

"Just leave. Go home. I don't want you here." He turned around and walked away from me.

I waited for a beat, then followed him back to the waiting room that was my way out. It would have been so easy to just keep walking, to leave, but instead, I turned around and asked if they wanted anything before I left.

Bryan's mom looked like she wanted to say something but Bryan beat her to the punch and he growled, "No." He sat in one of the chairs just outside of Anna's room next to his mom, giving me the cold shoulder. His arms were crossed in front of his chest and his head turned away so that he wasn't looking at me.

Bryan's mom mouthed an apology before I turned around and left. Tears were starting to sting the back of my eyes and I didn't want to be around him when they fell. A tear slid down my face when I escaped the building and broke out onto the sidewalk that led to the parking lot. I swiped at my face and took a deep breath, trying to keep the tears at bay.

I called my mom and asked if she would pick me up. I'd driven Cheryl's car so I didn't really have any other way to get home.

"What's wrong?" She asked.

I choked up trying to explain it to her — in as few words as possible because that was all I could get out. I didn't want her to know that she was right about Bryan, so I kept our little fight — the real reason for my tears — out of it. I wanted her to think that the tears were for Anna, the little girl with an open wound on her head. And then a whole new wave of tears swept me away as I hung up. I slid down the side of the hospital, pulling my knees close to me.

Eventually, I got ahold of myself and stopped crying.

The Game

It was a while later that a car pulled up and I got to my feet. Mom stopped in front of me and I wiped at my face and got in. André was in the backseat. When I got in, he looked at me with concern.

I waved them off. "I just want to go home. I'm tired and I want to go to sleep." And it was true too. We were silent on the drive back, but I could tell that they wanted to ask me what happened.

They both kept looking over and I could feel their eyes on me but I ignored it. I tried to not think about Bryan or how he looked when he'd yelled at me.

At home, I was the first one out of the car. My mom and brother just watched me, frozen in concern. Mom started to say something but I jumped out of the car before I could hear it.

I got ready for bed and crawled under the covers. I was ready for today to end.

But sleep did not come easily.

In fact, it hovered just out of reach as I ran over the scene in my head, again and again, a new ache in my chest igniting. But the tears didn't fall anymore; I had run out of tears to shed.

I don't know when but at some point, I must have fallen asleep because I awoke the next morning with my heart racing in my chest and my eyes seeking out my alarm. It was still around six in the morning. I was too afraid that I would oversleep if I went back to bed so I pulled myself up, away from my syren pillows and hypnotic blanket.

I was so physically and emotionally drained, all I wanted to do was go back to bed and back to sleep. I didn't want to go to school today. But if I didn't go just because I didn't want to, then I'd probably never go.

I had plenty of time so I went over my math notes; anything to distract me. I studied until my alarm went off and I was forced to get dressed. Shorts, plain white tee and a thin but comfortable sweater. I brushed my hair and put it in a French braid. I applied some makeup (mostly to remove the evidence that I hadn't slept much) and then I was done.

I know I should eat, but as I headed downstairs and smell the bacon that mom was cooking or had cooked, I felt nauseous. Clapping a hand over my mouth, I went into the kitchen and grabbed a banana off the table.

"I'm gonna walk to school," I told André. "Are you going to be okay to find your own way?"

He nodded. I could tell he wanted to say more, even mom looked over at me, worried. I had never withheld information from her for very long. If I was in her position, I would be fearing the worst. I gave them both a smile that I hoped would ease their worries and peeled my banana. Then I tossed the peel in the compost and walked out.

I nibbled on my banana, wondering if Bryan would be in school today. If he wasn't, I'd understand. If he did come to school, what would I be able to expect from him? Probably not an apology. I'm sure the way he saw it, he wasn't responsible for what he said out of anger. I could understand that he'd been angry, but the way he'd made me feel was not okay.

I pulled my phone out of my pocket and went right to his contact. My finger hovered above the **CALL** button and I really wanted to press it. I wanted to call him and ask if we could talk. I wanted to explain to him that what he'd said last night was not fair and that I deserved an apology. Maybe I had overstepped a bit when I gave his mother a ride, but I'd just been trying to do a nice thing for her. It was obvious that she'd wanted to be there.

I closed my phone and slipped it back into my pocket.

I stared at the ground.

And what about Thomas? Why was he back? I thought he'd left for good — or so I'd hoped. It was almost like he'd only come back to remind me that I am *not* and never *will* be free of him. But showing up at Bryan's house for a family barbecue; how did he even know where we would be?

I got to school in record time. As I stepped into the parking lot, my phone *dinged* in my pocket. I pulled it out to see a message from Bryan.

The Game

BABE: I won't be going to school today. I'm not feeling well.

Of course, he's not coming today. I wondered how Anna was doing. I even crafted a message to find out but erased it. Instead, I just said: **Ok. Feel better.**

I didn't need to make a stop to my locker, so instead, I just headed toward the cafeteria and sat at my table. I pulled out my notes and continued studying, trying to think about anything but Bryan right now.

I'd just moved onto my second page of notes when I heard the shuffling of feet. It was Melissa, walking toward me in a huff. She plopped down in the chair beside me. This was a very different look on her than I was used to.

"You know what I don't get?"

She just looked at me and it really seemed like she was waiting for me to guess. So I wracked my brain for something.

"Uh... why I'm here so early?" I guessed.

She shook her head. "Well, yes, but no."

"Did they mix up the streamers for prom?" I asked. I remember her having mentioned something about being on the planning committee.

"No, but now I need to check to make sure," she said, already digging through the bag on her shoulder for her phone. "No, what I don't get is why it's so hard for someone in this school to prove they have school spirit and put their voice on loan to us."

"Ah," I sympathized. She'd already asked me once if I would sing for her, just to see if I had chops, but I'd said no. I knew I had a great voice but that would mean giving up my prom night to sing to a bunch of my peers.

"Are you sure you can't do it?"

"I'm sure," I told her.

She sulked further in her chair. "Okay, fine," she relented. "We'll figure something out. See ya?"

"Uh huh," I said, but she was already speeding out of the cafeteria.

I watched her for a minute and wondered how I'd attracted the most social of people.

First Natalie, who was adored by all of the student body — except Megan, who didn't like anyone but Bryan, apparently — and the captain of the cheerleading squad. She was always after me to attend parties with her, being social is just how she connects with other people. I prefered to stay out of the line of fire.

And now, Melissa. The bubbliest person that I have ever met. I'd caught her bounding, jumping, or skipping down the hall with a big smile on her face. It was like she woke up every morning and realized that she'd won the lottery. She wasn't as talkative as Amy, but she did always have something on her mind.

And somehow, I attracted them and they both seemed to *actually* want to be my friend. Me, little miss boring, always with her nose in her notes, studying.

For the first time since last night, I started to feel a bit lighter, not so overwhelmed or as though I were carrying the weight of the world on my shoulders.

I'd always known that Natalie I would be best friends for life, but now I feel like I might just have another.

Last night, it almost seemed as if Bryan had been trying to push me away; as if he was afraid to have people in his life that cared about him. But maybe having people around wasn't as big a burden as he seemed to think, maybe there really was strength in numbers.

And for the first time in my life, I really believed that.

❦ Sixteen ❧

Math class came and went and I felt pretty good about the test.

There were still presentations that needed to be done for English, and still would be until we started practice essays for our exam. I started doodling in the back of my notebook, presentations had never been my favourite thing to endure, but I loved doing my own. Slowly but surely, English ended and I broke free and headed to the bathroom.

Natalie hadn't been in English so I didn't really have anyone to talk to so I put in my earbuds.

In the bathroom, I went about my business and when I was sure that no one else was around, I even sang a little. Just a little, as I was washing my hands, lathering them with soap and then drying them. But then, one of the bathroom stalls opened and out walked Melissa. She had a grin on her face and I knew *exactly* what she was thinking.

I pulled out my headphones.

"No," I stopped her, hand in the air.

"Oh, come on, we *need* you. You sound *so* good."

I hadn't even realized I'd sung that loud. I thought it was just barely above a whisper. I was already shaking my head, dismissing the idea. "No, I'm not even going to prom."

"So you've told me, but please, please, *please!*" She begged, clapping her hands together. "I am desperate. We need you. No one else will do it."

I promised her I would think about it and I did. And I realized something, I didn't like it. At all.

"I'm sorry!" I said. "But I *can't*. For one, I don't have a dress for prom."

"That's okay." Melissa waved her hand, dismissing the issue. "We can go shopping tonight and get you something sexy to wear."

I inhaled sharply. "I don't have a date."

"Neither do I. We can go *together*." Now she leaned against the sinks and grinned at me. "What else you got?"

I gave her a '*You've gotta be kidding me*' look. "Oh, yeah," I said, "I don't wanna."

She looked almost offended as if she were the reason that I didn't want to go when, in actuality, that wasn't true. I had many reasons to not go.

For one, I'm pretty sure I had a dress in the back of my closet that I haven't worn in years, but I didn't wanna get dressed up.

Two, I didn't have a date — and I didn't want one.

Three, I didn't want to get dressed in some fancy, expensive dress just to have drunk teens spill on me. Whether on purpose or not.

But when the offended look morphed into one of hurt, I felt bad. I wanted to change my mind to make her feel better but I just wasn't willing to sing in front of all my peers. I didn't want to look over the mic and see my boyfriend dancing with *Megan*.

"So, you won't even give it a chance?"

"Melissa, I wasn't even planning on going. I was planning on staying in and practicing my valedictorian speech," I admitted. "I want to do this for you, I really do, but at the same time I really don't."

She stuck her lower lip out in a pout. She stayed like that for a minute and I was really fighting the urge to cave. But then she relented. "Fine. Fine, this is the last time that I will ask you."

"Thank you."

Twenty minutes later as I was walking toward the cafeteria, the PA system crackled and a woman's voice said, "Would Janessa Reynolds please report to room 213? Janessa Reynolds to 213." I looked over at Melissa, walking beside me today and she just shrugged, looking as confused as I did. At the same time, she must've known that 213 was the room the planning committee met in.

Too bad I learned that a little too late.

I knocked on the door and was invited in to find the teacher in charge of the committee, the principal— Miss Jamison, Mr. Jackson — and right behind them, my least favourite person, Megan Lee. Her perfect blonde locks were pulled back in a gorgeous messy bun that looked meticulously styled. And she looked at me like she always did; like she'd *won* something.

I turned my gaze away from her toward the adults. "Hello? What's this about?" I asked.

They both gestured to a table. Mr. Jackson pulled out a chair. "Have a seat," he said in a gruff and authoritative voice.

I did as I was asked and waited for them to continue. Anyone of them. Except for Megan, her stupid face was enough to rub me the wrong way. I didn't need to hear her voice too.

"So, we've been told that you can sing," Miss Jamison said, pulling out a chair and sitting down across from me. She'd turned the chair around so her chest was pressed against the back of it. "You have no idea how long we have been searching for someone with the ability to carry a tune."

"Oh, how long has it been?"

"Since April."

"Oh, good. So not that long then."

No one thought it was funny so I had to hold back my own nervous laughter. Mr. Jackson pinned me with a steady stare while Miss Jamison just looked at me with a dumbfounded expression. Megan was just sitting back, uncaring.

"Besides, I don't know what you're talking about," I lied. "I can't sing to save my life."

"Oh, please," Megan said. Had her voice always been that whiny? "I heard you in the bathroom. You have talent." I glared at her but she ignored it. "In *fact*, since Miss Jamison is here, why don't you sing a little for us?"

"Yeah," Mr. Jackson agreed. "Just a little something. It'll only be a second."

It would have been easier to say no to singing if it was just Megan asking. But this was the principal and a teacher; two people that had authority over me. I'd never gotten into trouble before and I most certainly didn't know what Mr. Jackson's office looked like. I didn't know if refusing to sing would warrant a trip down there or not, but I really didn't want to find out.

So I opened my mouth to start, but my voice cracked. I cleared my throat to remove the lump that had lodged itself there. "Excuse me, I'm just going to get a sip of water."

Mr. Jackson gave a slight nod and I turned and practically ran out of the room. I found the nearest water fountain and took a minute to gulp down as much as I could. I wasn't surprised that Megan would do this to me. It was just the kind of stunt she'd pull. Force me to be at prom so she could torture me by dancing with my boyfriend.

I felt like my right to say 'no' had been taken away. Sure, if it was just Megan and Melissa asking, I wouldn't have a problem. The single word was easy to say, but throw in the principal and the teacher and it got a little harder.

When I went back into the room, the adults were chatting amongst themselves and Megan was staring at her phone — probably Twitter or Snapchat or whatever. Megan glanced at me, then went back to her phone. I didn't care; it was the adults that I was focused on. They both looked up at me and smiled.

They sat on the edge of the table and I began to sing *Genie in a Bottle*. It was the first song that came to mind and the only one I really knew by heart. They both listened. Even Megan. She set down her phone and listened. When I finished, I kept my gaze on Mr. Jackson and Miss Jamison so that I wouldn't stoop to Megan's level and give her a snooty look. Not that I was *proud* or *happy* to be singing for my peers on their oh-so 'magical' prom night, but it *did* feel good to wipe that silly little smile off her face.

Both Mr. Jackson and Miss Jamison agreed that I was a perfect fit for the band and they thanked me for accepting the role. Then they both turned their backs and I was free to leave. It all felt kind of anticlimactic.

＊＊＊

I was waiting in line in the cafeteria when someone nudged me from behind. "Hey," they said. At first, I thought it was Natalie, coming to tell me where she's been and that she was alright. It wasn't. It *also* wasn't Bryan or Melissa. It was someone else; James. The last person I'd expected.

"Hey," I greeted.

Yeah, he and my best friend were dating but that didn't mean I knew him well or that he and I hung out. I barely talked to the guy. But he was pretty handsome, I guess. He had a dark brown crop cut, warm brown eyes and a very athletic physique that resembled Bryan's. He wore a blue muscle shirt, jeans that hung loosely on his hips, Nikes and, around his neck he wore a band of dog tags. I wondered where they'd come from and why, every once in a while, I would catch him playing with them.

Just then I realized I had the chance to ask him something. I could find out what was wrong with Bryan but I figured that I probably knew more about his home life than James despite their many years of friendship. If Bryan was anything like me, he probably would have started by keeping James at an arm's length. And even if he wasn't like me, I'd come to realize that Bryan could be pretty secretive. I'm sure if my past didn't resemble his even a little bit, he wouldn't have shared his dark secret.

Instead, I asked about Natalie. I *should* know the most about my best friend and *he* should be coming to ask *me* about her but I knew deep down that that just wasn't the case right now.

"There's just a lot going on with her right now," James told me. Even though he'd already told me more than I'd expected him to I couldn't help but feel like he was keeping something from me. I nodded and thanked him for the info, though it wasn't much. It also didn't help to ease my worry. In fact, I was even more worried now.

I got to the end of the line and my total was rung up by the lunch lady. I started digging through my bag but it didn't matter what I moved or pulled out of my purse, I could not find my wallet anywhere. I'd started to think that maybe I'd left it in my bedroom when James strolled up and handed the lunch lady enough to pay for both meals.

I was ready to object but he just smiled and said, "Can't have you starving, now can we?" Then he picked up his tray and walked away, but not before flashing me a playful wink.

I promised myself that I would pay him back as I picked up my own tray and walked over to my table where Melissa was waiting for me. Then the most cliché of moments happened: Megan and I collided and my food was dumped all over my chest. The pasta sauce plus my white shirt was not a good combination. But Megan was more worried about her phone, which had fallen to the floor. She picked it up and cradled it to her chest.

I was dimly aware of the rest of the student body laughing at the scene, especially when Megan stood up, walked over to me and jabbed her finger in my shoulder. "You better hope that my phone isn't broken, or so help me God, I will ruin what is left of your senior year."

I watched as she pressed the **HOME** button on her phone and the screen lit up, revealing a surprisingly boring background.

Then she turned to me, glared and walked away.

❧

Melissa and I started our search for prom dresses in the Thrift Store in town. It may be unconventional but you can usually find some pretty decent clothes for cheap there.

I knew for a fact that Melissa was happy with how the situation in room 213 turned out because she got what she wanted. Once I'd told her what happened — after she gave me a ride home to change my shirt — she was beaming from ear to ear.

Now I've just decided to make the best of it, which was how we ended up in a Thrift Store looking for something cute. I had a few options thrown over my arm. And Melissa had a couple that I'd already ixnayed but she refused to put them back until I tried them on.

By the time I closed the dressing room door behind me, I had about ten dresses to try on. I tried on so many that I'd started to get annoyed with the unzipping — of which I had to invite Melissa inside because I couldn't reach. Eventually, I tried on a light purple dress with thin straps that formed an 'X' at my back, a neckline that showed a little, but not too much, cleavage, and a flowy skirt that hung around my knees. The bodice hugged my body and there was a little sash around my waist that I just adored.

Melissa agreed with me when I stepped out and showed her; it was the one.

"Give me a second to pick my jaw up from the floor," she said, giving herself a little smack. "You look *beautiful*. It's perfect."

I just smiled and looked down at myself and tried not to think about Bryan.

Before I could say anything, my phone rang and his caller ID lit up my screen. I debated for a brief second to reject his call, the briefest of moments and then my finger tapped the **ANSWER** button. "Hello," I answered, but when I heard his voice all I could think about was how insignificant my past was to him. That was enough to piss me off. I hung up in the middle of his greeting.

I felt bad but the damage had already been done.

I peeled out of the dress and pulled my shirt and shorts back on. I slipped my arms through the sleeves of my sweater and carried the dress to the counter. I was behind three other people, so Melissa and I chatted a bit about prom. She told me what to expect. I was just glad that they hadn't gone with 'Winter Wonderland' because that was so overdone.

Bryan called again before I got to the front of the line, but this time I didn't bother answering. I assumed it would just end the way it had before.

Bryan texted me asking me why I wasn't answering and saying that he needed to talk to me. I ignored them because I couldn't deal with that yet so I slipped my phone into my back pocket and stepped up to the counter. I laid the dress down and waited while the woman scanned it and rung up my total.

I was glad I'd come here. I'd gotten a great dress for cheap; something the other girls couldn't say about their own dresses.

As I was paying, I remembered my promise to pay James back for his generosity today. So I made a point of going to Bryan's house after dropping Melissa off.

I knocked and waited. From the other side of the door, I heard yells of defeat and betrayal. Even some hollers of death and I just assumed they were playing a violent video game.

Finally, Bryan's mom, Cheryl opened the door and I asked if James was there. She looked shocked for a minute and then nodded.

"Yeah." She turned slightly on the spot and looked into the living room. "James? It's for you." Just as Cheryl turned back to me to ask me something, I saw Bryan walk out of the kitchen behind her. My breath caught in my throat at how good he looked, even how *healthy* he looked; he did *not* look like he had spent the day in bed because he'd come down with a stomach virus.

James came out then, (thank God), and he stepped out onto the porch. "Hey, what's up?"

"I just wanted to thank you for what you did for me today. Not many people would have, and I just wanted you to know that I appreciate it," I told him, putting a smile on my face.

"You're welcome.." He said almost hesitantly.

Could he tell that there was more?

"Um… Also, I wanted to pay you back." I reached into the front pocket of my shorts and pulled out two crumpled five dollar bills and held it out to him. He looked at it like he didn't want it. "Please," I urged. "I'd feel bad if you didn't take it. *Please*."

"Okay." James surrendered, taking the money. "You didn't have to do this, you know."

"I know," I told him. "But I wanted to." Then I hugged him; which he seemed surprised about because he awkwardly returned the hug. "Thanks for being a good friend."

Unfortunately, my phone rang then and, because it was my mom, I answered.

"Janessa, where are you? André told me you're not home. I need you to watch him," she said, frantic.

I wanted to remind her that he was fifteen and that he didn't need a babysitter. Then I thought about Thomas and quickly promised to be home in a few minutes. Not that either of us was safe from him but, you know, safety in numbers. I hung up, thanked James again then turned and headed toward my car.

❧ Seventeen ❧

"What do you wanna watch?" I asked about an hour later.

When I'd gotten home, I had found André in the basement. I hadn't heard anything at first but that's because I'd gone upstairs to check his bedroom. When I'd found it empty, I tried the middle floor again and that was when I heard tool sounds downstairs; as if he was sanding something down.

I opened the door, called out his name and made it halfway down the stairs when the sounds stopped. Next thing I know, I'm being ushered upstairs and André's locking the door behind us. The key of which he slid into his pocket.

"Don't go down there," he tells me.

As if I could without that key, I thought glumly, folding my arms across my chest. Again, I had to wonder what mom and André were doing down there and why they were acting as if it was a surprise for me.

Maybe it is a surprise for you, my subconscious said.

I tried asking him what was down there that was so secretive, but he zipped his mouth and threw away the imaginary key.

"I'm gonna shower," he said. "Do you think you could order us a pizza?" He didn't wait for a reply.

An hour later, I set a bowl of popcorn on the coffee table and waited for André.

"Pick something you wanna watch," he called back from the kitchen. "Just nothing cheesy, like *the Notebook*. Yuck."

"So, I'm guessing a rom-com is out of the question?"

"Definitely."

There was a knock at the door and I was amazed at how fast the pizza was delivered. I called out, "One second," and got the money from the kitchen. When I threw open the door, I stopped in my tracks. "You're not the pizza guy…"

"No, but I *do* need to talk to you," Bryan said.

I *was* curious about what he wanted to talk about. Did he actually want to apologize for last night? Because I had *not* expected him to, at all. Maybe he *was* more mature than I'd given him credit for. *Me, on the other hand...* I thought as I set the money down on the stairs. Bryan followed me in, but I stopped him with a hand on his chest.

"Uh uh, out," I told him. "We can talk outside."

Yes, that meant we were alone and I was breaking one of mom's rules but if we talked inside than André was guaranteed to overhear and I didn't want him throwing punches.

I closed the door behind us and sat down on the porch swing set, waiting for him to talk. *He'd* come *here*, so *he* should start this conversation. But he was just leaning against the pillar on the porch, his hands in his pockets; watching me. His eyes took in my closed off position.

I sat with my legs up and my arms wrapped around them, trying to get as small as possible. When he didn't talk, I urged impatiently, "Well? What do you want?"

"I want to talk to you."

"Well, then talk," I snapped. "Or are you expecting us to have a conversation with our eyes?"

I heard him blow out a breath of air and then pushed off from the column. He came and sat down beside me. "Why did you come to see James and not me today?" He asked. "I've been trying to get in touch with you but you've been… avoiding me."

"Seriously? That's what you want to know?" I got up in a huff. I didn't get very far before I stopped and turned around. "I was looking for James because he did something nice for me today and I wanted to pay him back."

"Ness, about last night," he said. "I just wanted to say I'm sorry."

"Why? We both know you're just gonna do it again," I said.

"Look, I freaked out last night, okay?" I looked between him and the door. I didn't want to listen to him try to justify what he said and why, but at the same time, I needed it. I sighed and sat down beside him, just as I'd been before. "I'm supposed to be my sister's protector, the one person that she can count on and, last night, I failed. I spent the whole ride to the hospital kicking myself for not being the one to take her to bed. Then I was angry with my mom because *she* could've and then Anna wouldn't have needed stitches.

"And then I thought about you and your own dad," — *he's not my dad*, I thought, annoyed — "and what if it was you and I'd failed you.

"So when I saw you at the hospital, it was easier to make you hate me; to push you away. Just as long as it meant keeping you safe... from me."

"You mean, easier on *you*?" Now I was angry with him. Not hurt, just angry. "Bryan, with Thomas constantly lurking around every corner, I could be hurt with or without you in my life. So pushing me away isn't about my 'safety'. It's about *you* because *you* don't want to feel *responsible* if I get hurt."

I jumped off the porch swing. I was so done with this conversation and... where the *hell was* that stupid pizza guy?

"You're right," he admitted; which surprised me. "I don't want to feel responsible if you got hurt because I failed to get to you in time."

"It's not up to you to save me. This is the twenty-first century; I can save myself."

The way he was acting almost made me think that he shared his father's outdated belief. That he was supposed to be some sort of Prince Charming, swooping in to save his damsel in distress. Well, I was no damsel in distress.

"Whether you can or can't isn't being questioned," he said defensively. "I just came here to say that I was sorry for what I said last night. I didn't mean any of it. I was just angry and freaked."

"You really hurt me," I said, leaning against the column like he had when this conversation started.

"I know." He said softly. He walked over to me and took my hand. It was like last Friday when he told me about the game he'd recently quit. This time, instead of pulling my hand away, I gripped his hand and squeezed. "I'm sorry."

Something flashed in his eyes — *desire?* — before he leaned forward and gave me a small kiss. As a test, I realized. When he saw me softening, he kissed me again and I kissed him back, my hand snaking around to the nape of his neck. This kiss was gentle and rough all at once, his arm wound around my waist as he pulled me tighter against him.

Then we heard someone clear their throat. I looked over, it was the pizza guy. Why couldn't he have come before? I pushed away from Bryan and went back into the house to grab the money. I didn't find it on the stairs, where I'd put it. I asked André about the disappearance, and he told me he had moved it to the kitchen. I went back, and sure enough, it was on the island. I grabbed it just as the door opened behind me. Bryan walked in with the pizza.

"Please tell me he didn't leave," I pleaded with him, "because I haven't paid yet."

"Sorry, babe, he's gone," Bryan said and André groaned. Bryan laughed and handed André the pizza. He sauntered over to me, put his hands on my waist. "If I stay on my best behaviour, can I stay?"

"Your best behaviour? I'd like to see what that looks like," I joked.

"Hey!" He exclaimed but he laughed and kissed my cheek.

"Best behaviour," I reminded him.

"That was as innocent as they come."

"Not with André around."

Bryan looked over at him, and sure enough, André was watching and gagging. I chuckled and went to pick out something that I was sure would be liked by everyone. "How about *Taxi?*" I asked, holding up the movie. It was about a taxi driver and a guy who can't take no for an answer, fighting female robbers. I loved this movie.

They both agreed and I popped it in.

"You know, maybe you should talk to your mom," I suggested to Bryan later that night.

André had left us a few minutes ago, creating another commotion downstairs that I desperately wanted to check out. What were they hiding? But Bryan was still here so I couldn't just up and leave.

We were both still snuggled on the couch, his arm around me and my head on his shoulder. For the few minutes of quiet we'd had before André started disturbing the peace, I thought about what Bryan had said to me outside. I thought about his mom and how he'd been mad at her.

Now he just looked at me like I was crazy. He seemed like he wanted to shout as he told me about how he'd started talking to his mom once; only to chicken out because she'd started talking about her marriage to his father. And he just didn't want to hear about *any* of that.

"I'm just saying that I heard my mom out a few years ago when she talked to me about Thomas, and it eased my mind *and* strengthened our relationship," I told him. I took his hand and squeezed. He just stroked the back of my hand with his thumb, drawing little circles across it. It sent a shock wave through my body and I loved it. It did a great job of distracting me.

I lifted my other hand to his cheek and heard him exhale; his breath hit my shoulder.

"Just think about it, okay?"

He looked at me then, lifting his gaze from our hands. "Okay, but only because you're so strongly suggesting it."

Before I could say or do anything else, the Jaws theme song filled the room.

"I didn't know you were a Jaws fan."

"Not anymore," I grumbled, pulling the back of my shirt up slightly to grab Thomas' phone from my back pocket. Before answering, I put a hand over Bryan's mouth and said, "Just shut up for a minute," and then answered the call.

"Do you have any idea where I am right now?"

"No," I said in a bit of a clipped tone. He probably didn't notice.

"I'm with your mother and her *lawyer*," Thomas said.

"Okay?"

She could be getting André's last name changed, which must have been decided last night when I was preoccupied. Or she could be trying to get Thomas' parental rights removed, something she'd talked about doing once or twice. My mom had some serious guts to be doing either of those things in Thomas' presence.

Thomas paused, annoyed. "Can you convince her that taking my kids away is not a good idea?"

"Why?" I asked. I genuinely wanted to know. "I mean you don't even want us. You tried to kill me, and you tried to kill André." Bryan stiffened beside me when he heard the first one. I moved a finger to his lips to shush him.

"I don't need to explain myself to *you*," he snapped. "I may have asked before as a courtesy but now I'm telling you, talk to her."

Then the dial tone in my ear sounded. He was gone, leaving me with the hideous demand of talking to my mother about *not* taking away Thomas' parental rights. I thought it was a great idea to legally get him as far away from us as possible, so talking to my mom about *anything* but how it was going, did not sit well with me. I put the phone back in my pocket and looked at Bryan.

"Why didn't you tell me?" He asked softly.

"It's not that easy."

"Maybe, but at least I would've known. Then last night could have turned out *way* different."

I just looked at him. He really believed that. But I didn't. "Bryan, you were emotional yesterday, you would have said anything without thinking about it."

"Would that have been such a bad thing?" He asked. He ran a hand along my arm, gently and softly. "If you'd told me, then maybe someone could've overheard and called the police."

"Bryan..." I wondered what it would take for him to drop this. Yes, I almost died because of Thomas. Yes, I still had that threat hanging over my head. And, yes, now Bryan knew but all I wanted was for Thomas' threat to be forgotten. "Bryan, just let it go, *please?*"

He finally agreed to let it go. Reluctantly.

Bryan stayed for an hour longer and I managed to convince him to talk to his mom. I hoped he did it tonight so I could ask how it went tomorrow. But I had a feeling that Bryan might put it off.

Once Bryan left and mom was back, André and I went to bed.

☙❦❧

The next day as I was at my locker, I heard a voice. Someone that I hadn't spoken to in days because she'd been nowhere to be found. "Janessa," she sang. "Guess what we're doing today?"

"Not dress shopping for prom," I told her.

"I know, for some reason you're *insistent* about staying home and working on some little old speech," Natalie said, shaking her head in disbelief. "And no."

"Good, because I did that yesterday with Melissa," I told her. I was hoping she would clue in as to what I was saying, and she did.

Her eyes widened. "You're going to prom?" She asked to clarify. I nod. "With who? Who are you going with? Did Bryan ditch Megan to go with you?"

"No." I rolled my eyes. "Those two are still going together."

"Then who are you going with?"

"Why do I have to be going with anyone?" I asked, closing my locker and locking it. Spinning the dial up to zero.

"Because you just *have* to, especially now that *I* have a date and we can't go together. Then again, that was before I thought you were so dead set against going," she commented, which was punctuated with a dramatic eye roll.

"Yeah, well, I did put on my list that I'd do something I wouldn't normally say yes to, so when Mr. Jackson and Ms. Jamison asked me to audition to be the singer at prom, I did. Also, because Megan just *had to* put me on the spot," I told her. "I still don't like the idea of going but now I am... with Melissa."

"Janessa!" I heard from behind us.

"Speak of the devil," I whispered, turning around to find a beaming Melissa standing right in front of us. "What's up?"

"I just wanted to remind you about practice today, at lunch, with the band," she told me, linking arms with me.

"Right, I almost forgot, what with the excitement of dress shopping."

Natalie groaned from beside me. "I wish you guys had invited me. I mean, I don't even know what your dress looks like."

"Oh, here," Melissa said, pulling out her phone and scrolling through her camera roll until she found the single photo I allowed her to take of our final choice.

"It's so pretty," Natalie gushed. "You're going to look amazing."

"Thanks," I said. "Anyway, what were you gonna say before I mentioned prom?"

"Oh, just that I thought we could go get our piercings today during your free period."

"Okay, I have that at the end of the day today."

"Great."

Then the bell rang and we all bolted in separate directions. I ran for my math class, ready for review.

There was one final presentation left for English class, so we finished that and then we moved on to practice essays for our exam.

Then I had lunch and I met the guys in the music room where they were already setting up their drum, guitar — acoustic and electric, apparently, he was going to switch between the two between songs — then a piano, and a violin.

Johnny was about my height of 5'5", a little curvy and sat on a piano stool. He wore jeans and a tee and his shaggy blonde hair hung in his face. He was actually kind of cute. He played with the keys a little and smiled at me when he saw me looking.

Then Johnny introduced the tall, dark and very handsome Damon. He had blue eyes and black hair, and he wore a black v-neck, dark jeans, and black Converse. His style reminded me so much of André. Damon was the one that would be on guitar. I really felt bad for him, and I assumed it would be a lot of switching.

Jessie was a redhead with a faceful of freckles that made him look a little younger than he probably was. He had a beautiful smile which he flashed when I looked over. He was on drums and had a drumstick in each hand. One of which, he lifted in a wave.

Aaron was tall, blonde and wore jeans, a white shirt under a leather black jacket and grey Converse. He was sitting on a chair, too distracted to look at me as he was tuning the violin in his hands.

They all looked like a good group of guys interested in music. I could tell just by the way that Johnny let his fingers dance over the keys. By the little beat, Jessie created with the drums. By the riff that Damon produced with the electric as if to warm up. And the way Aaron tuned his violin.

I introduced myself.

Once we all knew each other's names, we started practice. It didn't take very long for Damon to realize how much of a hassle switching between two instruments was, especially when we wanted swift transitions between songs.

"Okay," I stopped them. They all looked at me, startled but I focused my attention on Damon. "Hand me the acoustic."

He looked a little confused so I explained to him that I could play and that it would make the transitions easier. After that, we all had an instrument and by the end of practice, *I* thought we all had what it took to make prom great for everyone.

Jessie, Aaron, and Johnny left first but Damon stayed behind and just looked at me from underneath his lashes. "You're pretty good," he said. It wasn't the first thing he'd said during lunch but it was the first thing he'd said that made me blush a little.

I looked away. "Thanks."

Then he left the room too and I followed him.

ᴇ𝓢 *Eighteen* ᴈᴠ

I had completely forgotten about the piercing that Natalie wanted to get after Chemistry until the last bell rang signalling the end of the third period and I noticed the message Natalie had left me.

NAT: Meet me in the parking lot. Bryan and James are coming too.

Great, I thought. I typed back a quick message telling her I would be there soon. Then I went to my locker, grabbed my math textbook and dropped it into my backpack. Then I met the three of them in front of Bryan's car. He greeted me with a hug and a kiss. I hadn't seen him much today or even really heard from him and I didn't realize how much I'd missed him until now.

"Ready to go?" Natalie asked.

"As ready as I'll ever be."

James and Natalie climbed into the back of the car; their hands seemed to be locked together the entire time. I just smiled and got in too. Though every nerve in my body was a tangled mess, I was actually really excited about this. I haven't had a piercing since my twelfth birthday.

"Oh! Ness, how did practice for prom go?"

"Good," I said, turning in my seat to look at her. "All the guys are really nice and welcoming. Though I'm pretty sure they had no choice. Though the one guy, Damon, has a bit of an *I don't care about anything* attitude." I pretended not to notice the way that Bryan tensed up at the mention of Damon's name.

"I wouldn't worry about it," she said, just waving it off. "Besides, with you in the band, they're sure to be *so* much better."

"Don't tell Johnny that," I said with a little half-scoff, half-laugh, "because he seems to think that he had everything under control before I swooped in. And Jessie and Aaron are really the only guys that would agree with you."

"Okay, what is it with all these guys?" Bryan suddenly snapped. I couldn't help but laugh at his expression. "Aren't there any girls in the band?"

"Yes, me."

"I mean *other* girls."

"Awe, is someone jealous?"

"No," he denied. "I don't get jealous."

"I think he's jealous," James said from the back seat which only invited Bryan to show him the finger. We all laughed, except Bryan.

When we parked, James and Natalie got out and headed inside. I took Bryan's hand. "Hey." I waited for him to look at me. "You have nothing to worry about. You know that, right?"

"I know, I'm the best thing that's ever happened to you," he joked.

I laughed. "But seriously, you don't have to worry about any of them, okay? You're the only one I want."

"Good," he said before he leaned forward and kiss me a little. He broke away too quickly for my taste. "Let's go inside."

I nodded.

He got out and I followed.

The tattoo/piercing parlour looked the same as I remembered it from last time. Three chairs in the waiting area, a counter next to it where two of the employees sat talking and eating something out of takeout containers. On the other side of the room, Natalie and James were waiting next to a glass counter that had a bunch of jewelry on display.

Bryan and I walked in beside them. Natalie was filling out a sheet of paper that I don't remember filling out last time. She handed me a clipboard and a pen. I started filling it out with the most basic of information — my name. I finished the sheet in a matter of minutes, flashed my ID, paid — since Natalie had paid for our tattoos, it was only fair — and then the four of us were ushered into a room in the back. Natalie sat down first.

∞ℰ∞

It happened so fast and then we were leaving the building.

The ten minutes it had taken to pierce our ears, was a moment that existed in the past now as we all climbed back into the car. Natalie got so excited about her new wave of freedom that had come from this trip, that she invited Bryan and me out on a date with her and James tonight.

I couldn't say I was entirely eager for it, but just thinking about it seemed to excite her, so I shrugged and agreed.

Bryan slowed in front of Natalie's house; James and Natalie got out, practically running up the porch steps and stumbling into the house, Natalie was in a sudden fit of giggles. I had never seen her like this before, not even with Christopher, *especially* not with Christopher. I wondered if I looked as happy with Bryan as she did with James. I know how I *feel*, but how do I *look* from someone else's point of view?

"You look happy," Bryan commented, a grin on his face as he backed out of her driveway.

"What?"

"You asked your question out loud," he told me.

"That happy?" I asked, gesturing to Natalie's house.

"Maybe the first few days; now you're just *really* comfortable with me," he said. He scrunched his face up a little, in a cute way, "I *think*."

"Maybe because I don't have to hide anything anymore." I smiled.

"True."

I didn't live that far from Natalie's, just a couple right and left turns here and there so it didn't surprise me that after a couple more minutes, Bryan pulled into my driveway and cut the engine.

"You wanna come in?" I looked from the house in front of me to Bryan. "But I *am* warning you that my brother may not be home yet, which means that we could be completely *alone.*"

He laughed. "What? Are you worried that I might try to get in your pants?"

"Would you?"

"No." Pause. "Not yet."

"And how will I know when you *do* want to?"

"Trust me, I already *want* to."

I swallowed, blood rushing to my cheeks. My nerves fluttered. "Fine." I groaned, and rephrased, "how will I know when you do *try*?" My cheeks were red. My heart was beating loud. My skin was warm. And I couldn't seem to catch what he was saying so I leaned toward him to hear him better.

He leaned toward me too. Bryan raised a hand and stroked my tomato red cheeks, grinning. "You'll know," he said a little huskily before bringing his lips to mine.

I smiled against his kiss.

Just as he started trying to pull me onto his lap, the gearshift jabbed me in my side; my pained groans ruined the mood.

"Sorry," he said softly, as much as his shallow breathing would allow. "Are you okay?"

"I'll live." I kissed him one last time, just to tease him, and got out before he could grab ahold of my wrist. He reached for my wrist but missed before climbing out of the car and following me up the porch steps.

Once inside, I went upstairs to grab a cardigan from my closet.

I felt his presence before I saw him. Bryan walked in behind me and stopped in front of my wall. He stared at the loose sticky notes and papers with pretty calligraphy. I could hear him whisper the quotes to himself and then suddenly, he turned to me. "Powerful stuff."

For some reason the casual response made me laugh. I don't know what I'd expected from him when he saw it but that *hadn't* been it. There weren't many people that I'd let in my room and the last time he was here, it had been dark and we'd sat in one spot for most of it. Then the next morning, I'd ushered him out in a hurry. He hadn't really had time to look around and take it all in.

Now that he did, I felt completely exposed. The quotes were there for when I was feeling low, or completely uninspired, or just downright insecure. Now knowing that he's seen them, I felt a little self-conscious.

He walked over to me and snaked his arms around my waist and pressed his forehead to mine. "It's you; I like it."

"Thanks." I smiled and kissed him just as I heard the *Jaws* theme song. I groaned and stepped away from him. Thomas' phone was on my desk. I hadn't heard from him for a couple days so it felt strange being comfortable with the silence. I should have known that it was too good to be true.

"Who's that?"

"Thomas," I said before I answered the call.

"Get the flash drive," snapped Thomas.

"What flash drive?"

I was *also* not surprised that the first thing he said to me in days would be an order of some sort. First, it was to spy on my mom for him (apparently he really doesn't want her to be happy, or so I've concluded). I mean, why else would he care if she's dating anyone? And now, some mysterious flash drive?

"It's a flash drive. It has something I need on it and your mom has it. I need you to find it." He sounded like he was losing his patience with me. Well, I was losing *mine* with *him*.

I sighed, impatiently. "What does it look like?"

"It's small, black, and it's a USB flash drive."

The only time I had ever seen a black USB was when it was mine and I used it to save projects and transport them from school to home. I have never seen one that mom would think was worth hiding.

"Just find it," Thomas shouted when I didn't say anything and then promptly hung up.

I turned off the phone and stuck it into my desk drawer. "He is impossible."

"What does he want?"

"A flash drive. Apparently, there's something on it that's important," I told Bryan. "I wouldn't even know where to start looking."

"How important can it really be?" Bryan asked, wrapping his arms around my waist and pulling me close. The warmth of his body surrounded me and the dulled forestry scent of his aftershave was all I smelled. "Can't I take you on a date first?" He asked against my neck.

"Right, the date. Don't you need to go home?"

"Nah, I've got everything I need." He waved his hand dismissively.

"Okay, then let's get out of here. I'll just lie and say I tried looking for it." I pulled at his arm and we both walked downstairs just as my brother opened the front door and stepped inside. "Hey."

"Hey..." He trailed off when he saw who I was with. "You're not supposed to be alone together."

"Gee, thanks for the reminder," I said sarcastically. "We wouldn't have been *alone* if *someone* didn't take forever to get back."

"Says the person that left school before the final bell."

I ignored him and then left mom a note telling her where I was going and who I was going to be with and that I'd be home for curfew. I filled André in and then left hand-in-hand with Bryan.

◦◦◦

"What do you mean we're not sharing a theatre?" I asked Natalie when she told me. It wasn't that I was afraid to be alone with Bryan; it was more that I was afraid that, if I took the risk, we'd get caught and I'd never be allowed to see him again.

"Well, you didn't *lie*, James and I are here too; we're just not watching the same movie. Relax," Natalie told me. She got in line behind a middle-aged couple who stood together in silence. One was on her phone (Facebook) and the guy looked like he was going to fall asleep on the spot. "Your mom won't find out. I promise."

I wasn't entirely convinced, but I nodded. I would have been fine sharing the same row as Natalie and James but if they insisted, fine. They would be the ones to blame when my mom eventually found out. Natalie and I both stepped up to order just as the guys came back. I got a package of Twizzlers along with a small popcorn. I wasn't going to eat a lot of *theatre popcorn* considering all the fat it contained.

Bryan and I got a couple drinks and I stuffed the Twizzlers in my purse, giving me an extra hand to carry something else.

Once inside the theatre, Bryan and I got our seats and sat down. I started to snack on the popcorn. I couldn't help it, they were right there.

"Can I ask you something?"

I looked over at him. Surprised that he'd asked for permission rather than just asking whatever was on his mind. "Sure."

"About your dad almost killing you."

My whole body tensed up as I looked around us. There weren't that many people around to overhear but I still didn't want to talk about it; I had thought he'd let it go. He'd promised. "Seriously? You're choosing *now* to bring that up?" I asked, my tone harsh but I didn't take it back. "Here? In a public place?"

"Maybe now isn't the best place to bring it up but I can't stop *thinking* about it," he said through his teeth. "Why didn't you just tell me?"

I fell silent. Just because he now knew what had happened (sort of), didn't mean he needed to know what would happen if Thomas knew our father-daughter secret was out. I wasn't about to tell him. It wasn't just that I didn't want to tell him but that I was *scared* to tell him.

"I thought you said you were going to let it go." I glared at him.

"I was, but like I said, I can't stop thinking about it."

"Well, you're going to have to." I focused my attention on the screen in front of me.

During the whole movie, I did everything I could to avoid him; his touch, his gaze. I grabbed popcorn only after he did. I used the other armrest so I'd be leaning away from him. And I refused to reach for his hand because with his touch came security. As much as I wanted to know I was safe, I also didn't want to delude myself into believing it.

He asked me about the movie as we were walking out and I just gave him mumbled, incoherent responses. I'd barely paid any attention to the movie. I was too busy thinking about whether Thomas had figured out I'd been with someone when I said that he'd tried to kill me. And, if he did know, then it was only a matter of time before he'd come for me.

We hadn't been watching a horror movie but I suddenly felt just as paranoid as I would be if we had.

Suddenly, a pair of arms snaked around my waist and pulled me towards him. It startled me out of my horrifying reverie. Then his lips were at my ear. "I'm sorry. I'll let it go, I just... I wish I knew why you didn't tell me before."

I leaned into him, letting that feeling of complete security fall over me. "If you care about me at all, you'll keep that promise."

I felt him nod into my shoulder before I noticed James and Natalie walking toward us, laughing. I wondered what they'd watched but I didn't ask. They seemed so engrossed in one another that asking them anything seemed impossible. Dinner was no better. They sat at the other end of the table talking and laughing. Worst of all, the only thing Bryan wanted to talk about was Thomas.

When I invited him to my next band meeting, however, he seemed thrilled. But not in the 'I'm a supportive boyfriend' way. But rather the 'I'm going to kill anyone that looks at my girlfriend' way. It was not comforting but at least he had his mind somewhere else that wasn't going to put me in danger.

Even Natalie and James seemed eager to come to practice.

My attempt to give Bryan something else to focus on had become a crowd pleaser.

So the next day, I walked into the music room just as the guys were starting to stream in. I smiled and waved, getting the guitar I had taken from Damon yesterday. He smiled at me this time when he saw me coming and, appeared to, *gladly* give me his guitar. Then he gave a small bow.

"Anything else you plan on taking from us?" He asked. "Like our masculinity?"

"Since when is your masculinity the same as a guitar?"

He froze for just a second, then his face broke into a grin. "I like you. You're funny."

"Thanks. I think."

I found a chair and played a little tune with the guitar just to make sure it was still okay from yesterday. It was.

"So listen, the guys and I are going to a party tonight. You wanna come with us?" Damon asked, leaning over the guitar in his lap.

The door behind us opened then.

I looked back once to see that it was Bryan, James and Natalie and quickly answered, "Sure, sounds fun."

"What sounds fun?" Bryan asked as he slid a chair up close to me.

"A party," Damon answered before I could, glaring at Bryan.

Did guys and girls, alike, have a problem with him? I wondered.

"Where is it?"

Damon gave the address, a little smirk on his face. I guess he knew he'd hit a sore spot with Bryan.

"I know where that is."

"Great. Starts at 7."

"Great, I'll be there."

"Great."

The rest of us just watched the exchange between Damon and Bryan. Damon was the first to start practicing, playing the tune of a very familiar song. The rest of us joined in.

It was a very tense practice. And I wasn't the only one who noticed. Natalie, James, Jessie, Aaron, and Johnny kept glancing between Bryan and Damon. Finally, the practice was over. The other members of the band put away their instruments and picked up their backpacks, and then left. Natalie and James followed.

It wasn't long before Bryan and I were the only ones in the room.

"I cannot believe what happened at the beginning of practice."

"I know, he has a lot of nerve," Bryan said, thinking he and I were on the same page.

"I meant you. You can't go around being possessive of me like that."

"I wasn't being possessive."

"Yes, you were," I insisted, hard. "When we graduate, I am going to move away, and I am going to live with people you don't know. And I can't have you telling me who I can or can't be friends with. Either you trust me to be faithful, or you don't."

I grabbed my backpack and I stormed out of the room, not even bothering to see what his response would be.

❧ Nineteen ❧

Since Natalie had to work, James and I went to the party together. I texted Bryan as I was getting ready that I would see him there and that I was going with James. He wasn't happy about that and insisted that he could drive me. But I wasn't in the mood to be his possession, so when they both showed up, I got in James' car, despite Bryan's protests.

At the party, I walked in behind James. When I spotted the guys by the drinks, I walked over and they all shouted their 'hello's over the pounding music. Johnny leaned in a little closer and yelled, "Want a coke?"

"Excuse me?"

"Coke. Like, a drink?"

Oh.. "Yea, yes please."

Johnny dug through the cooler and handed me a can of Coke. Someone else grabbed it before I had a chance to. Bryan. "I've got it from here."

"What's your problem?" Damon demanded from where he'd been standing, behind the table. "It's just a drink. From an unopened can."

Bryan ignored him and looked at me, seeming to plead with me. "Come with me?" He waited about two seconds before he pulled on my arm and grabbed something from the table and led me to the kitchen.

"Bryan, stop." He stopped at the kitchen counter. "What is wrong with you? Is this really because I came with James instead of you?"

He looked like he was having a hard time ignoring me as he poured a bottle of vodka into a cup and then filled the cup the rest of the way with the Coke. He handed it to me. "Drink it."

"No."

"Ness, please, I'm trying to keep my promise to Natalie. Please drink it."

That promise felt like a forever ago. A forever that existed back in a local McDonalds after a story about a fake I.D. and an out of town club.

He remembered promising Natalie that he'd help get me drunk?

Tasting alcohol *was* on my list, I hadn't forgotten that. I took the cup and already had a bad feeling about tonight. I should probably have learned to trust my gut but for some reason, I ignored it and finished the whole drink in one go. Which wasn't as bad as I thought it would be but I still didn't want to do it again.

Bryan tried to offer me another, I shook my head. Once was enough. I looked around and saw — what seemed like — the majority of our peers dancing very seductively in the living room. The furniture was pressed against the walls to make room. The kitchen and dining room were refreshments central. A bunch of people at the refreshments table were fighting Damon to get the last bottle of rum.

Wasn't there supposed to be a keg?

When I asked Bryan about it, he nodded toward the backyard. I looked out of a nearby window and sure enough, there was a crowd of people surrounding a keg. There was a loud cheer and then someone's legs went up in the air and I looked away.

Behind Bryan, there was now a girl laying on the kitchen counter, her head in the sink. Ugh. Suddenly, a group of girls bumped into me, shoving me hard into the counter. They didn't seem to notice as they rushed towards the girl by the sink in concern.

Just looking around at the chaos made me miss my room; my comfortable room where I didn't have to worry about getting injured by a hoard of girls crashing into me.

The Game

Bryan took my hand and pulled me toward the so-called dancefloor as the song changed. I loved the melody but I didn't want to risk accidentally bumping into anyone. But I was silly to worry about it. No one else was. Bryan stopped in front of me and put his hands on my waist, his eyes on me. He mouthed something like, "Relax."

Easy for *him* to say. This was his scene. It *wasn't* mine. I shouldn't be here.

We started swaying despite the song's rapid pace. I didn't mind it so much, being close to him was better than, well, whatever everyone else was doing. *Can they even really call that dancing?* I tried not to pay attention to anyone else as I closed my eyes and placed my head against Bryan's chest. He held me closer then as he pressed his lips to the crown of my head.

The music was so loud that it vibrated against the walls and pounded against the floor beneath me. In order to talk to anyone, you needed to shout whatever you wanted to say. I thought I heard Bryan try to say something to me but he didn't shout it so I wondered if I'd heard it at all. I *thought* he said he loved me and that he was sorry for everything. But I wasn't sure.

I wanted someone to turn down the music so that I could, maybe, get Bryan to repeat whatever he'd said. I looked up at him and I noticed the way his face had morphed from relaxed to stressed and apologetic. I reached up to cup his face and he seemed to visibly relax beneath my touch. He closed his eyes. I moved my fingers to trace his cheeks, lips, chin, then I moved my hands around his neck and pulled him down for a kiss.

This kiss was a little different than all the others. It was rough but gentle with a little too much emotion, both of us wanting more but me, wondering if I was even ready for it. I knew right then that I loved him. It was like a lightbulb had gone off in my head. I loved him. He could be mean, possessive, and he was known for horrible things, but with me, he could be kind and gentle and caring. With me, he showed a side that others didn't get to see. I loved it. I loved both sides of him, and I loved him.

I wanted to tell him but I didn't want to say the words *here*. So I let my lips do the talking, matching his emotion and passion until it left us breathless. We had to break apart, panting.

"Wanna get out of here?" He shouted.

"And go where?" I asked.

"Outside, maybe."

Well, it definitely would be easier to talk, I thought. I nodded and the two of us pushed our way through bodies until we made it to the door. We walked out and went to his car. It was reasonably quiet out here, so I decided to try and get him to repeat what he'd said in there. He seemed hesitant to and maybe even a little embarrassed, but eventually, I wore him down.

"I said that I was sorry for how I've been acting lately." He sat on the hood of his car and patted the spot between his legs, inviting me to sit.

I sat and looked at him. "And how have you been acting lately?" I wanted him to say it, really own up to it, not just say he was sorry.

"You know... You just want to hear me say it, don't you?"

I waited.

He sighed. "I've been acting possessive and incredibly jealous and I'm sorry if it seems like I don't trust you." He leaned back against his car and kept his gaze on me. "I lied."

"What?" I asked, curious. "Wait, so you're not sorry?"

"That's not— I *am* sorry. I mean, I lied to you when I met you, for the first time, in that bathroom," he said, amused. "I told you that I'd never seen you around school before. I lied."

Just as soon as we were on the same page, he flipped back to the beginning. What did he mean?

"On the first day of high school, you and I had our lockers in the same hallway and I noticed you struggling with your lock. I remember thinking that I could go and help. But you were so focused that I didn't, so I just watched instead. Completely mesmerized."

As he talked, I listened, remembering that day. And especially that stupid lock.

That was the day I found out I wasn't very good at remembering lock combinations. I'd gone that whole day thinking that I knew what my combination was. At the end of it, I was so frustrated that I was just about ready to kick my locker when Natalie came over and told me my combo. I was just glad that I'd let it slip to her because that would have been a waste of a good lock.

I also remembered looking up just in time to see Bryan, a good ten lockers down, with his lips locked with some girl; his girlfriend at the time. I'd been completely disgusted by their show of affection. I ignored them in favour of listening to Natalie, going on and on about some movie she wanted to watch. Or rather, *re*-watch.

It went on like that for a few minutes, Bryan telling me about times when he'd been watching me from afar, admiring and falling in love with 'the way that I carried myself' without me ever knowing.

He even remembered the first conversation we ever had, as short as it had been.

It was exam week, at the end of that first semester and I was at my locker, running late. I could have sworn I'd remembered my pencil case but I was wrong. I'd searched my entire locker, even my backpack a couple times and I'd come up empty-handed when this gorgeous stranger — at the time — came up to me and knelt beside me.

"Looking for something?" He'd said, holding out a brand new pencil, already sharpened.

"That's not mine." But I was so scared of being late that I itched to just grab it, shout 'thanks' over my shoulder and hurry to my exam. But, somehow, I kept my composure.

"I know. It's mine, but you can have it."

"Thanks," I told him, taking it. I promised I would give it back to him, but he told me not to worry about it and then he left me there. I was grateful for his kind gesture but haven't thought about it since.

"Say something," Bryan said now, his hand stroking my shoulder. The whole time he'd talked, he seemed to have felt the need to touch me. My hands, my face, my arm, my leg. His hands hadn't left my body and it felt good.

I sucked in a breath. "I still need to give you that pencil back."

He laughed. "You still have it?" He asked, taken aback.

I nodded. "Yup. I never used it except for exams and tests and *only* when I thought I needed some luck. It's the size of my thumb now." I smiled. "No one uses it but me."

"Well, you can keep it. We still have a couple exams to go."

He leaned back across the hood until I was sitting in between his lap, resting against his chest and looking up at the stars. A few people had come and gone past his car, crashing into each other with the inability to walk in a straight line but I didn't pay much attention to them.

All that mattered was Bryan and this moment.

※ ❦ ※

It was around nine when Natalie arrived at the party. She dragged Bryan and me back inside before she zeroed in on James. When she found him, she kissed him in greeting. It was short and sweet but I think it said all there was to say at that moment.

I looked away to give them a minute and glanced around at the lively party. I crossed my arms and leaned against a doorway when Bryan stepped up beside me. He kissed my cheek and said in my ear, "I'll be back. Get drunk, let loose, have fun, will ya?" Then he kissed my cheek once more and disappeared upstairs.

I looked around to find that Natalie and James had also disappeared and I was in a sea of people that I would normally never talk to, or people that I just didn't know at all. I didn't even know who the host or hostess was.

"Janessa!" I heard before I felt a hand come down on my shoulder.

Turning around, I saw a brunette with warm brown eyes that looked so familiar. And beside him was a girl, her arms around his waist. Long brown hair and a big smile as she looked from the guy to me. This girl I knew. She was on the cheerleading squad with Natalie. Her name was Chelsea. So that must mean that… *Oh!* "Hey, Reggie," I said. "Where's Melissa?"

"She's in her room. Something about needing to study for something."

"Not sure how she could with the music as loud as it is," I commented.

He smiled. "That's what she said the last couple times when she asked us to turn it down."

"Are you going to?"

"Where's the fun in that?" He shrugged. "Besides, she's always studying, so I'm pretty sure it's just an excuse."

I nodded, though there was nothing I wanted to do now then to go and study with her. I wish I had brought my books. I was feeling very unproductive.

"Oh, where are my manners?" Reggie replied rhetorically. "This is my girlfriend, Chelsea. Chelsea, this is Janessa; Bryan's girlfriend."

"Yeah, I know," Chelsea and I said at the same time. She seemed more bored than anything else but still managed to smile at me.

"Good to see you again," I told her. Then I pointed behind me to the stairs. "I should go check on Melissa. Have fun, guys."

I took the stairs two at a time.

The first door was the bathroom and occupied. I heard the water running like someone was washing their hands. Or, rinsing their mouth.

In the next room, I knocked and pressed my ear to the door. When I heard moaning, I stumbled back and continued to the next door. I visibly shivered in disgust as I knocked on the next room.

Melissa opened the door. Before she realized it was me, she looked ready to beat anyone who disturbed her into a pulp. And then, suddenly she beamed at me. "Janessa! Hey. Come in." She grabbed my hand and pulled me into her room, slamming the door shut behind us. "You here for the party?"

"I was," I nodded. "Then my boyfriend disappeared and then my best friend disappeared with her boyfriend. Which was when I saw your brother and he told me you were here."

"Oh, so he *is* good for something," she said annoyed, going to her bed. It was unmade but looked super comfy. Suddenly I felt very tired and just wanted my bed to look that inviting.

I helped her study for a while before I realized that it was time to go home or my mom would be pissed.

But when I walked out of the room, I was not prepared for what I saw. Coming out of the sex dungeon next to Melissa's room was Bryan. He leaned into the room for a second and then backed away, grinning. Quickly, so as to not be caught, I went back into Melissa's room and closed the door.

"What? What happened? Are you okay?"

I wanted to know the same thing.

At the same time, I didn't. I wanted to believe that my eyes were playing tricks on me. I wanted to believe that the boy that had left the bedroom next door was *not* Bryan. But if it *wasn't* Bryan, then who the hell looked that much like him? There was no one that I knew.

Melissa was staring at me, still waiting for an answer.

I shook my head and left her room again.

I found Bryan downstairs with Natalie and James. He lifted a can of pop to his lips. He was looking around and when he spotted me on the stairs, he broke away from the nauseating couple. The way he was looking at me made me think that my mind was messing with me.

Maybe it was the alcohol.

But… was that even really possible? I'd had one cup. Not even enough to make me dizzy.

I met him on the bottom step. He looked tired; like he'd just run a mile.

"Hey, ready to go home?"

"Yeah," I told him.

I was confused. I wanted to believe that he'd been honest with me when he'd told me that he was willing to give up the game. But with everything that had happened tonight, it was getting harder to believe it; to believe him. Was he lying this whole time? Did he only tell me about the game so I'd trust him?

The Game

Was I just being naive when I'd decided to trust him?

I didn't want to admit it out loud but, yes, a part of me truly believed all of that. I'd just been too blind to believe it before. Now, however, my eyes were open.

Bryan hadn't changed and I wasn't sure if he ever would.

⚜ Twenty ⚜

I made sure to give my two weeks to Natalie's mom when I went to work the next morning.

She was surprised because I'd told her that I would be working till the end of the summer; but after what happened last night, I just wanted to get out of town as soon as possible. Maybe running wasn't the best decision and definitely the coward's way out, but the fact was that there really wasn't much in this town for me anymore. Everyone around me would be moving on.

Natalie and James would spend every waking moment together before they went off to their separate schools. And I didn't want to be their pathetic little tag along.

I wasn't sure what Melissa was planning on doing but whatever it was, I was sure it wouldn't be hindered if I left town earlier than planned.

I hoped that Mom and André would be fine when I left. Not that I was my mom's sole protection — she did have a gun hidden under a loose floorboard in the living room — and I knew she would be fine, but it was André that I was a little more worried about. He could take care of himself but I didn't want him to think that I'd just abandoned him when he needed me most.

Everyone was accounted for and none of them needed me to stick around. So why not get a head start on my life?

Natalie came into work four hours later, looking quite rested. When I asked about it, she just mentioned that James '*may or may not have*' stayed over. In other words, her boyfriend stayed the night and her mother didn't know. I rolled my eyes and smiled. The smile quickly disappeared when I remembered the time when Bryan slipped through my window and spent the night. My mom hadn't known and she'd been pretty upset when we'd talked about it later on.

Natalie almost laughed when I mentioned to her that I thought Bryan had cheated on me last night.

"If you'd told me that three weeks ago, I'd have believed you but now? No way. He's totally in love with you," she said.

Great. He had her *completely* fooled.

Annoyed and frustrated, I picked up a damp rag and walked around her to the tables. I realized how oblivious I'd been. How foolish and naive! He'd never change and *that* hurt more than anything. I wanted to slap him and yell at him and call him names and mean every word. I wanted to hate him. Loathe him, even. I didn't *want* to love him. But I *did* and that made it so much worse.

He'd played me like a violin and I fell, jumping in and believing everything he said. I was naive and stupid and he just sat there and watched. Took pleasure in it; *revelled* in my pain. He was probably thinking about it right now. Thinking about last night and how he'd done it, *again*; tricked a too-trusting girl that would believe all the crap he spouted.

Well, not anymore.

I told myself that, right after work, I would go to his house and talk to him. Get him to admit it and if not, it was over. I couldn't be with a liar and cheat. I was *not* going to believe anything but the truth, and the truth was that he'd cheated. He kept playing the game, playing my heart; manipulating the strings to get the results he wanted.

But that night, I changed my mind.

I'd stopped at his house, even parked on the curb and gotten out of the car. But then raindrops started to fall and the steam defused. I didn't want to go into that house and have what I already knew, be confirmed. I didn't want to give this up; I wanted to work at it. If I could just give it the chance it deserved...

But at the same time, I *didn't* know what I wanted anymore.

I wanted the truth yet I couldn't get myself to walk the rest of the way up to the house to get it.

So I got back into my car and just watched as each dropped hit my windshield. A few minutes later my phone dinged with a message; I almost chucked it out the window when I saw who it was from.

BABE: Do you want to come in?

I answered 'no' and drove home.

❦

"Mom?"

She was in the kitchen, cleaning a pot and scrubbing *really* hard. She looked up when she heard me and smiled. "Hey, honey, you okay?"

"Can we talk for a minute?"

"Sure, what's up?"

Mom set the pot in the sink and dried her hands. We both took a seat at the island and I told her what happened last night. She listened. She didn't approve when I got to the part where I had accepted a cup of vodka/Coke from Bryan but didn't say anything more. She kept listening and when I told her what I thought I'd seen, she became very sympathetic.

"Oh, honey."

"I don't want this to end but at the same time, I can't be with him if it's true."

"You *need* to talk to him."

"I was afraid you'd say that," I grumbled, sinking into my seat.

She chuckled. "I know it's not the most appealing thing to do in this situation, but you need to. You need to get the facts straight and then, make a decision."

"And if he lies?"

"If he lies, then you know it wasn't meant to be."

"Okay. But first I'm gonna take a shower," I told her and headed upstairs.

Like raindrops on my windshield, water needled against my skin. I thought about what mom had said and knew she was right. I needed to talk to him. I needed to get the facts. Without the facts, I couldn't make a sound and sane decision. Maybe nothing happened last night and I was just overthinking what I'd seen. Or maybe I just wasn't willing to accept what I *knew* I'd seen.

I tried to call him but he didn't answer the first or even the second time. When I tried a third time, Thomas' phone rang. I quickly hung up on Bryan; grateful that he hadn't picked up. I still didn't know what to say to him; so I answered Thomas' phone instead.

"Did you talk to her?"

"I haven't had a chance," I told him.

Why does he always sound so angry with me? I wondered. *Not impatient, or in a hurry, or anything; just angry. As if he knew I was gonna disappoint him and he didn't want to feel hopeful.*

"Well, talk to her *now*. Get that flash drive."

Then, dial tone.

Conversations with him were always short and bitter and demanding, but at least they were short. Yet, they also left me feeling disgusted with myself. Like I was doing something wrong, something that should be reported to the police. I didn't know what was on that USB stick but I also didn't want to take the chance.

❧

Later that night, when I talked to mom, she looked like she was already half asleep. I felt bad but at the same time, I just wanted to get this over with.

From what she said, the meeting with her lawyer was fine until Thomas started yelling. She'd known since she found out she was pregnant with me that he didn't want to be a father. When they'd gotten married, she'd suspected that it was out of obligation so she didn't understand where his sudden need to have his children close was coming from.

I was a little confused myself. He'd practically beaten André almost to death until a teacher made a call that changed everything and then almost smothered me in my sleep. With those terrible parental acts, how could he possibly believe that anyone would think he should be allowed to keep his parental rights?

The more questions that I asked, the more awake she pretended to be. When I asked her about the box that we kept in the basement with Thomas' things, she couldn't fight it anymore. She managed to tell me that she'd stuffed it into the back of a closet. She didn't say which one so I'd have to check them all.

I draped a blanket over her and got to work.

I went to her bedroom first, hesitating at the door but eventually got my feet moving. Her room was the biggest in the whole house, which gave her a lot of space since she only kept the essentials near her. A bed, dresser, vanity, and her closet which added about a couple more feet in the room. It was also the cleanest part of the whole house, her bed meticulously made, her makeup arranged in a particular order.

I'd learned *that* the hard way. Once, when I got really into wearing makeup and wanted to stand out to people (for about five minutes), I'd snuck into my mom's room and borrowed some eyeshadow. I didn't think she'd find out, but she did.

I walked past her vanity and opened the closet door. Jackets and sweaters, things that were too bulky to be kept in her dresser, hung up in the closet on either side of the door. I checked the shelf above her clothes and started pulling boxes down. I didn't remember what Thomas' box of things looked like; I vaguely remembered some writing on it but I couldn't remember what.

That box didn't have anything useful in it and neither did the other two that she kept up there. I put everything back, hoping I'd put them all back in the right spot and then left her room, quietly closing the door behind me.

"What're you doing?"

"Jesus!" I hissed, hand over my heart. "You scared me."

"What're you doing?" André repeated.

"Nothing. I just have a top secret mission, that's all," I said, semi-sarcastic.

"Anything I can help with?"

I almost considered it. *Almost.* I shook my head and walked past him, and downstairs to check some more closets.

There were a couple of possibilities... I opened one and pulled out a box. I didn't realize Andre had followed me so when I glanced behind me, I jumped. "God, you could work for the CIA; you're *freakishly* quiet."

"Thank you." He took it as a compliment. Personally, I thought it was horrifying the way that he could walk around here and not make a sound. Especially with our creaky stairs. "Now, what are you looking for? I can help. It would go by faster, whatever this mission is that you have."

"It's *very* nice of you to offer but I can't say anything, okay?" *My life depends on it.*

"Yeah, yeah. 'Top secret'," he said, rolling his eyes. "You really don't think I haven't noticed the way that you move around here?

"Or how jumpy you are? It's like you're afraid someone's gonna jump out at you." He said, following me into the kitchen, an open box in my arms.

"I get it; you're super observant and quiet. Feel free to join the Justice League. Now leave me alone."

"I've been there."

"Been where, the Justice League?"

"Where you are; being scared of your own shadow."

"I'm not scared of my shadow." I snapped. Why couldn't he just leave? Go to bed. Read a book. Something. Anything.

I took a photo from the box and knew that *this* was it. This was the box I was looking for. It was a picture of my mom and Thomas. Thomas' arm was around her shoulder and her arms were around his waist. They stared into each other's eyes and looked insanely happy.

Thomas was actually quite handsome *way* back when. But that must have been before he went batshit crazy.

Mom was beautiful. She still was but it was a different kind of beautiful; she wasn't a kid anymore. She had wrinkles and laughter lines and two teenage children of her own. And yet… she was more beautiful now than she'd ever been.

In the photo, they both wore uniforms that would easily fit in at any fancy and super expensive private school.

There was another photo in the box; of just mom, posing for a picture, a big smile on her face and a gleam in her eye. She'd been happy then, with him. He had *made* her happy. What changed?

"Wow.." André said. He took the picture from me so he could continue examining it.

I rifled through the box, moving aside planners and big yellow envelopes and folders with titles on them in big lettering and permanent marker. Finally, down at the very bottom, there it was. A little black USB stick that Thomas was desperate to have.

"What are you gonna do with that?"

"Nothing," I told André, stuffing the USB stick into my pocket and putting the pictures back. I closed the box and shoved the box back into the closet.

"You don't know what's on it."

"Consider me curious," I said, taking the stairs two at a time.

A little while later, my laptop booted up and slipped the USB stick into it. I really *was* curious to find out what was so important. I grabbed Thomas' phone while I waited and texted him to let him know I had it. I also told him that mom was being stubborn and wouldn't listen to me about his precious parental rights. The last text was obviously a lie because I hadn't really tried to convince her that what she was doing was wrong, as he seemed to believe.

His response was what I'd expected, **Good.** No 'thanks' or any other form of gratitude from the man. Sometime in the middle of his fancy schooling, he must have lost the ability to say 'please' and 'thank you'. I'd never heard him say it before, and I wasn't sure how long it'd been since mom had. Thirteen years, at least, but who knows? Maybe it was longer.

When my computer was finally ready and I got it open, I looked through it. He'd probably punish me for this if he ever found out, but I was curious.

It was just filled with plans for grandpa's business; to make it better and more profitable. By the looks of it, it was quite normal and I wondered why Thomas had made such a fuss.

When I'd had enough of snooping, I pulled it out of my computer and slipped it into my purse.

◈

James came over the next day.

I answered the door and was surprised to find him there. But only because I assumed it'd be Bryan. Especially after his five denied calls.

"What are you doing here?"

"I need to talk to you about something."

"Which best friend? Mine or yours?"

He laughed at his own predictability. "Both, I guess."

"Okay." I sat down on the porch swing and waited for him to get to the point.

"I know this may be a little premature but what are you doing August fifth?"

"That's a little more than a month away," I said.

"Yup." He popped the 'p'.

"I probably won't even be in town in July."

"What?" He blinked, surprised.

"I haven't mentioned any of this to Natalie yet, so please don't say anything," I told him. "It's just with you and her dating now, I just don't want to stick around if I'm just going to be a third wheel."

"Sure, I get that, but what about Bryan. Don't you think you'll still be together?"

I looked away and didn't say anything but he got his answer anyway. I'd never been very good at keeping my feelings a secret. "If I'm being honest, I'm not even sure we'll last the week, let alone a month."

"What happened? What did he do?"

"What makes you think *he* did something? Maybe I just decided to cut my losses."

He gave me an *'oh, please'* look. "I've seen how he is with you. He's different. You're different from all the other girls. Trust me, he really likes you. If you end it now, you'd just hurt him."

I scoffed. I couldn't help it, it just came out.

"Is it really so crazy to think that you have a good influence on him?"

It was pretty obvious that Bryan hadn't told his friend about his little fling two nights ago. But the memory was burrowed in my brain; I couldn't stop thinking about it. And, last night, I'd had a dream that didn't really make me feel better about the situation. I knew it was because I'd been putting off our talk.

"All I'm saying is that he's different with you. And different with me and the other guys," he said when I didn't say anything, "*you* have something to do with that."

"Great," I said. "But *I'm* saying that there are some things about a person that can't be changed."

"True, but you *could* give him the benefit of the doubt."

"Whatever." Now I was getting annoyed. It wasn't that long ago when I was defending Bryan to other people. But, since then, things have happened that have opened my eyes and made me realize just how blind I've been.

"I know Bryan isn't the easiest—"

"Can we talk about someone else now?"

I hated that I was being so rude to him, especially since he'd been nothing but nice to me for so long. He really was the nicest person I'd ever met and definitely right for Natalie but he was pressing an issue that I'd prefer to just let go.

James threw his hands up in surrender. "Okay."

"Thank you."

"Now the other thing I wanted to talk to you about: I was wondering what you thought of me and Natalie."

"Excuse me?" I wasn't exactly sure what his question was. Did I miss something?

"I mean, do you approve of the two of us being together?" I felt my brows furrowed in confusion. "I just mean that you're Natalie's best friend and your opinion means everything to her."

"Right, well, I'm not really sure what this is about," I said. "And she doesn't really seem concerned..."

"Well, it's just that I— Never mind. I was just wondering." He started walking away.

"I *do* like you." He stopped and I went over to stand in front of him. "With her, I mean. She seems happy with you and that's all I want for her. So, I do approve; don't worry about that, okay?"

"Sure." His face broke out into a grin. "Whatever you say. I'll see you around."

"'Kay. Bye."

❧ Twenty-One ❧

A few days later, I didn't see Bryan until after school. I ran out with my Chemistry test, a big grin on my face and, out of gratitude, I shouted, "Bryan!" and ran towards him. His back was turned to me but he turned around in time to catch me in his arms.

"What's this for?"

I noticed how his friends, Reggie, Evan, James, as well as Natalie, moved back to give us space. "It's my way of thanking you," I said, stepping back a bit to show him my test. "I aced my test; the one you helped me study for."

He smiled, looking at the big 'A' at the top of the page. "I knew you could do it. You knew the information." He handed it back to me. "I'm proud of you."

"Thanks." I took back my test and slipped it into my backpack. "Hey, how about we go out for ice cream? Celebrate? Or maybe, talk?" I asked. I could feel the tension between us and I knew I couldn't let this go on any longer.

"I really can't," he said, "I have to go to work tonight. In fact, I should get going."

"Oh, okay."

He stepped around me to his car.

Fortunately, I didn't have time to dwell on how quickly he'd dismissed me because Thomas' phone beeped with a message; a rare occurrence.

THOMAS: Where are you? I'm waiting. You better have the drive.

Last night, he'd contacted me, again, and asked to meet, insisting that he needed the flash drive as soon as possible. It looked pretty innocent so I didn't understand why it seemed so important; but I agreed to meet him, at a popular fast food place a town over. I told mom that I was going to be at Natalie's and I told Natalie that I couldn't hang out today because mom needed my help with something. I knew that the lies would probably backfire on me at some point but I really didn't want to get anyone else involved.

I said goodbye to Natalie and James before heading out.

❦

When I got there, I realized that I'd been wrong about something. This place wasn't popular. The parking lot wasn't full. Aside from my car, there was only one other vehicle present. A black Honda. Had to be Thomas'. I dug through my purse to make sure that I still had it and got out, locked my car and shouldered my purse.

The whole walk to the entrance, I felt the urge to turn around and speed away. It was a sinking fear that I couldn't quite choke back.

With my hand on the handle, I inhaled, steadying myself. *Let's get this over with.*

The smell of burgers overwhelmed and nauseated me when it mixed with my nerves and fear as I looked around. Thomas was seated at a table, looking like one of those cool dads that wear a leather jacket, dark tee, and jeans. He was fingering something on the table that looked about the size of a business card. His dark hair looked windblown as if he had driven here with the windows down the whole way.

When his eyes found me, I knew it was too late to turn around and pretend I wasn't here. Then again, I didn't want to find out what my punishment would be for not following through with the meet.

"What took you so long?" He demanded when I sat down across the table from him.

"Oh, gee, I'm sorry. I don't want to get a ticket for speeding," I said, sarcastically, barely able to bite it back, though I regretted it immediately. "Sorry."

"Where is it?"

"If I give it to you, can I ask you a question?"

"No, just give it to me."

"It's just a question," I said, "what's the worst that could happen?" I held the drive in my hand and waited for him to relent; I hoped he would. He didn't do it often so I wasn't sure if he would now, but then he leaned back in his seat and crossed his arms.

"What do you want to know?"

"What happened to you?"

"What are you talking about?"

He leaned forward again, the brown in his eyes was cold and slippery. Like black ice; one wrong move and something dangerous could happen. "I just mean, when I was looking for the flash drive, I noticed some pictures of you and mom. And you looked happy."

"So?"

"What changed?" I looked into his eyes, waiting for them to melt, and they did, just a little. "Is it because of me? Because she got pregnant?" I told myself that I didn't care what his answer was, but a part of me did. I *did* care if *I* was the reason that he grew to be cold and abusive.

As much as I hated admitting it, he was my father. And I hated to think that he really did hate and despise me just for existing. I knew that he'd never wanted to be a father but he was, and he couldn't change that. He'd been in my life for all of five years and even longer for Andre. That meant he had to feel something for us, right? Even a little bit, in all that time?

"I never wanted to be a father." He confirmed. "But when your mother got pregnant, I thought I could do it. That it would be fine.

"Your grandpa, my dad, didn't think so. He beat into me all the reasons why I would never be a good dad. I'd never be able to provide for you and your mother, he'd tell me. That I should hope for her death so that it would take the pressure off of me to be good.

"I thought that if your mother and I married, then he'd see that I was serious, determined. But it didn't stop. And, eventually, I started to believe him. Nothing would ever be enough. I was making a mistake.

"I was angry. And then I started drinking and I became an angry drunk." He looked up at me from the spot on the table that he'd been staring at while he talked.

I shouldn't have believed him, let alone sympathized. But I did. For a second.

One moment, I was sympathizing and the next, I was doubting him. "Is that the truth?" I asked.

His face broke out into a malicious grin. "What do you think?"

"I think you're smart. You know what to say and you know how to make things up," I told him honestly. "I think you're the kind of person that never does anything without having a backup plan. I *also* think you're a manipulator and a liar. *And* I think you're evil." I pull out the flash drive from my purse and I held it out to him. "And I sincerely hope that, after this, you will leave us alone."

He reached out to take the USB but, instead of taking it, he grabbed hold of my hand — the one not holding the USB — and squeezed my wrist. "You really should learn to watch your mouth."

I ignored the pain and slid the drive toward him.

For a terrible moment, I thought he wouldn't let go. But then he did. He snatched up the USB and then took his time leaving.

I was afraid to get up and go before *he* did because that meant walking out of here with my back to him and I didn't know what would happen if I did that.

He pocketed the flash drive. "I want the pictures."

"What?" He *had* to be kidding me. This was supposed to be the *last* time. I didn't want to be his retriever anymore.

"The pictures in the box; I want them."

"What could you possibly want with them?"

"Doesn't matter. I want them and you're going to get them for me." He stood and looked down at me.

"Fine."

He smiled and walked away.

I left shortly after he did.

ண௳௺

The next day was the last day of school *and* a half day. Classes were shortened and before long, I was cleaning out my locker. Loose pages on the floor of my locker were thrown into the recycling unless I deemed them important.

It was at my car when I got the letter. The front of the envelope had my name on it, printed in sharpie:

Janessa.

I got in the car before I opened it and unfolded the letter to read what was inside.

> I am sorry for what I am about to do and I hope that you can understand that I never meant to hurt you.
>
> Everything I said before, I meant it all. You are the most amazing person that I have ever met and beautiful and smart and you have so much going for you. You have your whole life ahead of you and you certainly don't need me dragging you down.
>
> I would have said all this in person but I couldn't do it. That should probably mean something, right?
>
> I heard Bryan's laugh in my head. I could already see where this was going and I hated that I hadn't been strong enough to do it myself. But underneath all that, I could feel my heart breaking at the idea of going to school without him in my life.
>
> I am so screwed up, and it's probably my fault, you know? Maybe James had a point when he said the game was demeaning and demoralizing.
>
> For the last few years, I knew what I was doing was wrong, but I didn't care. I couldn't bring myself to care about that or the people that I hurt. I told myself that they would be fine, that it was just a little fun. And then you come along and you changed

everything for me. But you also made me realize that I can be more, and I <u>want</u> to be more.

I just need to work on myself first and, this way, you get to leave town with no strings attached.

I really am sorry and none of this was easy to write. I really hate to hurt you but I *do* think this is for the best.

I'm sorry.

.-Bryan

The more I read, the angrier I became. How *dare* he do this to me? How dare he break up with me *over a letter* and say that he was doing it for *me*?

I was at his house in record time. I knocked on the door — I'd have pounded if I didn't think about Cheryl and Anna. He wasn't gonna get away with this. No way!

Cheryl answered. I apologized as I pushed past her and ran upstairs.

"What—" was her startled response.

I searched for Bryan's bedroom. Only to realize that I'd never seen it so, of course, I didn't know where it was.

Finally, I found it.

I burst through the door and Bryan jumped to his feet. His eyes were wide with shock.

"What are you doing here?" He asked. "Didn't you get my letter?"

I lifted my hand to show the letter that he was talking about. "You mean *this* one?" He didn't say anything. Which just made me angrier. I didn't even think it was possible for me to be this mad. My hand was shaking with anger. My *whole body* quivered. "What the hell *is* this?"

I noticed the way he visibly swallowed.

"No. You don't get to do this to me," I said, tearing up the letter. Or at least, trying to. I was so angry that even the letter was afraid of me. Instead of tearing it, I just ended up with a partially crumpled ball of paper. So, frustrated, I threw it at him.

"Janessa…"

"No!" I shouted. "You listen to me." Even as I said that I didn't know what I was going to say. So I just froze for a second, choking back tears and angry, hurt words. I stared at him, gulping because, now, looking at him, it all came crashing down on me. I wanted to cry. I didn't want to break up with him but he was right.

He *was* screwed up and it *was* his fault.

It would be better for me to just leave, no strings and no loose ends. And that's *all* he'd be; a loose end.

But there was something that I *needed* to know.

"What happened Friday night?" I asked. My anger had dissipated into almost nothing.

"What?" He seemed confused; and tense like he was waiting for the shoe to drop.

"Friday night? You disappeared for awhile and the next thing I know, I see you walking out of a bedroom looking like… *ugh*," I couldn't even say it. But what I *did* say jogged his memory. He knew *exactly* what I was talking about.

"How do you know about that?"

"I was in the bedroom next door and walked out when you did."

He let out a sharp breath. "It's not what you think."

"Oh *really*?" I asked. He nodded. "Then what *was* it? Because it looked like you cheated on me." I waited for a second. "I mean, I wouldn't put it past you. You *did* say you did that stuff all the time."

"But not with *you*," he said quickly. He sounded offended like it was unreasonable of me to think he'd cheat on me. "You're different, okay?" Bryan came forward and put his hands on either side of my face. "I *never* cheated on you."

I glared, "You're *lying*."

"Why do you say that?" He was uneasy.

So I told him about the moaning I'd heard coming from the room that night.

He dropped his hands and looked at me like he knew what he'd given up and he regretted it. "I didn't mean to, Ness." Then, like it could possibly change how I felt, he said, "It didn't *mean* anything to me."

"'Didn't mean anything'?" I snapped. "That's how you justify your actions?"

"No."

I gave him a pointed look.

"Yes?" He asked. I scowled. "Well, what do you want me to do? Huh?"

I looked away, ready to throw my hands up, to give up. I hated it but it was what it was. He was a cheater and a liar, and I was done.

"Do you want me to get down on one knee and beg for forgiveness?"

"What I *would* have liked is to *not* be in this situation in the *first* place."

"I'm sorry," he said softly.

"Oh, you're sorry? I guess that makes us fine."

He looked away from me and sat down on his bed.

"You know what? Forget it, we're over. You said so yourself," I said, picking up the crumpled letter and flattened it, just to slap it on the bed. "I hope you and Megan are *super* happy together." When he didn't deny it, it was all the confirmation I needed. So, I left.

❦

James opened the door when I got to Natalie's house. Tears were streaming down my face.

We'd *both* decided to break up but that didn't mean it didn't hurt like hell. And to know that I was *right* — that first relationships inevitably end in heartbreak — it was like a slap to the face.

I'd started to think that *maybe* we'd have a shot. That, maybe, we'd last *beyond* high school; it crushed me to know that that wasn't gonna happen.

"Who is it?" I heard Natalie shout.

"Janessa," James said but he said it more to comfort me than to inform Nat. He stepped forward and pulled me into a hug. "I'm sorry. I'll talk to him."

"No. Don't," I replied. As my sobbing turned to hiccuping and, finally, hiccuping sobs. "There's no point. But if I could steal Natalie from you."

"Yeah, of course. I gotta get going anyway." He headed back inside, guiding me into the living room with him; his hand on the small of my back.

"Nessa, what happened?" Natalie said as she came forth and pulled me into her arms.

I wrapped my arms tightly around her but waited until the front door clicked shut to say anything. I told her what happened; that I'd been right about Bryan's unfaithfulness.

"Oh, honey," she said sympathetically. "I know what you need. Ice cream and lots of chick flicks."

I forced a laugh. That had been our solution for her split with Chris. It was our go-to medicine for a broken heart. "Yeah, that sounds great."

"Oh, shoot. We don't have any ice cream." She started rummaging around for her wallet. "I gotta go out and get some. Get comfortable. I'll be right back... Unless you want me to stay."

"No, go. Get enough for three."

"Three?"

"I'm going to invite Melissa."

"Okay." She nodded and hugged me again on her way out. "I am *so* sorry. This is *all* my fault."

"Why would it be your fault?" I asked, confused. She took too much responsibility for the hurt in my life. It wasn't *her* fault that Bryan cheated..

"I'll explain later," was all she said before she bolted out the door with the promise to be back soon.

I called Melissa and invited her over to Natalie's.

That night we watched movies, filled up on too much ice cream and junk food, and, most importantly, Natalie explained why she thought it was her fault that my relationship ended the way that it did.

"I would never have suggested that you date Bryan but James was so sure that this was his last chance to give Bryan a taste of his own medicine. I don't know *why* James picked you. I only did it because he told me to," Natalie said.

"James told Bryan to ask me out, didn't he?"

"I *assume* so." Natalie shrugged.

"I must be even more pathetic than I thought," I grumbled, staring into my cup of pop.

"No, you're not," she said. Melissa nodded in agreement.

"I actually thought he *liked* me. And, for a split *second*, I even thought he *loved* me too." Melissa and Natalie just listened as I continued. "I mean, *I* did."

"What?" Natalie couldn't believe it.

"Yup. I fell in love with him. And I can't believe I thought I meant *anything* to him. He didn't even *ask me out* because he *wanted* to; he just wanted somebody to hurt." Tears pricked my eyes again. And just when I thought I'd had enough… "You know, if he hadn't cheated and it was just him breaking up with me in a letter, I might've considered waiting for him to get to where I was. To be ready to be with me the way I wanted to be with him, but…" I trailed off, shaking my head. "God, I'm so stupid."

For the most part, they didn't try to correct me. They let me cry, hog most of the ice cream bucket and blubber on and on about the idiocy that I'd displayed these last few weeks. It was just what I needed.

Before going to bed, I made sure to call mom and pull her out of her hysterics. I let her know that I was staying at Natalie and I apologized for not telling her earlier.

Before bed, I'd been fine. The tears had stopped and I felt okay. But, later that night, they started up again.

So, like the time that Natalie cried herself to sleep after Chris, I now did the same.

❧ Twenty-Two ❧

The next day, I had one exam in the afternoon. I spent the morning cramming for it, my mind clear of everything except my notes. I even packed up the small items in my bedroom that I could live without for a little while and closed them into a box. I had a couple boxes packed when I decided that it was time to go before I was late.

I dug for my English books and packed them into my bag, making sure that I had my — or *Bryan's* — lucky pencil and an eraser. Then I headed out for my exam.

After the exam, I walked out past a group of people and only realized who they were when one of them grabbed my arm and pulled me back.

"Hey! Weren't you going to say hello to us... at all?" Natalie asked, moving back beside James, his arm wounding around her waist and pressing her to him. Melissa stood next to them, looking at me with concern.

"Of course I was going to say hello," I said. *Had I seen them.* "Did all of you have exams today?"

"I didn't, just the girls," James tells me. "But Natalie and I've been talking about doing something tonight and wondered if the two of you wanted to come along. As friends?"

"Um, I can't tonight."

"Nessa, are you going back into your shell? Hiding in your bedroom, away from the rest of the world?" Natalie asked; sympathetic and concerned.

"No, I just have to pack my stuff before tomorrow."

"What's happening tomorrow?" Natalie asked.

Her confusion reminded me that I hadn't told her my plans for the summer and it made me grateful that she didn't know because *I* still had a chance to tell her myself. I shared a look with James; he just shrugged and looked away.

I sighed. "I'm taking my things to my new place near my campus."

"But it's the beginning of summer."

She looked so wounded that I felt bad.

"Nat," I said slowly. "You have James now. You guys will probably spend all summer together and I am *not* going to stick around to be a third wheel."

She didn't like it but nodded anyway. I knew she understood but at the same time, I knew how she felt. This was our last summer before life really got in the way, and we weren't even going to be together. "I don't officially leave until next week."

"Ooh we got some time to hang out," she said. She moved away from James and looped her arm through mine, already walking away and talking about sleepovers and malls.

I looked back toward James and Melissa. James looked amused and not at all bothered. They both followed us until Melissa was walking alongside us with James' hand in Natalie's.

We made plans to meet up at my house that night so I hurried home to pack my clothes. Then I changed into a pair of sweatpants and a plain grey tee and ankle socks. I pulled my hair up and made a knot at the top of my head before heading down to find mom at the stove.

"Hey, honey. No plans tonight with that boyfriend of yours?" She asked when she took in my appearance.

I'd completely forgotten that not everyone knew about the split. But I didn't waste any time correcting her. Maybe it was because I was still angry with him, but I wanted to set the record straight. I told her everything that had happened; how Bryan had admitted to cheating on me and that he'd tried to break up with me with a *letter* instead of being mature and breaking up face to face.

"I'm so sorry, honey. I know you really liked him." I heard her mumble something that sounded like *'for some reason'*, under her breath which made me laugh.

"Yeah, I did really, *really* like him." Then just to mock her a little, I added, "For some reason."

She chuckled. "Okay, dinner will be ready soon."

"'Kay," I said. "Oh, I'm also having a couple friends over."

"Wearing that?" She asked, scrunching her face up the way Natalie would've if we were going out.

"Yes."

Then the doorbell rang. I went to get it. Natalie and Melissa were on the porch and they were each carrying a basket.

"So, James insists that I have to watch all of these before I see him next," Natalie said, holding up a DVD case. Harry Potter. "And I'm not doing it alone."

I laughed, letting them in.

"And I brought the snacks. All the essentials. Popcorn, Twizzlers, whipped cream," Melissa said, holding up a can of whipped cream and spraying some into her mouth. "Kitchen this way?"

I didn't need to tell her 'yes' because she'd already found it and started introducing herself to my mom.

That night, we watched one movie after another, stuffing ourselves full of candy and whatever junk Melissa had brought and, of course, mom's mashed potatoes.

❦

The next day, mom and I pulled up in front of a small white house that didn't look big enough for four bedrooms. It was cute with green eaves and flower beds. There was a driveway off to the side that looked like it could fit two cars side by side. I really hoped so because I needed to have my car come September.

Mom, André and I walked up to the small front porch and I knocked. At first, there was nothing, not a peep or even an indication that anyone was home. Then I knocked again and after we waited a beat, there was a voice from beyond that shouted, "Just one second. Garrett, get the damn door. I am up to my elbows in sugar!"

I chuckled and looked over at my mom, who tried to look happy but I knew that this was something she wasn't ready for; me leaving the nest. I gave her a small, reassuring smile as the door opened to reveal a boy in grey sweats, a baggy sweatshirt, sandy blonde hair and bright blue eyes that swept over the three of us and landed on me. He stopped to check me out.

Suddenly, I felt very self-conscious in my short shorts and light floral tank top, which I'd paired with a navy blue sweater. I slid my one leg up to scratch the back of the other, awkwardly, as he watched me.

"You guys must be Janessa and family," he said. He pointed at me first, then my mom and brother. His eyes followed his fingers. Then he stepped aside and let us in.

From where I stood, I could already see that the decoration was minimal. In front of us, behind him, was a short hallway and at the end of it, it split in two different directions; left and right. I wondered where they led. And at the end of it was a door, a closet? "Come on in, you guys. Meet the gang." He led the way and we followed. "There's three of us, Ronan and Ruth Abbott, and me, Garrett Thompson... Not that you needed to know our last names."

"Abbott? So they're siblings?" I quirked one of my eyebrows up. "They live together and go to the same school? How do you keep them from killing each oth— Ow!" I groaned, glaring at my brother. I rubbed my arm where Andre had pinched me.

Garrett just laughed. "Well, most of the time, I don't do a *great* job but we do have a system that tends to work. Ruth stays in the kitchen for the most part. She's kind of the mom of the group. She feeds us, she wakes us up so we don't sleep all day, she makes sure we're hydrated and have clean clothes. And then Ronan is the sloppy younger brother. And me? I'm somewhere in between."

I nodded, listening as he listed all this off. They really had an interesting dynamic going here.

Garrett led us into the living room where only a head with a patch of raven coloured hair could be seen above the back of the couch, until he jolted upright when his avatar was slaughtered unjustly by some opponent. I didn't even try to guess what game he was playing; I didn't really care. "This is Ronan," Garrett said, gesturing to the figure on the couch, who had, yet, to even notice our presence. Garrett waved his hand in front of Ronan's face and waited until he paused his game to glare at Garrett.

"What?"

"Can't you take one minute to say hello to your new roommate?"

"Well, not yet," I interjected. "There's still some things that I need to work out at home and then I'm here. By next week, it'll be official."

"Technicalities," the boys' said together in an eerie tone. Garrett waved a dismissive hand. To say I was stunned was an understatement. I stared at each of them and they just stared back for a moment. Then they shared a look and burst into laughter.

"Hey," Ronan finally said. It was a delayed greeting at best.

His eyes roamed over my body and I had to admit that I felt a little intimidated but I didn't back down. Instead, I kept my ground. I folded my arms across my chest and met his gaze. "Nice to meet you. I'll see you later then."

I gave him a nod and then he went back to his game, now completely ignoring us.

"Okay, well, that's that. Now the kitchen."

The kitchen was a little room that looked more like a narrow hallway where — I assumed — collisions happened when more than one person inhabited the space. On the left side of the space was a stove, counter space that was cluttered with appliances, a sink, and underneath that was also a dishwasher. Continuing down was more counter space that came out and curved toward us and left a 'doorway' for entry. Opposite that wall, there seemed to be shelves, a refrigerator with a butt sticking out of it, and more shelving. It almost looked like they were just moving in themselves.

"And that." Garrett pointed toward the jean covered butt and said, "is Ruth Abbott."

The butt slid out and up came rest of her. The girl — Ruth — stood up and walked over to us, her fingernails perfectly manicured and I wondered when she had the time to do such frivolous things. "Hi. You must be Janessa."

I smiled and shook her hand. "Yup, that's me."

"It's going to be good to have another girl around. These boys are just *way* too messy." Ruth gave a relieved grin, which I felt obligated to return. I wasn't entirely sure what that was like. I'd only had a full-time brother for a month and I hadn't noticed any typical messiness from him. "Especially Ronan. I swear he broke a bottle of Coke in the fridge and didn't have the decency to tell me about it. No, he had to cover it up with a clothe and pretend it didn't exist."

"So that's the sugar you were shouting about earlier?"

She nodded. "Anyway, Garrett will continue to give you the tour and we will have plenty of time to talk more later," she promised. Then she turned her back on me and continued cleaning the fridge with a disgusted look on her face.

⋅⋅⋅

The door I'd first seen in the house on first glance, had been a closet door, just as I'd suspected. There were three more doors in that hallway, down the left side, two bedrooms — decent sizes — and the last was a bathroom, which was wedged between the bedrooms. There was a bath and a shower in that bathroom and, in the bathroom in the basement was a single shower which Ruth and Ronan had dibs on. They basically had dibs on the basement, including the two bedrooms down there.

And then we were back in the living room. Ronan hadn't moved an inch.

"Alright, so there are some stuff we need to go over before you leave," Garrett told me as my mom and brother were already backing out of the house, not wanting to overstay their welcome. "Give me a sec and I will get you a key. We don't always lock that door but on occasion, a key comes in handy." He left the room as I stood there and looked around the minimalist place.

"Psst," Ronan hissed to get my attention. "So when you come back, wanna see my room? Up close and personal?" The corners of his mouth were upturned in a grin and his arm was slung over the back of the black leather couch as he leaned in closer. "Maybe I can kick the two of them out and we can have the place to ourselves."

I was about to answer when my phone rang in my pocket. I looked at it and immediately declined the call. It was Bryan. I didn't know why he suddenly felt the need to call me or what he could possibly want to say to me.

With tears pricking the back of my eyes and my heart aching, I sucked in a breath and slipped my phone back into my pocket. I glued on a smile and hoped it looked real; genuine.

"So, basically you're suggesting a friends with benefits kind of thing?" I tried to sound seductive or flirty but it didn't sound quite right.

"Sure, if you're into that kind of thing."

"Alright," Garrett said, coming back with the key and some sheets of paper. His gaze was completely fixated on the sheets in front of him so it gave Ronan and me a few extra seconds to act natural.

Just then there was banging and my mom's voice, "Careful, Andy." By the looks of it, he'd hit the side of the doorway with my bed frame.

"Let's go to the kitchen with this," Garrett suggested.

He went on for a few minutes talking about rules and regulations and stuff, he even gave me a few minutes for questions if I had any, which I didn't. The chair that I was sitting on looked a lot more comfortable than it felt and, by the time Garrett gave me the key, Ruth was back. She stood in front of us, scanning the sheet of paper. I waited as my phone rang again.

Bryan.

This time I declined and blocked any further calls he might make.

The Game

Mom and I spent the next couple hours unpacking the truck while André sat in the corner of my room and then we went home.

I spent that night with my family. My mom was the first to mention her dislike for me moving three hours away, especially immediately after the end of my two weeks at work.

But it was André's confession that I was the most surprised by. At first and maybe it really *was* just *at first*, but in the beginning I hadn't even thought that he would ever like me. And now, he couldn't stop going on about how he felt like he'd just found me and now he was losing me again. His confession brought me to tears as I slid over to him and wrapped my arms around his neck; I drew him close to me and just held him.

"You could never lose me," I told him. "I may be moving away but you and I are always going to have each other. Now and forever. You're my baby brother after all."

That seemed to ease him into the idea a little but his hold on me didn't weaken.

"I promise you," I tell him.

I did a bit of studying for my math and chemistry exam before I went to bed. I encouraged André to do the same. He grumbled and complained the whole time because his 'brain could not retain information' but an hour later, I got him reciting facts to me.

Then we went to bed.

ᵥₛ Twenty-Three ᶻᵥ

I had a couple exams the next day. Afterwards, I met up with the band in the gym; Johnny, Aaron, Jessie, and Damon and I had one last rehearsal on stage. Then, Damon invited me to ride along with them in the limo they'd rented for the night. I asked if Melissa could join us and they didn't mind.

When rehearsal ended, I went home and got ready.

Standing in a fuzzy bathrobe in the washroom, my mom helped me with my hair and makeup. She pulled my hair into a half-up, half-down do, curling the loose tendrils to hang down around my shoulders. I watched her reflection in the bathroom mirror as she twirled my hair around the curling wand.

My makeup was subtle and understated; purple eyeshadow to match my dress, some blush and lip gloss. My mom was telling me that she always regretted not going to her own prom for the sole reason that she was pregnant. She must've thought that hearing that would make me sad because she then said that even if she hadn't gotten pregnant, a part of her wouldn't have wanted to go.

I knew it was a lie. She'd wanted to go. What kind of girl didn't? Aside from me, I didn't know anyone that would have willingly chosen *not* to go to this thing so I knew she was just fibbing to make me feel better.

"There, all done," mom said, giving my hair one last spritz of hairspray. "Ready for the dress?"

"As ready as I'll ever be," I said, taking one last look at myself in the mirror, then heading to my bedroom.

Mom helped ease the dress over my hair and then zipped up the back of it.

Then the doorbell rang, which pulled mom away and I was left in my bedroom alone, trying to come up with something, anything, that could make seeing Bryan with *her*, worth it. There was nothing that came to mind and it gave me the urge to cry. My heart hurt, every piece; and thinking about him just made it hurt even more. It made the ache worse and, for a moment, I couldn't breathe; but at that moment, I had to suck it up and bite back tears.

"You okay?"

I looked up from the mirror to see André standing in the doorway. I nodded and lied, "Yeah, I'm fine." I forced a smile, slipped on a pair of wedges and headed downstairs. Mom had invited the whole group inside and she was holding up a camera. "Mom, I don't think we have time for that."

"So make time. Please? Just a couple?"

I looked at the others and none of them seemed to be in that much of a hurry; except Melissa, but she forced a smile and nodded.

"Fine, just a couple."

So mom took a couple pictures of all of us. Some were taken on the staircase and a couple more were taken on the front porch, but at that point, I just couldn't stand and smile anymore.

"Mom, seriously, we need to go."

"Okay, okay," she said, surrendering. "Have fun, you guys."

She waved at us as we all headed toward the limo. Jessie and Aaron went in first. When Damon got to the door, he turned slightly to let Melissa in first. "Well, well. Good to know at least *someone* has manners," Melissa whispered back to me.

I chuckled as I got in behind Johnny. Damon was the last to get in and then we were on our way.

❧

A few hours later, the guys and I took a couple of minutes from our set to get a drink. It was silent for a while until I heard the *click-clack* of high heels behind me. Without looking, I said, "You shouldn't be here, go back to the dancefloor."

"I would, but I wanted to see if you were okay."

Immediately, I straightened and came face to face with Megan. She wore a stunning, bold red dress that fit like a second skin and her hair was pulled up and out of her face, with little wisps of hair framing her face. Her voice sounded sympathetic, but her eyes were cold and cruel. "Like I said, you can't be here. Go away."

I got up to leave when she wouldn't but she stopped me with a hand on my shoulder. "I was just trying to be nice. I heard about what happened with you and Bryan and I just wanted to see how you were."

"I'm fine, leave."

The more times that I told her to disappear, the angrier I got. Somehow I'd been able to keep my voice level while I'd been singing; especially when she and Bryan had danced as close to the stage as they could, their bodies pressed so close to each other that they looked like they'd merged together. Not to mention all the times they'd kissed where I could've sworn she was looking at me.

I'd tried to train my attention elsewhere but that was impossible with him in my subconscious thoughts too.

"Maybe this will teach you to stay where you belong. Maybe *now* you realize that I was right," Megan said. It was funny how fast sympathy vanished when it came to Megan. "He belongs with me, he will *always* come back to me and there's *nothing* you can do about it."

"I don't care," I lied. My voice quivered; I prayed she didn't notice. "You can have him for all I care. Now, *leave*."

"I just wanted to be sure that *we're* okay," Megan continued.

"She said leave," Damon said. He came to stand beside me, and even wrapped a hand around my waist, pulling me towards him. I wasn't sure what he was trying to pull, but something about the way he held me didn't make me want to run or even fight back. Damon's eyes were focused solely on Megan. "I'm sure your boyfriend's waiting for you."

Seeming satisfied, she turned on her heels and walked away; but not before looking over her shoulder at me and smiling that superior smile of hers. I don't know *why*. She'd already gotten what she wanted: Bryan. And me out of the picture. Damon let me go then.

"How'd you know that Bryan and I broke up?" I asked. There was no other reason for him to hold me like that.

"Melissa filled us in on a few basic pieces of information," he said.

"I see." I looked away and had an idea. "Can you get the guys?"

I decided to change the set a little bit. I added a new song; something that Johnny didn't like very much. Aaron and Jessie weren't too happy either but Damon just looked amused. When we were all on the same page and Johnny, Aaron, and Jessie had caved, we went back out and took our places, starting anew with our added song, *I Knew You Were Trouble* by Taylor Swift.

I saw Bryan off to the side. I assumed Megan had disappeared into the bathroom or something but I didn't care. I just needed Bryan to know that no matter what he did, I *would* find a way to be okay again. To be who I was before him, or to be a better version of me. He could've been the guy to completely destroy me, but not now and I needed *him* to know that I would be okay without him.

> *Once upon a time*
> *A few mistakes ago*
> *I was in your sights*
> *You got me alone*

Like he was in a trance, he kept his eyes on me and I kept mine on him, until the very last chord and he broke it. He pushed himself off the wall just as Megan walked toward him and then he left the gymnasium. She saw me and her gaze hardened as she followed him out. I told myself I didn't care what he did with her, but just seeing them leave together, broke my heart.

It was around nine when Miss Jamison nudged me and the guys off of the stage and took the mic. I tuned her out as she gave the crowd what they were waiting for, prom king and queen. I pushed through the crowd, all anxiously awaiting the names, and went to the refreshments table where I found the punch. It had *definitely* been spiked. I could tell from my first taste.

There were water bottles backstage that I could drink so it turns out I didn't have to take the unnecessary walk to the back of the gym for refreshments.

When I turned to face the stage, I saw Natalie and James getting crowned King and Queen up on the stage and promptly spit out the punch that I'd sipped onto my hand. Natalie and James? How didn't I know that they'd campaigned?

I found a napkin to wipe my hand and watched as the pair held hands and smiled down at their audience. I noticed the way Natalie searched the crowd; when she found me, I gave her two thumbs up and she smiled. I smiled too but the truth was, I was confused. When did this happen?

The music started up again. This time from a playlist and speakers. James led Natalie onto the dance floor and took her in his arms. Then they danced their king and queen dance with everyone else watching. At first it was just them, then other couples joined in. I watched it all unfold with a numb feeling in my chest.

There was nothing I wanted more than to get out of these shoes and this dress — the straps were starting to pinch my skin — and just curl up in my bed. This nightmare had to end at some point, right?

"Wanna dance?"

I looked up to see Damon with an outstretched hand. He smiled innocently as he waited.

"I don't bite," he promised when I didn't say anything... or move to take his hand. "Unless you want me to."

I rolled my eyes, chuckling and finally took his hand. He led me onto the dancefloor and stopped, turned us so we were facing each other and pressed his hand to the small of my back. His other hand still held mine and he held it slightly extended as you would if you were ballroom dancing.

"Are we having fun yet?"

"As much fun as it's possible to have when you're dancing in aching feet," I replied. I laughed at his amused expression. "If I'm being completely honest, I just want to go home right now. I don't want to be here any longer than I have to."

"It shows."

"Excuse me?" A part of me *had* suspected that I might be the gloom and doom of the party, but I'd *hoped* that no one would notice.

"I can tell you don't want to be here," he said. "Would it have anything to do with Bryan?"

I shook my head. "I never wanted to be here. But," I shrugged, "I'm trying to make the most of it. As best I can, anyway."

He nodded. "Let me know if I can help."

"Thanks," I said. We swayed along to the music and I rested my head on his chest.

When we broke apart, all hell broke loose.

Bryan threw the first punch and it was aimed at Damon. He fell into a dancing couple and then landed on his butt. But Bryan wasn't done. He hit Damon again. Damon rolled them over and threw a third and fourth and fifth before I got ahold of him. Damon was stronger though and ended up slipping through my fingers. I fell on my butt, and they kept throwing punches at each other, rolling over each other to get the upper hand.

"Hey!" I pulled at him again, trying to get him to his feet when Miss Jamison broke through the eager crowd.

"What's going on here?" She demanded.

Damon was panting beside me, but it was Bryan's expression that caught my attention. He looked so hurt. He had a cut lip, blood dripped from his nose and there was a bruise forming just below his right eye. But it was more than that. It'd hurt him to see me with Damon.

His green orbs found mine and held my stare until a jerk on my arm broke the connection and I pushed through the crowd. I'd completely missed what Miss Jamison had said to the crowd and, especially, to Bryan and Damon. But whatever she'd said, Damon didn't care one way or another.

We left and, on our way out, the rest of the band caught up. Then they took me home.

❧❦☙

I was on the front porch in my pjs and guitar when André stepped out in cotton plaid pants and a plain white top. His only white article of clothing as far as I knew. I was just softly strumming the guitar when he came out and sat next to me. I figured that I wouldn't want to play anymore after playing so much tonight, but it was the opposite. I didn't mind so much.

"How was the dance?"

"It was fine."

There was a pause, where he waited for me to elaborate but I didn't.

"And? What happened?"

So I filled him in, omitting a few details. I told him about singing on that stage in front of so many people and the nerves — because I'd been plenty nervous — then Natalie and James being crowned, even though I hadn't known they'd campaigned. "It was fine."

"Okay." He dropped the subject and just listened to me play.

"How was your night?" I asked a little while later. "Did you and mom do anything?"

"Oh, yeah, we had a great night." It didn't take much to notice the sarcasm that dripped off of each word.

He told me what happened, starting with a mini grocery shopping spree followed by catching Thomas in the middle of breaking a window. I wondered if he was trying to get in to get the box. I'd started to wonder why he wouldn't just come in and get his stupid box himself. André didn't know. He hadn't caught any of the details between mom and Thomas. He *did* say that she'd been pissed. But he didn't know anything else.

I didn't press him and we were quiet after that.

A few hours later, we went to bed.

☙❦❧

That night was the first time I'd ever had a dream of Bryan.

He pleaded with me to forgive him, to give him another chance. I really wanted to believe that it was real. That he meant what he said and that I wasn't just being naive.

When I woke up the next morning, it took everything in me not to call him. To not pick up the phone just to hear his voice one last time.

It'd only been a month that we'd been together. Scratch that, it'd been *shorter* than a month but it *still* hurt and it was *still* hard to believe that the next few days to come were my last chance to see him.

I went to work the next day, the dream still on my mind, stealing glances at my phone to check for missed messages and missed calls. But there weren't any... Then I remembered blocking his number and understood why.

After work, Natalie and James decided to take me out.

I had no idea what they were planning until we ended up at the convenience store in town; the one Bryan worked at. Just remembering my dream from the night before brought on urges to run to him and apologize to him and tell him that I forgave him. The look on Natalie's face told me that she was banking on that, the feelings I still had for Bryan.

"I'm not going in there," I told them. Stubbornly, I planted my foot down against the car's flooring, my arms crossed in front of my chest. "You guys can go in there all you want, but I am staying *right here*."

James and Natalie shared a look and then James got out of the car, leaned against the hood. Natalie turned around in her seat and looked at me. "Is there anything I can get you?"

"No, I'm okay. I think I just want to go home."

"But, James and I had something planned for tonight," she whined.

"I know, and I'm sorry that I'm messing with your plans but, I'm just not in the mood tonight," I told her. "Why don't you two go on ahead? Have the night to yourselves."

Reluctantly, she agreed and got out of the car. I waited until both of them had gone into the building before I slipped out of the vehicle and walked around. I kept my head down, pulling the hood of my sweater over my hair. I didn't even notice Bryan leaving the convenience store. We collided and he grabbed my arm to steady me.

Just looking up into those green eyes brought my own to tears and made my heart thud painfully in my chest. For a second he just stared at me and I stared back. Then I pulled my arm out of his grip and muttered a quick, "Thanks," before I got away from him and then I ran.

I ran all the way home.

By the time I got there, my heart was beating painfully in my chest — for a whole other reason. My lungs ached and burned and beads of sweat matted my face and arms. I was panting, my throat raw as I dropped down onto the porch steps.

Then the tears started to spill; just when I thought I'd shed enough tears for that boy, my body proved me wrong. I waited until my eyes dried before I got to my feet and went to bed, avoiding mom and André just in case they'd be able to tell that I'd been crying.

My room was quiet and the emptiness clawed at my skin. It was hard to sleep and when I finally did, my sleep was restless. But it was sleep and I needed it.

❧ Twenty-Four ❧

I didn't hear from Thomas until the morning of my graduation.

He called me and gave a time and place to drop off the box of his momentos just inside an abandoned warehouse. It sounded creepy and cliché.

The warehouse was just outside of town but if I went, I wouldn't be able to get there and back before Natalie was expecting me at her place.

"Would it be possible to do this tomorrow?" I asked him.

"Either you come on your own *or*," he paused. I rolled my eyes. What a drama queen. "I'll have someone go over there and *get* you." *Click*. He'd hung up.

I went downstairs to find the box that he kept asking for and just looking at it, made me feel frustrated. With him. With this back and forth. With the never-ending demands. I would always be his delivery girl if I didn't draw the line somewhere. Well, I was drawing it right *here*. I slid the box back in the closet and went back upstairs to grab my car keys.

A few hours later, after I'd been beautified, I headed back home, promising to meet the girls at the front of the gym. They hadn't heard my speech yet and I didn't want to have to read it out loud any more times than necessary; I was nervous enough as it was. I got home, with the help of the sunlight flooding through the windows, I found a note in the kitchen from my mom that said she would meet André and me there.

"André!" I shouted into the silence of our house, taking the sticky note with me up to my bedroom. There, my cap and gown lay on my bed, ready for me. I took a deep breath. This was it. The end of a chapter, a long-awaited chapter. I couldn't *wait* to get away from here.

Still, my brother didn't answer and I was getting annoyed with him. "André? Hello?" He refused to acknowledge me but I called out to him again anyway. "Are you here?"

I picked up my cap and gown and headed downstairs; I heard footsteps. I assumed it was André, waiting for me. But the living room was clear. I looked outside and there he was, putting something into the trunk of my car. *Or taking something out..?* I didn't remember *having* anything back there but before I had time to open the front door and yell at him, someone or something hit the back of my head — *hard!* — and my vision went dark.

⚜

I heard two voices talking. They were both gruff and low and neither one sounded very friendly. My head hurt as I tried to lift it to see if I could get a clear image of what was in front of me. Maybe even focus better on what they were saying.

"Wouldn't it just be easier to kill her and be done with it?" I heard one of the voices say. It sounded familiar, like I'd heard it somewhere before but at that moment, my mind was too foggy to even try to remember.

"Are you questioning my orders?" The other demanded. That voice I knew. I'd certainly heard it enough times in nightmares and reality combined.

I heard some scuffling, like the first guy was moving away from the second — Thomas — and then again, more scuffling as someone advanced on me. I could *feel* them getting closer.

My attempt to open my eyes was met with some success. My eyelids were heavy and droopy, like I'd been drugged, but they did the job as I met Thomas' gaze.

"Well, well. Look who finally decided to join us."

My back was firm against a pillar, my arms pulled back almost painfully and tied in place. I could feel the rope biting into my skin. Though the joints in my shoulders ached, it was the piercing hit that I took to the back of the head that grabbed my attention. As vulnerable as I was, I figured it would be best to just keep my mouth shut, so I did. I figured that the least offensive thing I could do was look around and I took advantage of that freedom.

Behind Thomas was Mr. O'Donald, Bryan's dad. I recognized him from the barbecue that we had at his place that one time. His arms were crossed in front of his chest impatiently as he watched Thomas. If he hadn't voiced his disapproval of this plan — whatever it was — I would have been able to guess it just by looking at him.

I realized that we weren't the only ones in the room. André was there too. Sitting by a table with his elbows on his knees. I couldn't tell what he thought of this situation because he wouldn't look at me. His gaze was fixed on a small part of the floor in front of him. And beside him on the table was the box that — I assumed — was filled with Thomas' office belongings. *So he got it after all.*

"Oh, thanks for bringing me my box," Thomas said. He clasped his hands behind his back and paced in front of me. As he walked, he watched his feet. *Was he trying to show me how sober he was?* If he was, I didn't care. No matter how many times he walked a straight line, I knew that there was at least one shot of alcohol in his system.

"I didn't really have a choice, now did I?" My voice came out a little weak; like my mouth was too dry to form words.

I hated it. I'd hoped that, if I just refused to do what he said that this would be over. But I guess I had underestimated him.

He chuckled a cold, evil sound that echoed in the large space. "I suppose you're right about that." He stopped walking and turned to face me. "You know, I'd thought about just taking the box and leaving town, but that just seemed too anticlimactic to me. And, *again*, blackmailing your brother into coming with me when I left *also* felt too anticlimactic. I couldn't just leave you *alone*. Your mother would've thought I'd gone soft."

"Where she's concerned, you have. *Haven't* you?"

It happened so fast that I almost didn't have time to hiss a reaction when he pressed a sharp blade into my neck.

"Shut up," he hissed.

But I couldn't help it. I cursed myself for every word I spoke but I couldn't keep my mouth shut. "André was your eyes and ears in our house when you left, *wasn't* he?" I didn't need a verbal confirmation to know that I was right. Andre's shame was obvious. "All he had to do was keep me and mom believing that he was just an innocent victim in whatever plans you've concocted, and I would do the rest, hm?" I said. "You just needed someone to do your—"

"I said, 'shut up'," he snarled and, this time when he pressed the blade further against my neck, it broke skin.

"Go ahead. Just do it." I dared him. I'd rather die than let him keep dragging me into his mess. And, dead, I was useless to him. I'd finally be free of him.

I just wanted to be free of him.

Thomas stopped, narrowed his eyes at me, and then laughed. He stumbled back in hysterical laughter. When he whipped around and slapped me with the back of his hand, I didn't expect it. Just like that night that Bryan had shared his secrets with me; I tasted blood in my mouth. I spit it to the concrete flooring as he walked over to Bryan's dad.

They talked amongst themselves, looking back at me every so often but it was André that my attention strayed to. He still wouldn't look at me but I couldn't figure out *why*. I struggled to free myself from my bonds but the more I tried, the tighter the knot seemed to get.

I jumped when a phone started ringing. Thomas went over to it and answered the call; he went further into the building so that I couldn't make out what he was saying. At about the same time, Mr. O'Donald left out of the big double doors to my left. That must've been where they hauled my sorry butt through.

With their attention divided, André looked up and came over to me. He looked guiltier than I'd ever seen him; there was no doubt in my mind, he'd had a hand in this. In my kidnapping. And he was sorry about it. But he was also scared.

"Janessa," he said softly. His voice quavered as he came to stop in front of me. "I just want you to know that I would've never helped... kidnap you if I'd had a choice, if I hadn't been threatened."

"What threats?" I asked. "What are you talking about?"

I figured that Thomas must've threatened to kill André if he didn't do as he was told. Whatever Thomas was planning, it was obvious that Andre was just a pawn. And me? I didn't know. I just hoped that I'd get out of this in one piece.

"Did he threaten to kill you?" I asked.

"No. He threatened to kill *you* if I didn't do it," he said. "But he won't now, he promised" André sounded so sure but I had a feeling he was wrong.

"Oh, yeah. Of course. 'Cause dear old dad is *so* trustworthy," I muttered. I glared at him. "Don't be so naive, Andy."

He shook his head. "Fine. You don't have to trust him. But trust *me*; you'll make it out of this alive."

I snorted. "You're no better. I'm in this situation *because* of you.

"I'm missing my high school graduation because *you* helped kidnap and bring me here using my own car. *Away* from everyone... and now Thomas will kill me."

"He won't. I won't let him." It sounded like a promise. He truly believed that he could save me; it was too bad that I didn't believe a word he said.

"Good luck with that," I muttered.

Thomas came back and, a few minutes later, the big double doors opened. I just expected Mr. O'Donald but he wasn't alone. He shoved his son onto the cement floor.

Bryan! *What was he doing here?* I glanced over at André, wondering if he'd summoned him but he'd already turned his back and walking back to his table with his tail between his legs like the little coward that he was.

Bryan looked up at me, his face both icy and pained at the same time. But then he looked at me and the ice in his emerald orbs thawed; for just a minute, then he'd look at Thomas and his own father and they'd freeze once again.

"I got another one for you," Mr. O'Donald said, hauling Bryan to his feet and dragging him toward another pillar. Then he tied Bryan up the same way they'd tied me up. I tried to catch *how* he tied the rope so that I could figure out how to undo it. Unfortunately, I was in the wrong position to see much of anything.

"Well, well, come to save your little girlfriend, did you?" Thomas mocked. He pulled out the same knife he'd threatened me with and stalked over to Bryan.

No matter how mad I was at Bryan for what he'd done and for how he'd chosen to go about the events of the last week, I didn't want him to die.

"Wow. You're *really* out of the loop," I said, trying to direct Thomas' attention at me. It worked, because, he looked between the both of us and kept his gaze on me just a fraction longer than on Bryan. I continued, "Bryan and I aren't *together* anymore; haven't been for a while." *Not that it's any of your business.*

"Either way," Thomas grunted, shrugging. "You're both loose ends. And we can't *leave* until all the loose ends are tied up." He circled the two of us with his fingers.

"Murder, that's smart. *Real* subtle," I grumbled but Thomas didn't catch it.

"And now I'm bored. Louis? Kill them," Thomas said before he walked out of the building. Apparently, he was good at making threats but when he could pawn the actual task off to someone else, he would. Mr. O'Donald — or Louis — walked over to me first.

Out of the corner of my eye, Bryan struggled against his restraints and I saw André get up and walk away from his table, but I wasn't sure. I was more focused on the gun that was pressed to my forehead. It was ice cold and terrifying.

"Any last words?" Mr. O'Donald sneered.

It was just a typical thing to ask someone that was about to die but, still, I struggled for a moment to form a single thought. *Last words?* I opened my mouth to say something but then I saw a blur of beige and Mr. O'Donald stumbled toward me before falling to the floor, unconscious. Behind him was André, a big block of wood in his hands and a wild look in his eyes. The piece of wood dropped to the floor and, for a moment, our eyes met and I let out the breath that I hadn't realized that I was holding.

He'd saved me. Even when I'd doubted him, he'd saved my life.

André hurried to free my wrists and went to do the same for Bryan. I bent down and pressed two hesitant fingers to Mr. O'Donald's throat to find his pulse, it took a second but there it was. He was alive and that was all I needed to know. Then I picked up his gun.

I'd held my mother's gun many times — I'd never fired it — but this one felt different, awkward, in my hand.

The three of us went to the big double doors and peered out. There was my car, Bryan's and another, a black Honda. Thomas was sitting in the front seat, waiting. I could almost see the waves of impatience rolling off of him.

The rest of the parking lot was empty. One against three; the odds were in our favour.

"Alright, Bryan. you go first. Get to your car and get out of here; don't wait for us, just go. We'll meet at McDonald's, okay?"

He looked like he wanted to protest but I gave him a stern look that made him think twice about it. He nodded reluctantly and did as he was told. I watched Thomas and when he saw Bryan leaving the building instead of Mr. O'Donald, he reached for something in the passenger seat and climbed out of his car. I ran out just as Thomas fired his first shot; it was aimed at Bryan.

When I saw Bryan had been hit, I stopped, raised my gun and fired three shots. Thomas had the same idea. I didn't have time to see if I'd hit my target before I got struck. I stumbled back and my breath caught in my throat. I grabbed my shoulder, hissing through the pain as I pressed down on my wound. Blood seeped through and coated my fingers in a red, syrupy liquid. My head swam and I felt unsteady.

This time, when I looked up, it was to see Thomas lying on the ground, unmoving. I wasn't sure if that was a good sign or not. But, regardless, he was all I could stare at. I saw his blood pool around him and felt sick.

André and Bryan ran over, practically begging me to tell them that I was alright. I looked up and told them I was fine; then I examined Bryan. There was a tear in his shirt, the edges of which were stained with blood but, as far as I could tell, it wasn't too bad.

"Come on, let's get you to the hospital." Bryan lifted me into his arms and carried me to his car. Andre followed behind us, looking even guiltier than before. I could practically read his mind; if it weren't for him, I wouldn't have gotten hurt. But as true as that was, it was *also* true that tonight, he'd *saved* my life. I'd have to remember to tell him that.

Carefully, I got in the backseat of Bryan's car with André. He tried to make me as comfortable as possible. I didn't tell him how pointless that was.

A couple hours later, at the hospital, Bryan came into my little curtained off area as I was getting my arm bandaged up. The cut on my throat got cleaned and patched up with a Dora the Explorer band-aid.

I hadn't checked a mirror yet, but I assumed that a bruise was forming on my cheek from Thomas' slap.

When Bryan came in, he looked like he'd gone home and changed into a clean pair of clothes. He wasn't wearing the same suit he'd worn earlier when he assumed that he'd be heading straight to the school for our graduation. Now he had on a grey v-neck, a pair of jeans, Nikes, and a black leather jacket. It looked weirdly warm and cozy. *And* it looked great on him.

The nurse finished bandaging me up. "Alright, you are free to go."

"Thanks," I told her, hopping off the bed. She left.

It was silent between me and Bryan for a minute before I finally got up the courage to ask what he was doing here. I figured that someone would've filled my mom in on what happened and that she'd be here, a frantic mess.

"I came to pick you up."

But, I *knew* that there was more to it than that. He had an ulterior motive.

"I also wanted to talk to you," he admitted, after a minute.

"Right." I nodded. I wasn't sure *what* he wanted to talk about and I wasn't really in the mood to talk to him, but... "Fine, you want to talk, then talk," I walked past him and headed to the exit.

He didn't say anything for a while. We spent the whole ride back to my house in silence. Not a *word* until he pulled into my driveway and he took the key out of the ignition.

He cleared his throat. "Um, I just wanted to say that I'm sorry. For what happened between us. It was stupid." Pause. "*I* was stupid. I understand if you don't trust me. I just need you to know that after I confessed about the game, I never lied to you. Everything I said was the truth. Right up until..."

"You cheated?"

"Yeah." He turned in his seat and looked at me head on. His hand reaching across and gripping the back of my seat. "I really *do* care about you. Why else do you think I came when your brother texted me?"

I just looked at him, confused. I hadn't even thought about that. I'd *wondered* why he'd come and how he'd even known, but I just thought it'd been set up. Or that *I'd* been set up.

"I was trying to save you, Ness," he told me.

I remembered how that had all played out from the moment that he was thrown to the floor of that building. I couldn't help my snort of disbelief. "Yeah, what a bang-up job you did."

"Yeah. You ended up saving me instead." He waited until I looked at him before he added, "In more ways than one."

Like all those other times when we'd been in this car together, alone, he leaned closer and pressed his lips to mine. I wanted to fight him but I just couldn't; I *wanted* to kiss him. It was a sad kiss. I could feel it in the way he kissed me. So I kissed him back, because I, too, was sad that this was over. That *we* were over.

Unlike those other times that we'd kissed in this car, this was goodbye.

And I think we both knew that. And that night, when mom hugged me to her chest and repeatedly kissed my head, I could feel myself starting to cave. Starting to believe him. I could believe that he *did* care about me. That I *did* mean something to him. That I was more than just another girl. I really *did* believe all of that.

I just didn't care.

❧ Twenty-Five ❧

Melissa and Natalie came over as soon as they heard about what had happened to me. I didn't know *who* spilled the beans but I'm sure they'd have figured it out sooner or later.

I was a little scared of how Melissa would react or what she'd think of me when she found out about my past and about Thomas. But as I talked and explained everything — past to present encounters with him — she just sat there and listened. She looked at me with concern and worry but it wasn't the *'oh, you poor baby'* pity that I'd been expecting. They asked about my shoulder and I told them about how Thomas had shot me. About how the bullet had just skinned my arm and taken a penny-sized bit of skin with it as it disappeared into the warehouse. It ached like hell even now but it was stitched up so I was fine. I *would* be fine.

I swore I was fine before they each grabbed their purses, gave me a quick hug and left. As they were walking out the door, they promised they would see me in the morning before I left town.

"You know, no one would blame you if you took a gap year and just took this time to heal," my mom said. She sat down on the couch. André had gone to bed about an hour ago so it was just mom and me.

I sat down beside her. It wasn't hard to see the look of complete guilt on her face, as blameless as she was.

I could see where she was coming from; I was her baby girl and she felt like she'd failed me. For me to come home, patched up, a cut on my throat and a bruise on my cheek, was just a reminder for her.

It was one of the reasons why I couldn't stay here. If I took a gap year, I'd always see the guilt on her face. And I couldn't sit around like a snail in a shell because of something that happened to me.

I rested my head on mom's shoulder and nodded. "I know that. Really," I told her. "But I *want* to go." We were quiet for a while as she kissed the top of my head. "I know that isn't what you want to hear, but I'm okay. Honest. And I need to live my life if I expect to get better."

"Yeah, you're right." She held my head against her shoulder and for a minute we just sat like that.

I looked around the living room and the full weight of what I had just said really came crashing down on me. This was going to be my last night in this house. The last time, for a *long* time, where I got to just sit on the couch like this with my mom. Tomorrow night, everything would be different. The people I'll be living with, be myself with, will be different. My life was about to change and it was starting to scare me, the unknown.

Everything I always dreamed of was just out of reach and it used to comfort me. Knowing where I was going and what I was going to do; but you make dreams never *completely* believing that you'll live to see the day they come true.

I was moving in a direction I didn't feel ready to walk. My future, so clear before now, was fogging by the second.

"Hey, how about we go get your car? Huh?" Mom said, nudging my uninjured shoulder. "It's still back at the warehouse, right?"

"It *should* be."

So mom and I left. We went back to the warehouse to find that certain things that were there before, were now missing. The black Honda — gone. Thomas' body — also gone. I *hoped* that they were just gone because someone simultaneously took care of Thomas and stole his car. And then there was my perfectly good car — trashed.

The windows were smashed, both back and front windshields had spiderwebbed cracks in the glass. Glass was scattered on the ground and cluttering up my seats. When we looked closer, it was clear that someone had deliberately cut holes in my tires and let the air out. As if that wasn't enough, the top of my car was caved in, like someone had beaten it down with a tire iron. Someone had been *pissed*.

Mom stood a little ways away from me, watching me examine the car she'd bought for me. A sweet sixteen gift. I wanted to scream in anger. This car *meant* something to me. "Wha... What kind of monster would do this?" I asked aloud. My voice broke.

My mom came up behind me and put a hand on my shoulder. "We should go. It's getting late."

"But, my car... *You* got me that car," I said, stating the fact as if she didn't already know. My voice quavered and I could feel the tears coming.

"I know, sweetie. Come on, we should go."

I knew she was right. It was creeping up to midnight, but leaving my car here felt like abandonment. Eventually, mom got me into her car — a nearly impossible task. Then we drove back to our house.

Back at home, I took a short shower and headed to bed.

It took longer than usual for me to get comfortable enough to sleep. I usually slept on my side, switching every once in a while. Now I couldn't. For a while, I slept on my right side. It just didn't feel right. Eventually, I resorted to just sleeping on my stomach and, I don't know how long I lay there just staring into the dark, but I finally fell asleep.

⋯❦⋯

The next morning, while I was less than half awake, I turned onto my left side. And promptly bolted upright. "Ahhh," I cried out, clutching my arm in pain. I sucked in a breath through my teeth; it made a hissing sound like a cat whose tail has just been stepped on.

I hopped out of bed and went to clean and re-bandage my shoulder before I met my mom and André in the kitchen for breakfast.

"Breakfast." My mom called up as I was redressing my wound.

"Okay," I called back. "Just a minute."

"I'll leave you a plate, okay?" she called up.

Good, I thought. *No rush.*

Mom had set aside a plate of pancakes for me; I found that out when I came into the kitchen.

My shoulder was still throbbing; not as bad as when I'd woken up, but still painfully. I didn't mention it to my mom but a little while later, mom handed me a couple pills and a glass of water. I gladly accepted both when there was a knock at the door.

"Come in!" I shouted.

For a short second, my heart stopped in panic. Calling out that invitation was just a gut reaction, but what if I hadn't (accidentally) killed Thomas and he showed up on our doorstep to finish what he'd started yesterday? I was stiff as a board until the door opened and Melissa and Natalie came in. Natalie led the way into the kitchen and gave me a one-armed hug.

"Morning, everyone."

"Morning." Mom replied. "Pancakes, anyone?"

My friends both raised their hands with a cheerful, "Me!"

We all moved to the kitchen table for more room, and that's where we ate breakfast together, just the five of us. We chatted and Natalie confirmed what I'd already guessed — that she and James would spend the summer together — and gossiped about what I didn't know. She and James would be working full-time for the next two weeks and saving every bit of their pay, on top of what they'd already saved. From there, they were going to go on a road trip, starting here — Ontario — and going west to British Columbia. Natalie told me not to worry; she'd be back for my birthday.

Melissa, on the other hand, was just going to work the whole summer and get a headstart on her college reading. She'd already purchased her textbooks and school supplies. That was something she and the old me had in common. I'd already gotten everything I needed for school but after this month, I had no plans to crack them open any sooner than I needed to.

André had gotten a call this morning and had gotten a job. It was at the convenience store that Bryan worked at. He planned to work there for the summer and his first shift was later today. He was excited about his first shift but our mom was nervous. She wasn't too thrilled with driving me to my new place and leaving André all alone. She would just be dropping me off and then heading back but that was a three-hour drive, both ways: there and back.

André easily dismissed her concern for his safety, which didn't make her feel better until Natalie offered to stay and look out for him.

After breakfast, André headed into the basement and closed the door behind him. I was still itching with curiosity about what they were hiding but I wasn't gonna invade their privacy. Besides, I'd probably find out sooner or later; so I stayed put in the kitchen, stacking the dirty dishes.

"Hey," Natalie said with a smile, walking up behind me. "How are you?"

"I'm fine," I told her, with a roll of my eyes, smiling back.

"Okay," she surrendered, putting the stopper into the sink. Then she asked about the whereabouts of my car. She must've noticed the empty spot in the driveway. I looked up at her abruptly. "I thought you would've wanted to go back and get it because, you know, it's your car. You *love* that car."

"I *do*." I inhaled deeply. Then I told her what had happened to it. "I guess I'm just going to have to deal without one for a while." I shrugged.

Melissa came by a little while later and the three of us washed the dishes together; talking and listening to the music playing on Natalie's phone. Then Melissa had to leave, and frankly, so did I.

I put the last of my stuff — which fit in a duffle — into the back of my mom's car and went to say goodbye. I started with Melissa.

I promised I'd see her soon and that I'd text her when I could.

André waited until she left and then he wrapped me in a hug. I felt like a happy little sushi roll.

He let me go and said, "Nessa, I am so sorry for what happened." I was getting tired of hearing that.

He looked pained and guilty but he didn't need to be. He was an open book, couldn't hide his emotions all that well. I pulled him into a hug again and waited for his arms to tighten around my waist before I spoke. "I know, André. It's okay. I forgive you."

He pulled back slightly (again) and looked at me, unsure.

"You saved me, okay?" I told him. He nodded, sheepishly. "I love you, kiddo."

His laugh was between a chuckle and a scoff when he hugged me once more and whispered his goodbyes into my ear. Then he spun on his heel and walked back inside. Turing to wave just before he disappeared.

"So," Natalie said, coming to take his place in front of me, "this is it."

"Hey! This goodbye isn't forever."

She nodded, her eyes a little misty. "I'm going to miss you."

I cracked up. "You make it sound like I'm moving to Timbuktu or something."

"I'm still gonna miss you."

"Yeah, me too."

I hugged her and she hugged back just as tight. Holding on one last time, hoping to make the memory last until we could see each other again.

"Take lots of pictures on your road trip," I demanded, backing up and heading to mom's car.

"You know me, I am not a photographer."

"I don't care!" I shouted at her, opening the passenger side door. "Take pictures!" And that was the last thing I said to her before I got in and closed the door behind me.

❧ ❦ ☙

I ended up falling asleep during the three hours and was woken by my mom shaking my shoulder. "Honey, wake up. We're here."

Sure enough, when I looked up, we were parked on the curb just outside the house I'd started to move into. The curtains were open in the living room and I saw Ruth and Ronan going at it. I don't know what they were arguing about, but they were waving their arms comically. I could almost imagine steam bursting from their ears and the image was enough to make me chuckle.

There was one car in the drive but that was it.

The Game

Mom was wearing an overly large smile as she looked at me, that sadness of having to let her baby girl go was clear as day. It was almost enough for me to back out of my decision to leave early, *almost*.

"Mom, I'm going to be fine. I promise."

"I know you will be." She nodded. My mom rubbed my arm with the palm of her hand. "I know I don't have to worry about you so much, but I do. I know you're going to be just fine. You're clever and resourceful but if you need anything, *anything* at all—"

"I know," I interrupted. And I did know. I shouldn't hesitate to call her if I ever needed anything. My mouth twitched up into a smile. I leaned across her car to hug her. And, like I had with Natalie, I held on tight. Probably a little tighter than necessary because it would be a while until my birthday. A while until I saw her again. Probably

"I love you, Nessa."

"I love you too, mom."

Then I got out of the car and grabbed my bag from the trunk. She followed me and gave me one more hug, one that filled my chest with a warm, affectionate feeling. I hugged her back, no hesitation. But we were interrupted by the sounds of feet hitting the pavement behind us and I turned to see Garrett — the blue-eyed, blonde-haired roommate — jogging on the sidewalk behind us.

"Hi, Mrs. Reynolds," he said before he looked at me and stopped jogging. He looked shocked. I figured the bruise on my face was a lot more noticeable than I'd thought; because it stopped him cold. "Are you okay?"

"Yeah," I said, quickly. I tucked invisible strands of hair behind my ear in embarrassment. "I'm fine."

"Anyway...," mom said, "I should be going." She kissed my head once. Then she got into her car and pulled away quickly, probably wanting to leave before she changed her mind about letting me move out. I just watched her leave, and kept watching until the car disappeared around the corner.

Then I looked at Garrett, already jogging to the front porch of the house, and took it all in. The small white house with green eaves and the three people in it, the twins — Ronan and Ruth, and Garrett. I took in the block too, it seemed quiet. Safe. Undisturbed, almost. It was nice. This was going to be my life for the next few years.

It was still uncharted territory but now that I was here, it didn't seem quite as scary as it had last night. It was still frightening but it was bearable. Did I want to run back home? Back to my family? Back to my safety net? Sure. I wanted to do all of that. I wanted to call my mom back and get her to pick me up because although it wasn't quite as scary as it *had* been, I still didn't know what to expect from it.

But maybe that was a good thing. Maybe not knowing was the point. Learning as you go. Letting yourself out of that comfortable but confining box that you put yourself in.

So instead of calling mom and getting her to pick me up, I tucked my phone into my back pocket, readjusted the strap of my purse and carried my last duffle into the house.

End of Book One

⚜ Acknowledgements ⚜

I just wanted to take a moment to thank everyone who had a hand in making this possible for me.

First, I would like to thank my friends and family for their encouragements and their support over the years. It has been a long time coming and now that it's here, I can't thank all of you enough for being there for me and sometimes for listening to me talk about nothing else but this story. I love you guys!

Melissa, my editor, who had the hard job of going in and catching my mistakes, mostly grammar. You are the best. Couldn't have done this without you.

Also, the iUniverse team that has put in so much work and effort to helping me make my dreams come true.

And to God, for making all of this possible.

Thank you!

Printed in the United States
By Bookmasters